The Enchantment of Christina von Retzen

Antony Beevor

WEIDENFELD AND NICOLSON

London

First published in Great Britain in 1989 by
George Weidenfeld & Nicolson Limited,
91 Clapham High Street, London SW4 7TA

British Library Cataloguing in Publication Data

Beevor, Antony, 1946–
The enchantment of Christina von Retzen
I. Title
823'.914 [F]
ISBN 0–297–79523–6

Printed and bound in Great Britain by
Butler & Tanner Ltd, Frome, Somerset

For Artemis

Part One

1

Christina was incapable of dissembling. Her confession tumbled out like brooms from a cupboard opened by mistake. In the silence that followed, she sat motionless at the dressing-table, her shoulders naked above the bath towel and her tawny-gold hair piled in a makeshift chignon. The triptych looking-glass appeared to imprison her in endless images of herself.

James's arms had sagged to his sides, leaving the black bow tie undone and his shirt collar up. Standing behind her, he pushed his spectacles back into place.

Husband and wife stared at their joint reflection until the deathly seriousness of the tableau brought a disbelieving grin to his face. A twice-married woman of thirty-five with a sixteen-year-old daughter, and then out of the blue this schoolgirl passion for a man she scarcely knew. Instinctively, he put his hands on her shoulders, but she flinched at the touch and he withdrew them.

'Can we get things straight?' There was an edge of incredulous aggravation in his voice. 'You've known this character for years, but only really got to know him recently. And now you're flying home to Austria because he's going to be at this wedding next weekend?'

'I know it must sound mad. Perhaps it is I that is mad. Oh, James, I am so *sorry*!' The tormented note made him regret his tone. And her way of saying 'Chames' always touched him. Christina's English, unlike that of her German relatives, was untainted by prissy exactitude.

'So was this the reason for those strange moods you didn't want to talk about?' He shook his head as if to act out the

3

sense of dislocation. She did not reply.

'Have I ever met him?' he said.

'Please! Do not ask questions.'

'But having brought the subject up, surely the least you can do is to tell me a bit about him.'

Her eyes remained fixed on the oval dish in front of her. He attempted a light-hearted tone. 'Well, if the man in question is going to that wedding, then I can only assume he's a member of the Lumbering Procession. It's not Hugo von what's-his-name, is it? The one with the umlaut.'

'No! Do not tease. Not now!' The desperate note took him aback. 'I'm sorry, but *Tante* Sisi must be expecting us downstairs. The others will be arriving at any moment. James, I really am sorry! It was a very bad time to come out.'

'You can say that again,' he sighed. He ran a hand through his hair, then sat down on the end of the bed and frowned, although the significance of her disclosure had still not sunk in. He leaned forward, elbows on knees, to stare at the carpet between his feet.

After a few moments, he raised his head. Her hand faltered in the middle of applying some cream. Christina wore virtually no makeup and then only as a social requirement in the evening. She certainly did not need it. Contrived colouring could only detract from the warm honey glow of her skin which went with that marvellous hair. She looked so healthy that nobody could ever imagine her ill. The only time James had seen her pale was in hospital in Italy. He would never forget the sight. She had looked drained of blood.

Christina removed the pins to shake out her hair and then, head tilted, began to brush sideways. She burned under his gaze.

'Aren't you going to finish dressing?' she exclaimed.

'In a moment,' he said quietly and looked away at last. It felt as though he had been studying her for the first time, and yet he had sensed a few weeks ago, despite all her assurances to the contrary, that something must be wrong. Now he berated himself for accepting those excuses at face value. Perhaps he had not wanted to find out. Men were such moral cowards:

head in the clouds one day, then buried in the sand the next without acknowledging the difference.

He was surprised not to have felt a stab of betrayal at her announcement. Perhaps, as with physical injury, pain came later when the astonishment wore off. But for the moment, confused and empty, he felt only a numb weakness in his limbs.

Three years together must surely count for something, he reasoned, even if their attraction for each other had originally been one of opposites. Perhaps that was his trouble. He had always been fascinated by contrasts, as long as he could remember.

Christina came from another world entirely. Born into that bizarre European cousinage based on the great Austrian and German houses, she had grown up in the fairy-tale setting of Schloss Lotzingen in the Styrian Alps. In Vienna, the family retained part of the Schwanemberg Palace, whose baroque plasterwork had survived both the bombs of the US Air Force and a brief occupation by the Red Army. The resilience of their way of life still struck him as incredible.

James's own childhood, although also unusual, had taken place in the immeasurably less romantic surroundings of Norfield House near Harrogate. Built shortly before the turn of the century in red brick with slate roofs and monumental chimneystacks, Norfield later summed up for him the peculiar qualities of Britain's imperial age: both ugly and impossible to maintain.

In the two walled gardens, Carter, the gammy-legged handyman, carried on a dispirited rearguard action against weed, ivy and decay. The outbuildings behind, built in the same Edwardian brick as the house, were kept locked on the orders of James's father, a man of irrational rages. But one summer holiday, during the heavy silence of a Sunday afternoon, James crept to the kitchen, his heart thumping, and from the row of hooks inside the door he took the large iron keys attached by string to old cotton-reels.

In the dark coolness of those outbuildings with their smell of rust and damp stone, he slowly advanced, flashing his torch over the abandoned impedimenta, from garden tools to a pony trap with a broken axle, and into recesses where cobwebs had curled to a feathery soot. But the expedition was a frustrating failure. The door to the loft, the last remaining place where his mother's possessions could have been stored, was fitted with an extra padlock to which there was no key.

James's other area of interest lay just outside the property. Like a cavalry scout spying a Sioux encampment, he used to crawl to the edge of the old orchard and study life on the new housing estate through his father's binoculars. The contrast with the post-war decay of an almost servantless Norfield aroused in him a strange joy. He exulted in the crude energy of this tasteless new world: the tussle of teenage couples in the adjoining field, the gaudy curtains, the blare of radio music, and the chimes of the ice cream van – a burst of 'John Peel' broken off in mid-bar. They helped make the brash freedom across the frontier extraordinarily tantalizing. And knowing that Mrs Harding, their cook-cum-housekeeper, would scold him on return for the state of his clothes, he used to burn with rancour at the unfair lottery of birth.

The interior of Norfield had the shabby, masculine gloom so often found then in undistinguished country houses. This was emphasized by barometers, and heavy mahogany furniture, and sporting prints with tiny dead insects trapped under the glass, and, worst of all, a grandfather clock whose ticking in the stillness made childhood feel a life sentence.

With his father shut away in his study – nobody knew what he did there, except brood in egotistic melancholia – Norfield had the air of a run-down prep school from which all the other boys had been taken away by their parents. James later felt that, like François Seurel, the loyal classmate of Le Grand Meaulnes, he had been forced by fate to stay behind.

James's daydreams had focused on bringing someone into his life. At prep school, he would invent a heroic act of sacrifice to win the friendship of a boy or teacher he admired. At public school this changed to the rescue of a girl whose chaste gratitude was zealously segregated from any sexual fantasy. Influenced mainly by the other boys and the pervasive emphasis on hierarchy, the scenario of his daydreams had also become more snobbish. That earlier fascination for the housing estate was quietly forgotten.

Even after school and university, James's fantasy world changed little. His heroines retained a paradoxical perfection: challenging but soft, intelligent but playful, experienced but virgin. All those confused yet manipulative male dualities, as his first editor, a humorous and outspoken feminist, had put it. According to her theory, man's creation of artificial alternatives was the root of all politics. This was what had destroyed the ancient and far more stable trinities of early society.

With an unconvincing sigh of bravado, James pushed himself up to finish the struggle with his bow tie. It was true, he told himself in an attempt to keep calm. Christina really did have a terrible sense of timing.

At last ready, she nervously avoided his eyes. Turning, she asked him to fasten the hooks at the back of her dress which was cut generously in a dark, moss-green velvet.

'Apart from Andrea and your brother,' he said, striving to keep his voice neutral, 'is anybody else coming tonight?'

They were staying in Oxfordshire with *Tante* Sisi, Christina's aunt on her mother's side. The Lumbering Procession had a surprising number of members in England – an archipelago of Grand Mitteleuropa concealed in the stockbroker belt. A few, like the Kinskys, had owned houses from those days when the Empress Elizabeth used to come for a whole hunting season and a Newmarket thoroughbred was considered the finest horse in the world. But the majority had arrived in waves since the collapse of the Dual Monarchy in 1918.

Tante Sisi, a great-niece of Franz Josef, had decided with her husband after the *Anschluss* to leave Austria and take British nationality. Within a year, their adopted country was at war with Greater Germany, and she could only obtain news of her brother in the Luftwaffe through relations in Switzerland. There was something both magnificent and exasperating in the way the Cousinage managed to treat nationality as little more than a bureaucratic inconvenience.

'I am sorry,' said Christina abruptly. 'I don't remember who else is coming.'

He sensed she probably did know but was too tense for conversation at that moment. Under emotional strain, Christina found it hard to think straight or laugh. She certainly wouldn't find anything funny right now, James thought. Yet he failed to notice that his usual compulsion to make jokes in unpromising circumstances had vanished as well. [*This damage to both our senses of humour was more important than I realized. And for those first two days I also forgot how guilt, when bottled up, can produce its own baffled resentment.*]

The carpet in the corridor muffled their footfalls. His eyes were drawn to the line of Christina's neck. The moment had the feel of a clip from a French film, one of those hand-held sequences. He cocked his head to listen. By the sound of voices downstairs, someone had already arrived.

Tante Sisi greeted them from in front of a blazing fire. Her simple, long black dress was in wool. She claimed that the one thing she could never get used to in England was the damp in the cold. Seventy-four years old that day, and still a classic beauty, there was an ageless attraction in her low, smoker's voice and sleepy-looking eyes.

She brushed aside Christina's apology for coming down so late. 'There is still no sign of Sasha and this fiancée of his, whom he is supposed to be bringing this evening. Your brother really is hopeless.'

From the sofa opposite, Andrea de Bourbon Valdemar, another of Christina's cousins, rose more gracefully than might have been expected from his conspicuously unathletic appearance. With white hair and pudgy, albino flesh, he was saved from an otherwise unappealing sexlessness by his air of mischief. He loved to tease Christina, and with James he enjoyed a frivolous skirmishing. The fact that the *jeune couple*, as he still insisted on calling them, had met at a party of his in Paris apparently allowed him a proprietorial merriment.

Watching Andrea stretch out his jaw, a movement intended to reduce his double chin, James was struck by the possibility that such a connoisseur of gossip might already know about Christina's infatuation. Perhaps that was why she had blurted out her secret just before they came down. In any case, both Andrea and Sisi would be going to the wedding next Saturday.

James usually managed to avoid these incestuous occasions around which the Cousinage still revolved. His reaction to this particular invitation had been no different. When the instantly recognizable envelope arrived, he had passed it to Christina and, not bothering to wait for the sheaf of circuitous formulae, asked her to count him out.

Christina went over to her aunt and, with a shy laugh, handed her a small present. '*Herzlichen Glückwunsch!*'

Tante Sisi kissed her, thanked them both, then turned to throw her cigarette in the fire before starting to unwrap the neat little package.

'James darling,' she said, raising her head for a moment. 'Can you help yourself and Christina to drinks?'

From the tray he asked if anyone else wanted anything. *Tante* Sisi's welcome earlier had been so natural that he could not believe she knew, and yet she possessed that royal knack for refusing to acknowledge embarrassment in any form. But the real problem was Christina knotting into a defensive ball. To get her to talk when they finally returned to their room was not going to be easy. He wondered how on earth he was going to last the evening until then.

Once he had given Christina a glass of orange juice, James sipped his whisky and looked around in an attempt to keep his mind on other things. The sitting-room walls were covered in a blue watered silk and hung with four oval portraits and a pair of unusually fine Venetian mirrors. He had always loved this house, a well-proportioned Georgian vicarage, and above all, he admired the way *Tante* Sisi had subverted the quintessential Englishness of the place. He imagined Juniper Hall with Fanny Burney and the French émigrés.

After another twenty minutes of desultory chat between Andrea and *Tante* Sisi, the crunch of tyres on gravel provided a welcome distraction. Christina sighed in a mixture of resignation and apology. 'Late as usual,' she said.

'The unfortunate part,' her aunt replied, 'is that he still manages to get away with it. If only Sasha's very agreeable nature had been put to better use.' Andrea chuckled at some private joke. *Tante* Sisi gave him a look of indulgent reproof before continuing. 'I really cannot believe in his marriage to this latest girl ... Barbara what's-her-name. Honestly, what a boy. This will be his third marriage, and each one has been more unsuitable than the last.'

'Boy?' Andrea laughed. 'But Sasha's nearly fifty. Almost twice as old as Mademoiselle Barbara.'

With a small upward movement of the head, *Tante* Sisi dismissed the notion that age and maturity were necessarily linked. James, glanced over at Christina. Few could have been less suitable than himself.

Alexander Schwanemberg and his fiancée were shown in by *Tante* Sisi's devoted cook, Mrs Fraser. Sasha made a mime of contrition as he crossed the room. He lifted his aunt's hand in a quick, formal *Handkuss* before embracing her on both cheeks. He then turned to present Barbara, an immaculate blonde, dressed for Fifth Avenue rather than the English countryside. The twenty years between them might well have passed unnoticed.

The perfection of Barbara's figure and features struck James as exaggerated. Teeth, hair, skin and makeup showed an Olympic-class dedication. But it wasn't the sort of beauty to inspire much in the way of love or, for that matter, lust. All it could arouse was the challenge of possession. Even her expressions looked as though they had been carefully studied, no doubt at that finishing school in Bavaria which Andrea called 'the princess factory'.

Sasha eyed the dinner jackets and opened his hands to his aunt, asking for a decision on whether he and Barbara had time to go up to change.

'You have ten minutes,' she said. 'If you're not down, we shall go in without you. Otherwise it is not fair on Mrs Fraser.'

Once they were out of earshot, *Tante* Sisi commented in a low voice that they would almost certainly not be ready in time.

'What?' said Christina in surprise. 'Do you really think she will want to redo her face?'

'*Mais non, ma chère,*' replied Andrea. 'Your dear brother may well be wallowing in a bath fifteen minutes from now, but *la belle* Barbara will be ready on the dot. Her looks have an alarming air of efficiency. In their way, I suppose, they are quite as efficient as her father's business empire. Almost what one might call an extension of policy by other means. Appropriately Germanic, don't you agree, James?'

James automatically returned Andrea's facetious smile. He was thinking how hard Christina would find it to welcome this new sister-in-law. That air of calculation made Barbara her least favourite type of woman, and yet in Christina's eyes, no woman could really be worthy of her beloved brother. As the baby of the family, her affection for the absurdly good-looking Alexander was to be expected, even though he had a feckless playboy streak of the sort she detested in other men.

To everyone's surprise, the sound of doors and voices upstairs came within the time limit. 'Perhaps Barbara is just what Sasha needs after all,' said Andrea. *Tante* Sisi gave him a look telling him to keep his voice down.

At the round dining-room table, *Tante* Sisi placed James on her left. He remained standing, ostensibly until everyone else was seated, but his movements were unnaturally slow. The prospect of food dismayed him. He wanted to be away from there, to be alone with Christina.

Andrea began talking with *Tante* Sisi in Italian, and James found himself engaged in conversation by Barbara on the other side. But unable to stop watching Christina out of the corner of his eye, he missed her question. James apologized and again warned himself to put Christina from his mind.

'I asked how long have you and Sasha's sister been married?'

James told her and then, to escape a discomforting sequence of interrogation, began one of his own.

Barbara had done a course in dress design in Milan, modelled in New York and handled the public relations for a couturier in Paris. She had met Sasha in Marbella the previous May. James then attempted a few questions about the fashion industry and life as a model, but they sounded leaden in his ears.

At this point, Barbara deftly took charge. She asked what he wrote, and although he told her as briefly as possible, she frowned with concentration, nodded emphatically at the right moments and said that she would buy a copy of his latest book on returning to London.

They both glanced across the table at the same moment. Sasha was recounting a boar shoot during the winter. Christina sat with her head turned towards him, apparently spellbound, but James suspected that her thoughts were far away. Barbara craned forward as if about to join in, but then changed her mind, and returned to the subject of books.

James had to revise his earlier cynicism. Her comments indicated at the very least a competent filleting of English and American reviews. She also displayed a good knowledge of world affairs and British politics. Where does she find the time? he thought, finding it hard to picture her on Sasha's round of idle restlessness – shoots and travel in the winter, Rio for Carnival, skiing in the spring and then a summer-long zigzag around the Mediterranean from yacht to house party.

Suddenly, he felt certain he had guessed Barbara's plan. Her future identity as a Princess Schwanemberg would be perfect for launching a fashion house, particularly one aimed at the American market. Without thinking, he longed to ask Christina what she thought, but that brought him painfully back to the question of his own marriage.

He looked across the table. His thoughts about Barbara made him realize how much he loved Christina's spontaneity in spite, or perhaps even because of all those bombshells and conversation-stopping non sequiturs. For the second time that evening he had the impression of seeing her anew.

She was now trying to listen to Andrea's account of the latest political scandal in Paris, to which he had added several outrageous details. The turmoil behind her uncertain smile was also revealed in the way she kept twisting her wedding ring. She had a lost look, obviously failing to take in anything that was said.

The contrast with Barbara reminded James of Christina's estrangement from modern life. The youngest of her family by

far, and with elderly parents, she had some reason for ident-
ifying with a previous generation. But her isolation went
beyond that: it had an emotional depth which was hard to
fathom. Competitiveness she found genuinely distasteful,
above all she could not stand people who talked about money,
and her compulsive generosity could be unsettling for those
who did not know her.

Christina at last sensed James's gaze and her eyes flickered
in his direction. Conversation languished all round the table.

'An angel passes,' she said with a hurried laugh.

'It must be twenty past or twenty to,' said *Tante* Sisi.

Sasha checked his watch. 'Almost twenty to ten.'

Barbara smiled at this family ritual. Sasha turned to her
with a mock confidential air and, at the same time, put a hand
on Christina's forearm. 'Did you know that my extraordinarily
young sister here, has a daughter of sixteen? Even if others do
not find that hard to believe, it makes me feel quite ancient.'

'No, is that true?' said Barbara, leaning forward over the
table. 'She is really *sixteen?*'

Christina answered the polite astonishment with a look of
unconcealed scepticism.

Barbara, caught on the wrong foot, felt compelled to go on.
'And does she take after you, or ...' The question stumbled
and fell into an excruciating silence. Yet the only real gaffe
was her sudden confusion over Christina's former husband,
for it raised the question of what she might have been told
about him.

Christina clearly derived no satisfaction from Barbara's dis-
comfiture. 'Stephanie always resembled her father more than
me,' she said, avoiding everybody's eyes.

'Sasha,' said *Tante* Sisi, 'does anyone on your side of the
table need more wine? Yes, now that I come to think of it, I
have heard very little of Stephanie's news recently. How is she
getting on at school? She is such an intelligent child that I
suppose it cannot be long before she goes to university.'

James, having seen Christina's distracted glances around
the room, felt obliged to answer in her stead.

*   *   *

13

Soon after the move back to the drawing room, Christina pleaded a headache and James overplayed the role of solicitous husband. Although he should have allowed her to go up on her own, he was so desperate to be with her and to know the truth that he no longer cared what anyone thought. But on the stairs, his courage began to fail.

'Well,' he sighed as they approached their bedroom. 'Poor Barbara turned out to be fallible after all.' He leaned forward to open the door for her with a semi-ironic flourish. He knew he was making things worse, but could not stop himself.

Christina went over to the dressing-table to take off her earrings. Every movement revealed how conscious she was of his eyes upon her.

'Can you now tell me who he is?' he asked, unable to bear the tension any longer.

For several moments she studied the jewellery she had just placed in the china dish. She glanced up at him, then down again. 'Oh, James,' she said sadly. 'There would be no point in telling you anything about him. Only that the two of you have never met. Maybe it is something crazy in me that will pass.' But her voice did not sound hopeful.

'How have you been seeing him?' he heard himself say. 'Has it just been at all these weddings and family parties, or have you been stopping off on your way home to Lotzingen? Or even meeting him in London?'

'A mixture,' she admitted quietly. 'He comes to England on business from time to time. We have lunch together.'

'Just lunch? No more?'

She reddened. 'No.'

He continued to watch her, not knowing what to believe.

'Perhaps . . .' She gave him a tragic, apologetic look. 'Perhaps it would have been better if I had not tried to tell you yet.' She shook her head helplessly. 'I just do not know what else I can say.'

Eventually, to avoid his uncomprehending gaze, she began to pull the combs from her hair.

After she had disappeared into the bathroom, James, feeling both dazed and caged, moved aimlessly about. Although he was supposed to have given up smoking, he craved for a cigarette. To get Christina to talk about herself had always been an uphill struggle. She was the most private person he had ever known. Yet to allow a silence between them to set would be fatal. Some sort of dialogue had to be started before it was too late.

Teeth-brushing noises came from the other side of the door. He knocked lightly as he entered. Christina, turning in alarm from the basin, instinctively put an arm across her breasts. They stared at each other in mutual astonishment. James felt a void in his stomach as if from the punch of an invisible assailant. He turned back in confusion. Her reflex had been that of a woman surprised by a stranger.

Long after the light was out he listened hard, wondering if she too could not sleep. The other bed was no more than a few feet away, yet, staring up into the darkness, he might easily have been alone. As in his childhood at Norfield, the night felt both cavernous and infinite; claustrophobic yet deserted.

Rain began to fall steadily outside. Soon a hollow tinkling sound came from the gutter above their window. He lay frozen while his mind raced. An outburst of Sasha's laughter came from downstairs.

❧ 2 ❧

At the end of the short drive James leaned forward over the steering wheel to check that the road was clear. He glanced at Christina. Her eyebrows rose noncommittally. She hated stratagems, even white lies like their excuse for leaving soon after breakfast and her telephone call to Stephanie's convent.

'Honestly, I'm sure *Tante* Sisi didn't mind,' he said. Christina did not answer.

The day was one of those peculiar to late spring, a restless mixture of bright sunshine, wind and sudden storms. Winter had gone on so long that the blossom blown from apple trees could easily be mistaken for flurries of snow. Sealed from the weather, they drove without speaking through the neat suburban countryside of Berkshire. Sunday morning in the Home Counties, he thought. The Conservative Party at golf.

When he pulled out to overtake a rented van an oncoming car appeared, forcing him to pull back suddenly. Christina's foot jabbed at an imaginary brake pedal.

'Sorry about that,' he said, tilting his head. She glanced at him from behind her tortoiseshell dark glasses, worn as much to hide the tiredness of her eyes as to protect them from the brittle glare. He too felt light-headed from lack of sleep. His mood was as volatile as the weather. Dejection would be broken up by a febrile certainty that she would never actually leave him, then banks of doubt would gather on the horizon again.

Having parked on the forecourt, James once again took in the rhododendron bushes, playing fields, red brick buildings and the protruding chapel with its neo-Gothic windows. The architecture of schools struck him as uniformly depressing.

16

This religious barracks bore an uncanny resemblance to his prep school, which had been housed in a Victorian mansion built to the glory of Mammon.

The iron-studded door was opened by Sister Bona, an ancient, straight-backed nun still in the traditional habit. She greeted Christina, an eminent old girl, with a smile of warm approval. Once again, she managed to ignore James, who suspected that her beaky nose could sniff out a heretic at fifty paces. Sister Bona's views on the more relaxed regime at the convent were not hard to guess.

While she spoke to Christina in her turkey-gobbling voice about Stephanie, James wandered off along the corridor past a print of the Pope, an elaborate crucifix, a leaflet dispenser for the Catholic Truth Society and a Della-Robbia plaque of Madonna and Child. Whitewashed and barrel-vaulted with a floor of terracotta tiles, the Italianate style appeared doubly inappropriate on reaching a window. The view of rhododendrons, and the Wellingtonia towering against a slate-coloured sky, was discouragingly British.

He turned to the noticeboards and found that even the announcements about tennis competitions and music practice held a fascination. Like the echo of shrill cries in swimming baths, they could still trigger a masochistic nostalgia.

Sensing a presence at his shoulder, he found Stephanie waiting for the discussion about her to finish. He made a face of commiseration, to which she replied with a movement of her eyebrows very like her mother. The similarity was startling mainly because of their contrasts. Stephanie, with her long dark hair, had the delicate yet resolute profile of a young Edwardian beauty. She was already as tall as Christina, and the nuns had drilled her into holding herself well.

Eventually the three of them hurried out to the car, hunching instinctively against the incipient storm. From just inside the door, Sister Bona raised a hand in what looked like benediction on the meal.

Half way down the drive, Stephanie leaned forward between them. 'Well, this is an unexpected treat. I thought you weren't coming till this afternoon.'

'Er, yes,' said James. 'In the end it all fitted in rather well.' The car came out from under the trees and he had to raise his voice above the rattle of hailstones. 'So where would you like to have lunch?'

'Not round here if that's all right. There's nothing worse than going out and then finding lots of other girls with their parents. Particularly in that *dreary* old hotel.' Stephanie had picked up the intonation of the English schoolgirl to such an extent that it almost sounded incongruous when she broke into German with her mother.

He twisted his wrist on the steering wheel to check the time. 'Well, where we go rather depends how much of a hurry everyone's in to eat.' He looked across at Christina. She indicated with a careless, nervous gesture that she did not mind.

'Do you get on well with Sister Bona?' she asked her daughter, turning round as far as the seatbelt would permit. The attempt at conversation was painfully transparent, but Stephanie did not appear to notice.

'Not much. She's such a snob. And she's so disapproving. We call her Sister Crossbones.'

James looked up at the rear-view mirror and grinned. But then, out of the corner of his eye, he noticed Christina's frown, more of unease than disapproval. He remembered her express a fear that Stephanie was becoming cynical, yet he had not really seen enough of her during the past year to judge. At almost every opportunity Christina would take her back to Lotzingen. And to allow mother and daughter as much time together as possible, James usually stayed in London or went down to the cottage to work. He had probably been unnecessarily scrupulous about not coming between them. But then Christina's attitude towards her daughter was always rather defensive. He wondered whether this had anything to do with a lingering fear of Stephanie's father, perhaps even of some genetic legacy.

'I say, James. Have you decided where to take us?' Stephanie asked a few minutes later.

'What's the matter? Are you getting hungry?'

'*Star*ving!'

'It's not far now. I hope it'll be worth the wait.'

'I'm *sure* it will.' The ambiguous emphasis made him glance up into the driving mirror again.

When they had been given the menu, he told Stephanie to choose whatever she wanted since school food couldn't have improved much since his day. Christina eyed him for an instant. He was the one who usually disapproved of restaurants as a waste of money.

Stephanie raised her head, although her eyes were still drawn to the menu. 'James, what were you like at my age?'

'Me? Oh, spotty and awkward, I suppose.' Truth slipping past in the guise of the buffoon, he told himself.

Her mouth pursed in renewed contemplation of the choice. '*Impossible* to imagine now, of course.'

A few moments later she sat up, her decision made. 'You know, those spectacles Mummy made you buy look really rather distinguished. And they *even* manage to go with your standard uniform.' She raised her eyebrows. This time, the parody of her mother's expression of faintly humorous surprise could not be doubted. Christina was right about one thing, he thought. Stephanie certainly had changed.

'What do you mean, my "standard uniform"? I'll have you know that tweed jackets and corduroy trousers are never out of fashion. One's always seeing them in the glossies. Worn, it must be said, by young men who look distinctly ill at ease in the country.'

'Yes, James. But those jackets aren't quite like yours. They're a little newer for a start. And anyway, something that's supposedly never "out of fashion" can hardly be very fashionable in the sense of *à la mode*. Can it?'

'Has everyone chosen?' Christina broke in impatiently. James glanced across at her. She was even more on edge than in the car.

'Hang on, Mummy! A slight problem here. I'm afraid I've just had second thoughts about the fish.' She beamed an apology at the waiter.

19

The wine James ordered arrived with the first course. Christina refused and poured herself some water instead. He reached across, the neck of the bottle poised interrogatively over Stephanie's glass.

'Oh, yes please,' she said. 'By the way, Sister Crossbones was "most disappointed" you didn't manage to come to Mass this morning. I think she's worried for your souls.'

Christina avoided her husband's eyes. 'We could not have got away any earlier than we did.'

'Of course, it's probably a bit late to start worrying about your soul, isn't it, James? I mean you only became a Catholic to marry Mummy.'

'True. But she was certainly worth a Mass. And Paris too, if it had been mine to exchange.' He gave Christina an affectionate grin, but she looked away in discomfort.

Stephanie, who had been buttering her last piece of roll, missed this. 'You know, I never liked Henri of Navarre for changing his religion to become king.' At Easter she had announced her intention to read History at either Oxford or Cambridge. Christina's reaction, he suddenly remembered, had been rather evasive, as if their future in England were undecided. He quickly suppressed such thoughts. 'There were a lot of other things to dislike about Henri IV,' he replied. Then it occurred to him that perhaps Stephanie also considered him a turncoat for accepting a religion of convenience. The apostasy of an agnostic. In spite of his jokes at the time, the paradox had remained vaguely unsettling.

They went on to discuss the Thirty Years' War which she was studying. 'I can't see you getting an exactly objective account from the nuns,' he said as the waiter removed their plates.

'I wonder if your teachers were any better?' she shot back. 'I bet they thought Gustavus Adolphus was a thoroughly good egg.' He conceded the point, then asked if she wanted apple pie or one of the sorbets.

'By the way, James,' said Stephanie. 'There's something I've always wanted to ask you.'

'What's that?'

'You occasionally refer to all the relations as the Procession. Knowing you, it's bound to be some frightfully clever quote.'

'If you really want to know, it comes from Carlyle's description of the Holy Roman Empire: "That Lumbering Procession of heraldry and anachronism miscalled the Holy Roman Empire." But seriously, you must try him some time. Once you get used to his gargantuan sentences, he's great fun, though perhaps in rather an English way. If you like, I'll lend you *Frederick the Great*.'

'If you've got a copy, then yes please. I'd love to try him. Now tell me about the weekend. How was *Tante* Sisi?'

Lifted by the wine and Stephanie's high spirits, he replied without thinking. 'Well, your great-aunt is as amazing as ever and sent you lots of love. And so did Andrea. He, needless to say, was on typical form and wanted to know whether we were all going to stay with him in Greece again this summer.' He reached across to refill her glass. But when he glanced up at Christina, the expression on her half-averted face made him trail off into an awkward silence.

Stephanie at last sensed the tension between them. She looked at her mother with an earnest frown. 'What's the matter, Mummy?'

Christina's smile resembled an unconvincing denial of pain. He saw that she must suspect him of trying to forge an alliance with her daughter. An entente that threatened to encircle her. [*At the time, I thought this was just a defensive reaction on her part, but later I recognized that she had almost certainly been right. Christina possessed a remarkable instinct in that way.*]

When they returned to London at the end of the afternoon, they both felt uneasy, alone together in the house. James tried to pretend that this was little more than the usual flat, Sunday evening sensation on coming back from the country.

While Christina unpacked upstairs, he turned up the central heating, went round switching on lights and carried in logs for a fire in the sitting room; anything to stop the place feeling like a morgue.

After all the years in his scruffy bachelor flat near Notting

Hill Gate, he had never really grown used to this place, a Regency house on Brook Green in Hammersmith. Everything looked so large and smart and professionally done. The expanse of floorboard, polished to an amber glow, was broken with old Turkey rugs. The two large, eighteenth-century landscapes were in simple black frames against the white walls. The furniture, apart from a Biedermeier sofa, was French provincial in that smooth, caramel-coloured fruitwood which begged to be stroked. Curtains and cushions, all in plain cotton, were grey and an attractive dull green.

Except for his study on the top floor and Stephanie's room, Christina's stamp was everywhere. Consciously or not, she had imitated Lotzingen in a number of ways. All they needed, he had once remarked, were a few chamois horns in the hall. But the most important memento, and the one which James would have preferred to do without, was a large, silver-framed photograph of Prince Tassilo, prominently displayed on a writing table. Sometimes he felt the eyes follow him round the room.

Although neither of them was really hungry, Christina made a cheese omelette. They ate carefully in the silence. Even the sound of fork on plate seemed excessive. James felt hurt and alarmed. How could two people survive like this together? They so badly needed to talk, yet she hated any discussion of feelings, and in the confusion of guilt and resentment, almost any remark could be taken the wrong way.

Once they had both finished, he took their plates over to the sink. He disliked the dishwasher. Christina's belief in machines had always struck him as strange in someone so traditional in other ways. He turned round and saw her gazing at the table. Trying to keep a note of truculence out of his voice, he asked if he should sleep in the spare room. Christina, still staring down, shook her head sadly. 'It should be me, if anyone.'

They lay facing outwards. James stared at the shaft of light from a streetlamp. A fatalistic inertia prevented him from getting up to close the curtains properly. He felt drained, yet unable to sleep. He wondered whether his teasing had increased or even become aggressive. He had certainly been suffering from bad moods due to the lack of progress on his book. Evidently, there was a lot he had failed to see – or shut his eyes to for some reason.

In his desperation, a childlike penitence came over him. He longed to be able to turn back the clock. There appeared to be no way of avoiding the disastrous consequences of this obsession. Christina's passionately monogamous nature would compel her to treat everything in apocalyptic terms. And she might well start to burn her boats too soon. That was the most immediate danger.

James felt utterly bewildered. To feel sorry for her only created a perverse frustration. Anger or hatred would have been so much easier. His only straightforward emotion was an empty fear like that sensation of paralysis in a nightmare.

He froze on remembering that they had invited people to dinner the next evening. He raised his head from the pillow. 'Are you awake?' he whispered.

There was a pause. 'Yes, I am,' came the guarded reply.

'What about tomorrow night? All those people we've invited.'

'I know. That's what I was thinking too.'

'Do you want to cancel it? I could always invent an excuse. For example ring round saying you were ill.'

'No,' she said eventually. 'I think we had better leave things as they are.'

'Are you absolutely sure?' He felt her nod. Presumably, she was sick of lies.

A little later, he wanted to ask exactly when she intended to fly back to Austria, but his courage failed.

Part Two

3

The chain of coincidence which brought James to Christina had always been important to his personal mythology. He loved to dramatize in retrospect the improbable circumstances: they confirmed a belief that the marriage was blessed from the start with the vital element of good timing.

James's trip to Paris should have taken place the previous month, but the night before leaving, his flat had been broken into and passport, ticket and money were stolen. A subsequent attempt had been thwarted by a last-minute complication over dates. Eventually installed in a friend's apartment off the rue Jacob, he had sworn to stay in every night writing up notes from his day in the Bibliothèque Nationale. But one evening, an instant of loneliness led to the telephone call which brought him to Andrea's party and Christina.

Although he would not have acknowledged it, James at that time was quietly and indistinctly dejected. His previous book had been a disappointment. The sporadic nights with his girl-friend, an American publisher in London, no longer seemed such an ideal solution, for their affair of convenience had lost its appeal in theory as well as practice. And at thirty-six, he did not have many years left in the category either of young author or of young bachelor.

He had planned to cram his research in Paris into a week, but unable to face another evening alone, he looked up the telephone number of Stefan Valkus – or the Baron de Valkus, as he now called himself with a good deal of licence.

James had met Stefan through his father, a diplomat and soldier of the old school who had escaped to England during the war. Colonel Valkus was put up by James's aunt Margaret, then working for Special Operations Executive at their Baker Street headquarters. Twenty-five years later, he had appeared at Aunt Margaret's funeral to pay his respects. After presenting his condolences to James, her only surviving relative, he recalled her kindness during the war, and insisted that he get in touch when he next came to Paris. Colonel Valkus, a soft-spoken, courteous and utterly honourable old man, could hardly have been less like the son he introduced to James ten years later.

As James waited, partially mesmerized by the ringing tone, he felt a little ashamed of giving in to this sudden, vicarious urge. He had never come across anyone else quite like Stefan Valkus. His cynicism alone was enough to make most people feel they had led an unusually sheltered existence. The only excuse – a shamefully dubious one – for seeing such a character was the vague idea of using him in a novel, yet a faithful portrait would probably sound too appalling to be credible.

Stefan, who greatly exaggerated the family possessions lost to the Communists, had somehow convinced himself that any methods were justified to restore his rightful fortune. In addition to his ruthlessly opportunistic streak, he had a cruel sense of humour. And his views on politics and women were worse than reactionary, although one could never really tell which remark was intended merely to be provocative and which was genuine. They were all delivered with the same hint of malicious satisfaction.

Stefan guessed the reason for the call. 'Lonely in your little garret? *Ah! Comme c'est triste, la vie de bohème!*' He was incapable of limiting any conversation to a single language. This had amused James at first, then irritated him, but now he managed to ignore it.

'*Tu as de la chance,*' Stefan continued. 'There is a party this evening which might possibly be amusing. Come round here later on and we'll go together.'

'But what sort of party is it? And who's giving it?'

'You wouldn't know him. See you at around eight thirty, if you are interested.'

'What should I wear?'

'Oh, it's informal. *Tenue de ville*. A dark suit. *Ciao!*'

His eyes glittering in double-edged humour, Stefan parried James's questions with facetious mimes of mock emotion. Only in the taxi did he reveal the identity of their host.

'Andrea is a Bourbon Valdemar. He still finds his title very useful. In fact he claims to go down on his knees each day to thank the good Lord for providing snobs to keep him *hors de la misère*.'

'I'm glad to know he can make a full-time career of it.'

'You'd be surprised how full! The potential was first revealed to him when some ghastly American widow offered a million dollars – and this was over twenty years ago – in return for a *mariage blanc*. All the old harridan wanted was to become *Son Altesse Royale* and have the coat of arms for her gravestone. But with the pride of youth, Andrea refused.' Stefan flashed a sideways grin. 'Of course, now he says he's never regretted anything so much in his life.'

The apartment was impeccably traditional with Louis XV chairs, parquet floor, a faded Aubusson tapestry and a series of small eighteenth-century portraits. Stefan indicated their host and took James over to meet him.

Andrea, who could have been almost any age, had the rare quality of appearing to be both dignified and irresponsible at the same time. The combination gave him great charm. James could not help wondering how Stefan had become a friend, unless Andrea was another to be intrigued by his devious nature.

Apparently unconcerned at the extra guest, he gave James a drink and took him on a round of introductions. Several of those present belonged to dispossessed dynasties. Alongside their cousin, they appeared a rather humourless lumpen-royalty. A young Orléans Braganza princess, with an almost touching ingenuousness, urged James to visit Brazil as though her family still ruled the country.

Bemused by the unreality of the conversation, he extricated himself to refill his glass. After the atmosphere of the Bibliothèque Nationale and his solitary, studious existence living off sandwiches in the café opposite, this change in surroundings produced a strange sensation. It felt a bit like waking up in a wonderfully implausible dream.

Conscious of how little he had eaten that day, James's attention focused on the cold buffet beautifully displayed on a white damask tablecloth. Laid out alongside were plastic knives and forks and cardboard plates.

Stefan appeared at his shoulder. 'As you can see, Andrea takes great pride in his informality.'

'Where on earth did you disappear to?'

'Just having a private word with someone.'

James refused to react to his smug air of mystery. 'Well, since you're here, you can tell me about that little trio of immaculately groomed men. The ones in dark flannel suits. Are they also part of the family network?'

'No. They're the tame snobs. Property developers for the most part.'

Since Stefan dabbled in that field himself, the temptation to ask which category he belonged to was considerable.

'So how do they fit in?'

'They're the ones who provide Andrea's directorships – "all pay and no work," as he says – in order to have his name on their company stationery. Sometimes, like tonight, he invites them along to rub shoulders with his relatives as a sort of bonus.'

James nodded as if to acknowledge the logic of the arrangement when in fact it revived his Alice in Wonderland feeling. And that was the moment he caught sight of Christina.

She was glancing around with a slightly mystified frown to see who she knew. Somebody greeted her from across the room. The answering smile had an angle of sadness which seemed to contradict her healthy good looks. Tragedy or disillusionment, James instinctively wondered.

When she sensed his gaze, he quickly turned away. A

moment later, he slowly swung back, raising his glass to study her over the rim while pretending to sip. The air of physical well-being could have come from a week in the mountains and yet she did not look the sporting type. The heavy, tawny-gold hair, pinned above the ears with tortoiseshell combs, then falling to her shoulders, hardly gave that impression.

Her colouring and blue eyes had none of that cold Nordic hardness. James was drawn irresistibly by what appeared to be the bodily expression of an essential warmth and innocence. Her skin had the tone of evening sunlight, her flesh an innate cleanliness. She would smell of wild flowers and her mouth would taste cool and pure. The lyrical surge made him laugh at himself. He put it down to the effect of wine on an empty stomach and tried to make his scrutiny more critical.

For someone who looked no more than twenty-seven or so, her clothes were those of a woman at least ten years older. The simple dark green dress had long sleeves and a hem well below the knee. Next to the slinky Balmain or Givenchy creations worn by the tycoons' wives it looked even more old-fashioned.

'She's called Christina von Retzen,' Stefan murmured in his ear. 'Retzen was the name of her Bavarian husband. The title's very recent. Mid-nineteenth century, that sort of thing. She, *par contre*, is Austrian. A Schwanemberg Lotzingen, no less. The youngest daughter of Prince Tassilo. Anyway, husband Georg, you will be encouraged to hear, recently came to an abrupt end. He was flattened inside his Mercedes by a tanker on the autobahn outside Munich. No doubt one full of beer. *Viens, je te présenterai.*'

James, emerging from a daze, felt a wave of irrational panic as they approached. Christina regarded him with a puzzled air as if she had met him before but could not recall the circumstances. Quite plainly, she did not remember Stefan, for when he mentioned meeting at a previous party of Andrea's, she said: '*Ah, oui, mais bien sûr,*' almost certainly none the wiser.

'James is a very famous writer,' Stefan interjected with a parody of unctuousness. 'What was it, the title of your novel?

Something very amusing, I think.' Immoderately pleased with himself, he pretended to recognize somebody across the room, and left them, his '*Ciao*' accompanied by that Italian greeting in which a raised hand is opened and closed like a beak.

She answered James's exasperation with an amused lift to her eyebrows. 'Is he not a friend of yours then?'

'I'm not sure that's the way I'd describe him!'

'So, how did you get to know him?'

'Funnily enough through his father, who could not have been more different. He was a Balkan diplomat whom my aunt took in during the war when he escaped to England.'

'I see. And what is it that you write?'

'Novels usually, but at the moment I'm toying with the idea of a book about the way power and authority have been portrayed in art – literature as well as painting.'

'Where would you research something like that?'

'Well, here in Paris, at the Louvre of course, and right at the moment in the Bibliothèque Nationale. But even though it's an intriguing idea, I'm sure the whole thing's going to prove far too ambitious a project. For a start I'm no art expert.' He shrugged and asked what she enjoyed reading.

Her taste for French and Russian authors rather than German intrigued him. So did her preference for mainly nine-teenth-century passion. She loved Tolstoy, Balzac and Stendhal, and her two favourite books turned out to be *Madame Bovary* and *Le Grand Meaulnes*.

What a contrast, he thought. If not a contradiction. Then he remembered the look of sadness. Perhaps it was tragedy *and* disillusionment. Perhaps, like Emma Bovary, she found life demolishing all those romantic ideas which had appeared so beautiful in books. Yet she spoke with such feeling about the different characters, almost as though they had become intimate acquaintances, that he responded with equal enthusi-asm. And when Andrea came over to urge them to help themselves, James regarded him for a moment with surprise. The conversation had made him forget his hunger completely.

Everyone else was already seated or perched, eating with great caution off the flexible plates. Christina led the way to the buffet, and with a long-suffering smile at her cousin's eccentricity, handed James a plastic knife and fork rolled in a paper napkin. Since there were no chairs available, they remained standing near the table.

James dispatched his food so fast that when he turned back from putting down the plate, he found Christina staring in amazement.

He grinned. 'What's the matter?'

'Do you always eat so quickly?'

'Not always. But still too often, I'm afraid. Yes, I know, it's very bad for me.' He took off his spectacles and began to polish them with a paper napkin. 'What is it now?' he asked, amused at her interest in the operation.

'You have beautiful hands,' she said simply.

He laughed, taken off guard by the compliment. 'You know, I've never really understood why women seem to attach so much importance to a man's hands.'

She coloured slightly. 'Then perhaps you should use your imagination.'

'Ouch! I deserved that.'

'Yes,' she said, then looking round, she caught sight of somebody across the room. 'Ah, there's Fritzi.'

A tall man with light brown hair returned her silent greeting and began to make his way over. He had the angular, elusive look of a Pied Piper.

'So who is Fritzi?'

'Oh, he is another sort of cousin. His name is Friedrich Witzenbach. He works here in Paris for an international body. He's a brilliant economist – some sort of expert on Third World trade, I think.'

Fritzi von Witzenbach's speciality could hardly have been gleaned from his conversation with Christina. Almost immediately, they began to talk of family and friends. With nicknames like Poldi and Loulou, most of them had been to the same wedding in Württemberg or fancy-dress ball at a castle near Salzburg.

Next to them, James saw himself as gauche and provincially English. Theirs was a world in which everyone seemed to move effortlessly between half a dozen cities and almost as many languages. In spite of Christina's lack of guile and artifice, even in spite of her love of books, she would always have far more in common with a cousin like Fritzi. That something so obvious should come as a jolt was unsettling.

Christina's occasional attempts to include him in the conversation and the way they continued to speak English out of politeness made him feel even more of an intruder. Rebelling against his dumb show of interest, James decided on withdrawal. 'Can I get anyone a drink?' he asked.

Christina shook her head and Fritzi followed her refusal. 'I'm only here en route to dinner,' he said, then glanced at his watch. 'In the case of South Americans there is never any point in turning up until about this time.' He made a face of comic suffering. 'I don't suppose we'll sit down to eat for another hour or two.'

'*Poor* Fritzi,' said Christina. 'But if you are going to have such exotic friends, then what do you expect?'

'It certainly wouldn't be your cup of tea, would it, my dear *Aschenbrödel?*'

'I could not stand it!' she laughed and turned to James. 'He calls me Cinderella, because he says I have this reputation . . .'

'Completely deserved!'

'. . . for insisting on early nights.'

'She's famous for it – almost as famous as for her diplomacy. In German, the full medical term is *"Das Aschenbrödel Syndrom"*. Basically it represents a profound urge to be tucked up in one's own little bed before midnight.' He nodded towards the window. 'The pumpkin's probably waiting outside already.' He bent to kiss her goodbye, murmured something in German and chuckled. Then he bowed his head in farewell to James.

When Fritzi moved away, James felt at a loss. He longed to know her well, to be able to tease her too, yet at the same time he instinctively knew that to fall for her in a major way could be disastrous. He looked about the room feeling trapped and again drained his already empty glass. He searched for an excuse to escape. But then he noticed Christina gazing at him thoughtfully.

'Would you tell me about your childhood?' she said.

His astonishment was genuine. 'Why on earth do you want to hear about that?'

'Because it is the most interesting part of anyone's life.' She nodded towards two empty chairs. 'Shall we go and sit down.'

James, whose surprise was compounded by this unexpectedly nannyish streak, insisted on fetching some more wine first. He had no idea where to begin. 'Listen, are you sure about this?' he said, sitting down. 'It's going to be terribly boring for you.'

'Perhaps, but I do not think so. It is probably very Germanic of me to love other people's stories about how they grew up. As you must know, we have an obsession with folk tales.'

He nodded without immediately taking in what she said. He sipped his wine, wondering where to begin. Then he smiled into his glass. Her mention of folk tales had shown the way.

'Once upon a time – that is to say, shortly before the war – there were three sisters: Margaret, Marigold and Mary. In those days people often seemed to go in for naming a series of daughters as though they were a flotilla of corvettes. Although in this case it was perhaps slightly surprising, since the family they came from was an academic one. Anyway, the war was to bring tragedy to all three of them in different ways. The middle one died after a motor accident in 1941 during the blackout. And Margaret, the eldest, lost her husband at Anzio.' James reached down over the arm of the chair to put his wine glass on the floor.

'Margaret coped by working even harder at her job in Special Operations. She was a brisk, sensible person. A bit bossy in that well-meaning English way, but basically very kind. Curiously, the person most affected by the death of her husband was Mary, the youngest, then still at Oxford.'

'Mary was your mother?'

He raised both hands urging patience with a rather priestly gesture. 'Mary was also the prettiest, and probably the most intelligent of the three, even if it was in what Margaret termed "an over-imaginative way". But although greatly indulged as a child by their father, she was far from being spoilt or self-absorbed. In fact, as her reaction showed, she had this urge to take on other people's unhappiness.

'Almost without warning, she decided to leave Oxford to volunteer as a nurse. Margaret tried to persuade her to stay for her degree, but Mary's mind was made up. A year later, early in 1945, she met her future husband, Major Reginald Gaunt, at a base hospital in Belgium. He was one of her patients, though what he was suffering from, I never discovered. Probably a very minor complaint.' Christina glanced up with a puzzled frown, then returned to staring at his knees.

'Margaret was uneasy as soon as she heard of the engagement. She tried to put it down to a prejudice against the name Reginald and the difference in their ages. But when she invited them to supper at her little house in Chelsea, Reginald sent Mary on ahead and turned up late with a pretty condescending apology.' Andrea came over to see if they wanted more food, but Christina virtually waved him away.

'That evening, Margaret tried once again to persuade her sister to return to Oxford to finish her degree. But it was no good. Mary turned down the idea in her sweet, rather dreamy way, saying all she wanted now was to devote herself entirely to Reginald. And he just filled his pipe and nodded in approval.'

'How many years older than Mary was he?'

'Fourteen. Although it wasn't so much a problem of age but of mentality. In his case, a frightful combination of being old before his time while at heart remaining a spoilt little boy. Well, the wedding took place a week after the 1945 General Election which unseated Churchill. What with rationing and all the shortages, the reception could hardly be a very lavish affair. But apparently the whole thing was a nightmare. A series of embarrassed silences, usually filled with a crashing platitude from Reginald.'

'But why did Mary marry such a man?'

'Her sister, Margaret, always thought it was another perverse attempt to shoulder other people's emotional burdens.'

'And what do you think?'

'It's not very easy for me to judge. You see, I never knew her. She died giving birth to me.'

Christina took a moment to digest this. 'But then who looked after you?' she asked uncertainly. 'Your father?' His description of Reginald Gaunt had confused her.

' "Looked after"?' He made a dubious face. 'I'm not sure if you can call it that. My father never took the slightest interest. It was a strange childhood to say the least.' And he described Norfield for her in all its gloom.

'My mother, during her short time there, can't have been allowed to change a thing or spend any money. Not only was it very ugly, but the house had no central heating. My father subscribed to that curious English fallacy that discomfort was somehow morally superior. "Pampering", as he called it, smacked of something dubiously foreign, if not pansy. He was, needless to say, a complete philistine.'

Christina cocked her head sceptically. 'Was your father really as bad as you make him out to be?'

James looked straight at her. 'Yes, he most certainly was. He behaved as if my mother's death had given him a licence for unlimited self-pity. Once, I even heard him complain about the inconvenience of being left on his own with a child. Not that he ever lifted a finger. I was looked after entirely by Mrs Harding, our housekeeper, and her daughter Betty who used to read me stories at bedtime.'

'And did you fall in love with Betty?' she asked.

'Oh, passionately! At the age of six or seven, I asked if I could give her a bath for a change. "Ooh, you little monkey!" was her reply. But then came the saddest day of my life. Betty told me she was going to marry and live in Sheffield. It felt like the worst betrayal and desertion I could possibly imagine. My tears were boiling hot.' He smiled quickly. 'But what about you? Did you go through such powerful emotions when you were a child?'

'Perhaps. But I do not have such a good memory as you.' To his surprise, she looked away as if slightly disconcerted.

'Where was I?' he said. 'Oh, yes. Well, I used to spend part of each school holiday with Aunt Margaret, either in London or at her little cottage in Sussex, all of which involved an incredibly complicated to-ing and fro-ing by train. Having never had any children of her own, Aunt Margaret wasn't very good with them.'

'Was this the aunt who took in the father of that man just now? I have forgotten his name.'

'Stefan Valkus. Yes, that's right.'

'But what I would like to know is whether you managed to discover anything of your mother's life in this house you described.'

'Only a few tantalizing fragments. Just after I had gone up to university, Aunt Margaret was told she had cancer. I used to visit her in the Royal Marsden whenever I could. And on one of these visits, she suddenly remembered that my mother had once said something about attempting a novel.

'Not surprisingly, there wasn't a trace of it at Norfield. I'd already discovered from Mrs Harding that my father had got the gardener to burn all her papers and letters. I don't think he even went through them first. But in a room over the garage, there were two tea chests of books which I had just rummaged in before.

'The only one of real interest was an edition of Rilke's poems with her maiden name and the date May 1944 in pencil on the flyleaf. It fell open automatically at *The Song of Love and Death of the Cornet Christopher Rilke*. You probably know it – the one in which Rilke makes an ancestral hero out of a cavalry officer who died fighting the Turks.'

'It was my favourite poem at school.'

'Well then, you'll know what I mean by its romantic intensity. Anyway, for a start it was unusual that she should have been drawn to a German poem during the war, above all just after the death of her brother-in-law. But then I started to wonder whether she might have taken some of Rilke's ideas almost literally. All this probably sounds a bit far-fetched ...'

'Go on.'

'There were two really: that you carry your death within yourself, and that poetry and real life must be intertwined.'

Christina considered this for a moment. 'So what exactly is it, you think? That she may have thought of death as the greatest expression of self-sacrifice?' She made a doubtful face.

'It is of course possible. But if you are trying to link it to her own experience, then I would think it very unlikely. I cannot imagine any woman *wanting* to die in childbirth.'

'Perhaps not. Obviously I wouldn't know, and anyway, I'm only guessing in the dark about all of this. But I can't help thinking that in a peculiar way, she was born twenty-five years too late. She somehow seemed to belong more to that generation carried away in 1914 when poems about sacrifice and cavalry officers had such an effect.

'Just one other thing. At university, I read more of Rilke's work, and I couldn't help being struck by another saying of his – I can't now remember where from – that "the woman who loves, always transcends the man she loves, because life is greater than fate." I've never been able to decide whether that's romantic bosh or not, but I'm sure my mother believed it.' He noticed her faraway expression. 'What are you thinking?'

She looked at him without really registering, then across the room. 'Oh, it is nothing. The quote, by the way, comes in his novel, *The Notebooks of Malte Laurids Brigge*.'

James was impressed. 'So it does,' he said. 'It's such a long time since I read it.'

'Come on,' she said. 'Let's get some of that strawberry tart before it disappears.'

Once everybody had finished eating, Andrea came round holding open a black dustbin liner for the paper plates and napkins. 'It's the servants' day off!' he announced with cherubic glee.

An elderly French princess, uncertain how to react to such strange behaviour, kept repeating: '*Comme c'est original! Comme c'est amusant!*'

Christina began to grow restless. 'Yes,' James agreed, longing to be alone with her. 'I think it's time to be making a move.'

'Where has Andrea got to now?' she said, her neck extended as she looked round for him. He was tempted by an urge to kiss her throat. He pictured her twisting away with an embarrassed laugh.

'He's over there,' he said, surprised at himself, and above all at the complete reversal of his mood since Fritzi's departure. 'By the way, have you got your own transport?'

'Yes,' she said. 'My feet. It is not far to go and I love walking at night.'

'May I volunteer as bodyguard?'

'You make it sound like Paris in the time of Richelieu.'

During Christina's goodbye to Andrea on the landing, James held open the door of the old-fashioned lift cage. He was unsure how to react to their host's air of secret amusement. Luckily, Christina did not seem to have noticed.

Outside, the streets glistened. It must have rained heavily during the party. James inhaled the fresh, damp air and then breathed out. Twisting round for a couple of paces, he looked up at the apartment they had just left and thought how difficult it was to imagine from below.

As they walked along the deserted streets, their steps measured an agreeable, echoing rhythm. He regretted having done too much of the talking. Unfortunately, it was nothing new, but at the same time she had not exactly been forthcoming about herself.

'Have you any children?' he asked. Christina had stopped to peer in at the window of an antique shop. She nodded, her head at an angle as if her thoughts were elsewhere. They walked on a little, then she told him of her husband's death and her daughter Stephanie. James could hardly believe she had a child of thirteen. Evidently she was used to such a reaction. She said she was almost thirty-two.

They eventually came to a halt in front of a *porte cochère* in the rue de l'Université. 'But you haven't told me what you're doing here in Paris,' he said. 'I mean, are you here for a special reason?'

'Special? No. Mainly to see a few friends. And also to visit some exhibitions.'

'The exhibition part sounds exactly what I need. Could I join you for tomorrow's programme?'

'Don't you want to know what it consists of first?'

'I don't think I'll be disappointed whatever it turns out to be.'

She glanced at him defensively, then considered for a moment. 'All right. Do you have something to write with? I'll give you the telephone number here and we can arrange In the morning when and where to meet.' Having noted it down, he put a hand on her shoulder and leaned forward to kiss her goodnight slowly on both cheeks.

The heavy door closed behind her with the buzz and click of an automated lock. He continued to stare at it for a little while, then, still in a slight trance, he wandered by instinct towards the river. He felt a calm, glorious sense of weightlessness. Inflating his chest with a deep breath of night air, he gazed across the black, gleaming river to the lights along the far embankment. His heart seemed to swell in magnanimous pity for those millions asleep in the stone-clad buildings all around. Oh, the infernal arrogance of love! he thought, no less pleased with himself, and finally turned for home.

With tired legs he plodded up the stairs to the apartment. Five flights. The same number as to the room Malte Laurids Brigge rented in the rue Toullier. James grunted at the utterly irrelevant details that tended to stick in his mind.

Inside the door, he fumbled for the switch. The low table lamps cast strange upward shadows and circles of light on the ceiling. He lit a cigarette, and smoking with an unhurried rhythm, studied himself in the looking-glass over the chimneypiece. He removed his spectacles and went closer.

As a child, he used to pass long spells hypnotized by himself. This lonely narcissism had given birth to an identical twin whom he called David. He had soon come to believe that David really existed somewhere in the world. There were stories of twins split up at birth. His father – their father – could well have had his reasons for keeping them apart.

Only once did any hint of this private world slip out. He had been seated at the kitchen table in pyjamas and prickly dressing gown, hair brushed and parted, waiting for his supper from Mrs Harding. But it was Betty who handed him his poached egg on toast. 'Look!' she said. 'You've got a double yolker.'

The question blurted out of its own accord: 'Was that what happened to me?' The two women stared at him in a strange way. 'What on earth do you mean, young man?' demanded Mrs Harding.

His face felt as though it were on fire. 'Did *I* have a twin? A brother just like me?' The note of desperation halted her in the middle of drying her hands on a tea towel. She looked sharply at her daughter, who made a face of bafflement, then back at James. 'Now, whatever put such daft ideas into your head?' She knew all right. The way she'd glanced at Betty was accusing. She suspected her of having told him something she shouldn't. 'Eat up your egg, young man, before it gets cold!' she ordered. But, pushing the plate away in revulsion, he had run sobbing from the room.

The unexpected memory made him squirm inside. It brought back the fantasies of a 'real' father, grand and charismatic, coming to take him away from his dismal imprisonment at Norfield.

He crushed out the cigarette. Taken unawares by a yawn, he rubbed his eyes, then blinked at his watch. Time for bed and dreaming of Christina. He would ring her first thing in the morning before she could go out.

❧ 4 ❧

During the remainder of that week in Paris, James did little work. Every possible moment was spent with Christina, and when apart, he could not stop thinking about her. By the end, it felt as if he had seen more museums and galleries in three days than in the whole of his life. He knew she had to return to Munich, but only on their last day together did she tell him it was to prepare Stephanie for school in England. This was the point from which he really began to believe that fate, or its subsidiary, good timing, was at last on his side.

Ten days later he was at Claridge's, waiting for them down-stairs. The lift door opened and suddenly they were coming towards him. Christina leaned forward to kiss on both sides. At the last moment, he became confused. Mid-air collision was just avoided. Then she turned to introduce Stephanie who, to James's astonishment, dropped a curtsey. Instead of bothering with German-language cassettes, it almost felt as if he should have been practising heelclicks and *Handkuss*.

To describe the thirteen-year-old Stephanie as a serious child bordered on understatement. Her eyes were distrustful, and her expression disturbingly adult. Her father's death must have marked her.

'So, what would you like to eat?' he asked. Stephanie gave a little shrug to indicate that she did not mind. He could not imagine her going in for any coy shoulder-swinging. 'Italian? Chinese? French? Hamburgers? Or boring old English to get you used to school food?' James warned himself against slipping into the favourite uncle role.

'Hamburgers, please.'

43

[In those days, Stephanie's accent was unmistakably German, and there wasn't the slightest sign of her talent for mimicry which emerged later.]

He turned to Christina. 'Why not?' she said with a laugh of nervous release. Outside, James led them to his old Fiat whose rust and dents were accentuated by the Daimler limousine parked next to it. After a dubious look from Stephanie, they piled in.

Stephanie's presence inevitably made that intimacy from Paris difficult to resurrect. This was, after all, her evening, James reminded himself. But his attempts at conversation met with monosyllabic answers, and soon he was down to a routine of likes and dislikes. He regretted the laugh that had slipped out at her curtsey, but to apologize now would only make things worse. In any case, there was one thing she had to learn sooner rather than later – grown-ups were a callous, badly brought-up lot, and in England you simply couldn't go round startling people like that.

Mother and daughter spent most of the next two days in department stores and school outfitters, then James took them round sightseeing. Christina wanted Stephanie to see the National Gallery, the Tate and the Wallace Collection. He considered that a little tough at her age, but told himself not to interfere. She obviously had a streak of Teutonic thoroughness when it came to her daughter's education. At first he thought it a bit like a peasant insisting that his son make full use of opportunities he himself had never known. But on reflection the parallel did not ring true. She was trying too hard, probably afraid of not bringing Stephanie up properly.

On the first day of the summer term, James drove them down to Ascot. Stephanie sat silently in the back.

'How are you feeling?' he asked over his shoulder. She shrugged and returned to staring out at the motorway land-scape. 'I can still remember,' he said, inexplicably compelled to go on, 'how frightened I always was of being late, or of breaking rules out of ignorance. But I'm sure girls' schools are much more relaxed.' Their eyes met in the rear-view mirror. She regarded him for a moment, then looked out of the window again.

When they emerged from the trees, James had his first view of the convent. Being the first day of term, the rhododendron-lined drive and forecourt had the air of a point-to-point, only with school trunks unloaded from the large estate cars instead of picnic hampers. Groups of parents stood chatting with stiff-shouldered daughters at their side, and nuns moved amongst them, conspicuous as policemen. Having carried Stephanie's newly acquired impedimenta to the door and wished her luck, James returned to the car and his book to spare Christina any speculative glances.

He was determined that she should not feel under pressure. Often in the past he had spoiled things because desire could feel so certain while emotions remained confused. This time there was an even greater need for caution. Christina had still not recovered from the shock of her husband's death and plainly did not know what to do with her life. But self-restraint was becoming increasingly difficult. Even in galleries in Paris while she gazed at a painting, her head on one side, then leaning forward to study a detail, he had suffered an over-whelming desire to embrace and nuzzle her all over.

The book he had brought, Turgenev's *Fathers and Children*, had long been a favourite: at university, he used to fancy himself as Bazarov. Soon carried away by the familiar story and characters, he became oblivious to time and place.

Nearly an hour later, the sudden opening of the passenger door startled him. Christina climbed in quickly and burst into a jumbled explanation as to why she had been so long.

'Don't worry,' he said. 'I've been perfectly happy.' But the distraught apology started again. 'Hey!' he broke in, uncertain what could have upset her so much. 'I *wanted* to bring you both down. I knew I'd have a longish wait and I don't regret the outing one little bit, because I happen to enjoy being with you.'

She was now gulping for breath, but the worst appeared to

be over. 'What's the matter?' he asked. 'What is it that's upset you so much?'

'Please,' she said, stiff with distress and embarrassment. 'Please, pay no attention. I am sorry. I will be all right in a moment.' He started the engine and drove off slowly with sideways glances. Was it just sadness at leaving a child at a new school? Or did she suffer from some tortuous sense of guilt? At the end of the drive, she wound down the window and breathed deeply. He continued to watch her out of the corner of his eye. Strands of her hair began to dance in the breeze as the car picked up speed. She raised a hand to disengage one from across her face. A moment later, she forced a smile to show she had recovered. Not entirely reassured, he thought it better to drive on in silence.

She finally spoke after several miles on the main road. 'I was very silly back there. I want to apologize. I don't know what came over me.'

'Now, listen. If anyone's to apologize, it's me. So please, let's leave it there. I just wanted you to know for absolute certain that being with you is far from a burden. In fact by now you should damn well know *how* far!'

His words produced another look of grateful scepticism. In an instant he forgot what she had just gone through. And without checking for traffic behind, he braked and pulled off the road. The car bounced up onto the grass verge, making their heads nearly hit the roof.

'What is wrong?' she asked when they came to a halt.

He switched off the engine and turned to face her. 'Listen, what I said just then was *not* part of a Let's-be-nice-to-Christina campaign, but a fairly clear way of expressing what I feel about you. In Paris you always turned the mood away if it ever looked like becoming intimate. Obviously, I can understand a certain amount of defensiveness. But on the other hand it might help if you were to trust me a bit and tell me something of yourself.' Somehow this all sounded wrong. He stopped and grinned lamely. 'Things would be a great deal easier if I didn't want to kiss you so much.'

[I am not entirely sure about Flaubert's 'lengthened perspective

of memory'. My memories, I regret to say, tend to lapse pretty quickly into cinematic cliché. Her eyes open and enormous in close-up, lips at first closed, then parting. A surge of exultation . . .]

Confused by the unexpectedness of those moments, they regarded each other with a certain bemusement. Gradually, they became aware of their surroundings. Vehicles whizzing past, then the airblast of a juggernaut powerful enough to rock the car on its suspension. 'So that's what they mean about the earth moving,' said James before he could stop himself.

Christina frowned and turned to stare forward through the windscreen as if miles away. He leaned over to kiss her ear, hoping to efface the stupid comment. A rueful twitch of the mouth was her only response.

'What a *bloody* idiot I am!' he muttered. She gave a sad smile. The signal to drive on.

His despondency must have touched her in the end. At a traffic light on the Cromwell Road, she reached over to push back his hair. His face lit up.

She shook her head in wonder. 'Is it really so easy to make you happy? It's like pressing a button.'

'If it's you forgiving me . . . then yes!'

After a few seconds' thought, she sighed. 'But James, I've got to go back. First to Lotzingen, and then to Munich.'

'When do you have to leave?'

'I'm booked on the early flight the day after tomorrow.'

'You know,' he said. 'I've always wanted to see Austria. But never so much as now.'

❧ 5 ❧

To find himself on the British Airways flight to Vienna, wings glinting in an Ektachrome sky and Christina dozing beside him, seemed little more than an extension of his most optimistic daydreams. That remark about visiting Austria had proved to be one of those gambles which only came off against expectation. [*For once it even looked as if my fantasies weren't going to prove a self-thwarting prophecy.*]

Perhaps the sensation of unreality had something to do with the altitude. Idly he watched two stewardesses manoeuvre the breakfast trolley out into the aisle. Table trays snapped open like the beaks of baby birds. Perhaps it all boiled down to oral fixation. How depressing, he told himself, too elated to take anything seriously.

When the wheels hit the runway and the engines roared in reverse, the fact of arrival in a foreign land seemed rather abstract. His picture of Vienna was a bizarre mixture of the Schönbrunn Palace, art nouveau, Harry Lime, coffee shops and banks.

Once the aircraft doors were open, everything began to happen too fast to take in properly. The mechanical farewell smiles of the air hostesses, then long corridors of tinted glass, passport control, luggage carousels and a rapid advance through customs.

James, who was pushing the trolley with their bags, emerged from his reverie. 'Hang on. I must change some money.'

'But you will not need any, at least for the moment.' Christina found it hard to conceal her impatience. 'And besides, I can exchange you pounds into schillings whenever you want.'

The offer made obvious sense, but did not reassure him. To restrain her generosity had already been a struggle both in Paris and London. On home ground it would be virtually impossible. 'Sorry, I'm feeling obstinate,' he said. 'It won't take long.'

Outside, Christina led him straight past the rank of Mercedes taxis. The brilliant sunshine made him sneeze. *'Gesundheit!'* she said with the reflex of an otherwise preoccupied mother. For a moment he could have been Stephanie. 'Thank you,' he replied drily, but she failed to notice. Her thoughts were no doubt fixed on their destination.

As they approached an old but well-preserved estate car, a man sprang out to take their bags from the trolley. James's battered old suitcase was at least twice the size of Christina's soft leather grip. Indecision over what to bring made it look as though he intended to stay for weeks.

After a brief exchange in German with the man who had brought the car, she indicated the passenger side to James and took the wheel herself. Intrigued by the administrative details, he watched her put on her tortoiseshell sunglasses, start the engine and wind down the window to wave her thanks as they drove off. They did not go into the centre of Vienna, but cut across to the Wiener–Neustadt autobahn. Christina's concentration was undivided for the first half an hour. She might have been alone in the car.

'You certainly don't hang about,' he remarked. She glanced across, but then relaxed. 'Sorry. I am always a little tense when travelling. That is why I feel I have to be at the airport in plenty of time.'

'I had noticed,' he said. 'This morning must have been the earliest I've ever arrived for check-in. By the way, how far is Graz?'

'About two hundred kilometres, but we're not taking that road.' He nodded, although still not sure where Lotzingen was. She had told him the name of the nearest town, but there did not appear to be a map in the car.

As they left the industrial landscape around Wiener Neustadt and began to rise into the mountains, James was more than content looking out at the neat, prosperous fields with their wooden huts and haymaking frames stacked ready, and at the Alpine houses hunched under tortoise-shaped roofs. Watching over each community was a creamy yellow church tower, its baroque cupola like a chesspiece. Yet sadly, in this increasingly beautiful scenery of pines as tall as ships' masts, and mountain ranges receding distantly in paler tones, the most conspicuous landmarks were the Aral service stations in bright plastic blue.

After they had been driving for over two hours, the first twinge of hunger prompted James to glance at his watch. Twenty-five to twelve, English time. He wound on an hour. Having left the main road a long way behind, he felt it couldn't be much further. They were in a wide, ascending valley free of pylons or any other reminder of modern ugliness. Cloud shadows raced along, and the dark forest on the higher slopes contrasted with the nascent green of the meadows. Ahead, the snow-capped mountains acted as a reminder of how fast the seasons changed.

They passed a granite rockface with a ragged waterfall. Like a broken gutter in a cloudburst, he thought, enjoying the prosaic comparison. He looked across at Christina. She was craning forward over the steering wheel. 'There it is!' She signalled with her head. 'Lotzingen.'

His first sight was a heavy square tower capped with a pyramidal roof, rather like the castle of Vaduz in Lichtenstein. Situated on a grassy spur emerging from the mountain forest above, it looked far more solid and medieval than he had expected. He could imagine the cold, ancient smells inside of stone and iron and petrified wood.

But as they continued along the road on the other side of the valley their angle of vision broadened, bringing the main part of Lotzingen into view. Separated from the old tower by an open-ended courtyard was a large eighteenth-century baroque schloss in apricot stucco with stone quoins and elaborate hood-moulds.

The effect on Christina was captivating. Her excitement conjured up a picture of arrivals home from school nearly twenty years before. Such an emotional bond with her *Heimat* struck him as more Slavic than Teutonic. Influenced no doubt by the cupolas of the churches, the idea brought on an almost vertiginous sense of vastness – Austria, Hungary, the Carpathian mountains, and then the Russian steppes, for thousands and thousands of miles.

'I'm longing for my guided tour,' he said.

'This afternoon, I promise.'

'Of course, but just give me a rough idea of its history. For example, how old is the tower?'

'The first castle on the site was built around 1180 during the reign of Ottakar IV of Styria, but that was destroyed by the Hungarians less than a century later. The tower is early fifteenth century, and it held out against a Turkish force during Suleiman the Magnificent's invasion in 1530.'

'What's it used for now? I presume nobody lives in it.'

'No. We use it only for special family occasions like wedding celebrations. They take place in what is known as the Great Hunting Hall. As you might imagine from the name, the walls are covered in antlers.'

James smiled to himself as an image flashed through his mind of *schlager*-scarred huntsmen drinking toasts in a confusion of baying dogs.

They drove into the main courtyard, a cobbled rectangle with what looked like a chapel at the far end. Christina drew up by a short flight of steps and James got out, stretched and looked around, squinting against the glare. A magnificent baroque archway led to another interior courtyard with round arched loggias on three floors. He had forgotten the extent of Italian influence. The result – a Germanic north subverted by the south – had probably been one of the first elements in Austria's schizophrenia.

An elderly manservant in a collarless jacket of grey loden with horn buttons came out to fetch the cases. Christina greeted him gaily – he was called Josef – and introduced James.

Inside, a fat grey-muzzled old labrador waggled up to her. She crouched to ruffle its neck with both hands. When it tried to lick her face, she arched back out of range, then grinned up at James even more like a girl home for the holidays. Intended or not, one thing was clear from her expression. Nobody could know her properly without having seen her here. A corollary was also easy to imagine. She could only know someone by their reaction to this place.

James gazed up and around. On the immense white walls hung dark portraits and ranks of chamois horns mounted on plaques of polished wood. There were enough to make him wonder what the Hunting Hall must be like. Inside the entrance, pairs of rubber boots in different sizes were lined up on the flagstoned floor and firewood was neatly stacked beside a huge tiled stove. The mixture of grandeur and rustic simplicity was rather beguiling.

Footsteps made him turn. In spite of no immediate resemblance, the old man's identity was plain even before she cried 'Papa!' Prince Tassilo with his close-cropped grey hair, Edwardian moustache and Norfolk jacket might have come straight from a sepia photograph at the time of Franz Josef. James calculated that he could have been a page at court when the telegram arrived from Sarajevo.

After Christina's hug, he examined James, then stuck out a huge hand, veined, mottled and with the blunt fingers of a peasant. 'Welcome,' he said. No words were wasted in pleasantries about their journey. He looked down at Christina. 'Would your friend like to wash before lunch?'

Her arm through her father's, Christina squeezed hard. 'His name is *James*, Papa.'

'Oh, am I allowed to call him that too?'

'Of course,' James laughed.

'I'm just going to say hello to Mama,' Christina put in. 'I'll take you along to meet her later.' Considering her family's importance in her life, she had revealed surprisingly little about them. James had only guessed her mother to be bedridden from a chance remark.

After showing James the cloakroom, Prince Tassilo led the way to a sitting room lined with bookcases. Although fairly dark, it had a cheerful, well lived-in feel. Glancing out of the corner of his eye at the framed photographs on a side table,

James crossed to one of the windows. The view down the valley was magnificent.

'One could never become indifferent to such a sight,' he said.

Prince Tassilo regarded him speculatively for a moment, then nodded. 'Yes. It is beautiful.' He could have been talking of a picture that had always belonged to his family.

'But what about the snow. Are you cut off for long?'

'Very seldom, even though it can in parts be several metres deep. But then here we are used to it.'

'Well yes, of course. Meanwhile in England, a couple of inches brings the whole country to a halt.'

Christina came in followed by a weak-faced young man with thin, colourless hair. 'My cousin Heinrich,' she said introducing him, 'but we all call him Bong.' James could not get over the way her relatives seemed to have nicknames straight out of a tennis club in the Twenties.

The majordomo stepped inside the door to announce lunch with a wordless inclination of the head. Prince Tassilo led the way, first into the hall, then through a succession of unheated staterooms where much of the furniture was covered with dustsheets. Their footsteps on the parquet echoed like a diplomatic mission from long ago.

As they took their places in the grey and gilt panelled dining room, James ran an eye over the portraits. Opposite hung the profile of a sixteenth-century cardinal with the hooded eyes of an inquisitor. Christina noticed the direction of his gaze. 'I hope he doesn't put you off your food.' Her laugh had a faintly nervous edge. 'He always used to terrify me as a child.'

James smiled automatically and unfolded his napkin. The sight of Christina on her father's right renewed his speculation about the family. Were her middle-aged brothers and sisters jealous or indulgent towards the youngest and evidently favourite child? Tenuous comparisons ran through his mind from the prodigal's return to *King Lear*. The image of Christina as Cordelia was inspired by a suspicion that she possessed the same perilous combination – an acute sensitivity with astonishing lapses of perception.

The simple and perfectly cooked food came from their farms.

Offered wine by Josef, James accepted only to see the others take water. Everyone spoke in English as if it were their usual practice.

Conversation began with the recent spate of avalanches which had led to the death of three skiers at the resort beyond the mountains. Then Christina, after a hurried glance in James's direction, mentioned the strike in England.

Prince Tassilo mopped his mouth and cleared his throat in a rumbling preparation. 'Perhaps you as an Englishman can explain to me one thing about all these strikes in your country. It is a question to which I have never yet received a satisfactory answer. How did it come about that such a great nation could decline so fast?'

While puzzled at the way Christina had trailed the question, James sighed inwardly. The old man evidently clung to a vision of the England of his youth. A country of cheering crowds at coronations, dedicated craftsmen like tailors and gunmakers, well-drilled servants and cheerful beaters on shoots. A golden age which existed mainly in the memory of its beneficiaries. The idea of discussing the latest strike – what some commentators already called the death throes of the labour movement – felt more than ironic in such a setting. The alarm and horror of revolution expressed at this table in 1848 and again in November 1918 was not hard to imagine. Yet now it looked as if the political process had gone into reverse.

James gazed for a moment at his glass, then raised his head. 'Britain's decline hasn't been particularly rapid, if you consider that it began over a hundred years ago. Most historians point to the way the Victorian middle class wanted to ape the aristocracy. Nobody loved a lord more than the British merchant. And his wife usually persuaded him to let their sons acquire the tastes of gentlemen, instead of putting them on the shop floor to learn the business.'

Prince Tassilo pushed up at his moustache with the knuckle of an index finger. 'Would things then have been very different if there had been a revolution in Britain, like in the other countries of Europe?'

'Well, yes. Almost inevitably. But it's still very difficult to imagine a swarm of *sans-culottes* trampling over the flowerbeds of Buckingham Palace. Britain, after all, became the despair of Karl Marx – the only country where the working class was as bourgeois as the monarchy.'

Prince Tassilo grunted noncommittally. He straightened the fruit knife beside his plate, then looked up. 'And so now I suppose you would say it is the only country in which the workers as well as the middle class have acquired the vices of the aristocracy.'

James's mouth twisted in acknowledgement. 'That's certainly one way of putting it. In any case, it's the middle classes who bear most responsibility for perpetuating that ghastly petty snobbery which has been England's real curse.'

Prince Tassilo made no comment and began to dissect the fruit on his plate.

'But James,' Christina said suddenly, 'how *did* England escape a revolution?'

Suspecting a greater interest in keeping up the exchange than in his answer, and aware that his account was beginning to sound like a tutorial, James answered with reluctance. 'Basically because the British establishment managed to absorb most of its opponents. And on critical issues, like the Great Reform Bill, the threat of serious rioting made enough of the diehards recognize the path of self-interest pretty smartly. There just wasn't the same rigid immobility, even ossification, which led to the collapse of *anciens régimes* elsewhere.' Wary of straying into any more contentious areas, and also noticing that the others had finished, he quickly tackled his apple.

The moment the last segment disappeared into his mouth, Prince Tassilo raised his crystal goblet for a final gulp of water, then brought up his napkin for a double wipe at his moustache. They were on their feet before James identified it as the signal to move.

By the time they reached the sitting room Bong had disappeared, and as soon as Christina had poured coffee for the two men, she murmured something about sorting through a cupboard of Stephanie's clothes and left them. James, uncertain what was expected of him, took the chair opposite her father.

The old man gazed out of the window and began to talk of cows. But his discourse was to recount how a study of old landscape paintings indicated that the breed of red cattle known in southern Europe since pre-Roman times had died out in the late sixteenth century. It sounded as if this might have been his own project.

From paintings, he moved on to patronage of the arts and the greatness of Lorenzo the Magnificent. In his view, the major advances in civilization followed a freshening of the genetic pool by barbarian invasion. James, a little taken aback, felt tempted to ask if he would therefore welcome a Russian surge across the Elbe.

Prince Tassilo's theories appeared to come from farmyard observation. He disapproved of artificial insemination on the grounds that animals produced that way lacked stamina and courage. James could not resist wondering whether he saw the aristocracy as the human equivalent of prize bulls – there to improve the strain. At any rate, he thought, it would have been a more down-to-earth rationale for the *jus primae noctis*, or *droit de cuissage* as the French put it in their more graphic fashion.

The ancient telephone on the table began to ring in a jerky, hand-cranked tinkle. The Prince picked up the receiver with a curt apology. Christina, in one of her rare descriptions of family life, had mentioned that the castle's antiquated exchange was a standing joke. Her eldest brother, Eberhard, who owned an electronics company, had tried in vain to persuade their father to accept the latest system. Eberhard, James decided after another glance at the framed photographs, must be the tall, slightly flabby one. A high forehead and large spectacles gave him an owl-like appearance.

'Regrettably, I must leave you,' said Prince Tassilo after finishing the call. 'There is a matter I have to attend to. But first of all I will find my daughter for you.'

Christina was in an uncharacteristically skittish mood when she showed James his room. He sensed she was longing to ask how he had got on. After going to the window to look down the valley, he wandered round peering at the old prints and small oil paintings. He then opened the enormous wardrobe. The smell of mothballs joined that of beeswax.

He closed it and gazed at the bed. 'The furniture's so gigantic that if I wake up in the middle of the night, I'm going to feel I've shrunk.' He turned to her. 'Tell me, when you were a child, just as you fell asleep, did you get that sensation of finally becoming the right size in comparison to your surroundings? When nothing seemed claustrophobic or overpowering any more?'

'No,' she laughed. 'But then I don't remember much. Only of being frightened of the dark.'

'Well, I suppose a child brought up in a castle is bound to think of ghost stories.'

'No, that is not necessarily true. When you grow up in a place like this, you are used to it as your home. As a child you do not think it very special, because you do not at first know the difference. Come. I will show you my room. It is the same one I had when little. It isn't in the least frightening.'

As James followed her, a rush of male optimism made him wonder whether he might be taking the same route late that night. He even took note of the way. The idea of bursting in on her mother by mistake was too frightful to contemplate. Almost as bad as Guizot, lost in the corridors of Windsor Castle, trying a door and finding himself face to face with Queen Victoria in her underwear.

Christina's room was indeed cheerful with its smooth fruit-wood furniture. The sunlight poured in through the window at the far end and the counterpane on the simple four-poster bed had a freshly ironed whiteness.

'So what do you think?'

'It's a lovely room,' he answered looking around, then tilted his head to run an eye along her bookshelf.

'Do you always check on what people read?'

'Sorry.' He gave her a shamefaced grin and pushed his spectacles back into place. 'It's compulsive.'

'Do you really judge people by their books?'

'Oh, no. That would be very dangerous. But it can often tell you quite a bit about somebody. The best thing is when you discover you've got some obscure interest in common.'

She nodded thoughtfully and turned away to look out of the window. He realized that the libidinous speculation in his mind had vanished. Did that have something to do with the room's neat and virginal aspect? The contrast with the perfumed squalor of so many beautiful women was striking; he had never quite understood why they of all people should have a sluttish streak. But as far as Christina and his hopes for that night were concerned, it certainly looked as if he had misread the signals. He glanced regretfully at the bed.

On the side table in a leather frame was the photograph of a startlingly good-looking man. 'Was that your husband?'

She swung round and he pointed to it. 'Oh, no,' she laughed quickly. 'That's Alexander, my playboy brother. But he's getting a bit old for the parties. Come on! Let's go down. Mama should be awake by now.'

The meeting with her mother was little more than a token audience. The old Princess Schwanemberg lay propped on a landslide of pillows, her long white hair brushed out like in the deathbed scene of a nineteenth-century tableau. Christina did not appear concerned at the lack of response, and after a quarter of an hour of laborious conversation, she showed him the rest of the schloss.

When they had finished, she took him off to try on boots and find him an old shooting jacket. Then, accompanied by Malte, a grandson of the ancient labrador, they went out into the late afternoon sunlight. James smiled at the name. 'I suppose calling him that was your idea.'

'Rilke loved dogs. He would have approved.'

'Absolutely.'

He liked the lack of elegance in her stride and watched as she searched out favourite views. Her eyes, narrowed against the wind and brightness, were moist. Even allowing for the elements, he could not help imagining tears of happiness.

The emotional intensity both touched and disturbed him. What was going to happen when her father died and Eberhard inherited? Lotzingen would no longer be her home, and among the casualties of change would be the room to which she remained so attached. Now he saw that she could never have invited him into that bed. It would have been like the violation of a shrine. But a shrine to what? Her family? Her childhood innocence?

'How long has your mother been like that?' he asked. They had stopped on an ornamental stone bridge at the bottom of the slope.

'Almost as long as I can remember.'

'But what's wrong with her? Is it some form of paralysis?'

'The doctors don't really know.' She shrugged impatiently and turned to walk on. James made a doubtful face to himself. He rolled a twig with his foot before making a move to follow her.

Malte, knowing the path well, bounded ahead. Suddenly he halted and turned in surprise at their disinclination to keep up. Then he crouched playfully and pretended to ambush them in a ritual game.

'Stupid dog,' said Christina affectionately. She glanced up at the hillside ahead. 'This is my favourite walk. It's the one I follow in my mind when I can't get to sleep.' James nodded and swivelled to look back across the valley at the afternoon sun on the old tower and at the shadows cast diagonally on the hillside by the tall, straight pines.

'Tell me your thoughts,' she said. 'You've been very quiet.'

'A rare moment that should be treasured.' He gave a quick grin.

'Is Lotzingen as you imagined it?'

'I'm not sure what I expected. But certainly the scenery is even more beautiful than I could have thought possible.' He did not add that at odd moments he felt threatened by the pine trees above as though they were an army poised to march down into the valley. The mountain forest was far thicker than he had visualized. It reminded him of those dark spirits of self-destruction which haunted Nordic and Slav alike.

'But is that what you were thinking?'

'No,' he hurriedly replied. 'In fact I was thinking how much you must love this place . . . as anyone would who was brought up here. But I couldn't help wondering whether an attachment like that makes one vulnerable in a way. I don't know.'

She looked ahead. 'No doubt you are right. But if I had not had Lotzingen to return to in my mind, certain times would have been very hard to take.'

'You mean like when your husband died?'

She avoided his eyes and said nothing. A dozen paces further on, she finally spoke. 'I have to go back to Munich for a few days.'

'Soon?'

'Yes.'

'Can I come with you?'

She uttered a harsh, disconcerting laugh, scornful of herself, not of him. 'Are you sure you want to?'

❧ 6 ❧

On their arrival at Munich airport, James booked a hotel room and hired a car to emphasize his self-sufficiency. Christina had much to arrange with lawyers and the last thing he wanted was to be in her way. He did, however, insist on driving her home because he longed to see the site of her marriage.

'But James,' she said. 'I promise it would be easier if I took a taxi. The house is at Starnberg and that is a very long distance out from the hotel you have chosen.'

'That's no problem. Honestly, driving around on a day like this is a pleasure.'

There was clearly more to her reluctance than mere politeness, but the warm sunshine and successful arrival put him in a holiday mood. From the bridge over the river Isar he glimpsed the twin towers of the Frauenkirche in the distance. Soon afterwards he saw the first sign to their destination.

'Wasn't King Ludwig drowned in the lake there?'

'The Starnberger See. That's right.' Christina was in rather a distant mood. She's probably thinking of all the things she has to do, he told himself. Or else steeling herself for the house's sad associations.

Starnberg, some twenty-five kilometres southwest of Munich on the Garmisch road, turned out to be a very smart suburb. The low houses, mostly of modern design, extended in a semi-wooded setting. Creeper-covered walls gave an impression of deliberate camouflage from public view, even from attack, to judge by some electrified fences and closed-circuit monitors. Unable to picture her living in such a neighbourhood, he was about to make a flippant observation when she spoke.

'It's the next entrance on the left.'

He nodded, slowing down. The gates were open. He swung into the crescent drive to find a grey Mercedes parked by the wide steps. After switching off the engine, he eyed Christina inquisitively. She was staring at the car in anger.

'I do not *believe* it. What is she doing here?'

'Who?'

'My mother-in-law.'

The idea of such a stock figure causing the same reaction here as in a popular comedy struck him as somehow para-doxical. 'You can always pass me off as your chauffeur,' he said, but the remark was ignored. Christina's mood had been dramatically affected. James, bemused by the circumstances, gave a semi-apologetic shrug and climbed out to fetch her bag from the back.

The front door opened, and an elderly woman of formidable appearance in loden and Tyrolean hat advanced stiffly, yet briskly, down the steps. She was followed by a man in his mid-thirties. Another son, James presumed. Brother of the deceased Georg.

The Countess von Retzen hailed her in a voice accustomed to command. Christina visibly stiffened for the embrace. The Countess's attention then switched to James. She looked him up and down in such a way that Christina had to introduce him hurriedly. 'This is James Gaunt,' she said in English. 'He kindly gave me a lift from the airport.'

'So? You met on the airplane?' The implication of an in-flight pick-up left James momentarily speechless. Christina, blushing angrily, had to explain that he had been staying with them in Austria.

The old *Grafin* turned to James, studying him with renewed interest. 'How nice. Such a beautiful place, Lotzingen. You have known Christina's family long?'

'No, not very,' he replied cautiously. 'But you're absolutely right about Lotzingen. It's a really magnificent setting.' He searched for an exit. 'You must know it well, of course.'

Some sort of gaffe was immediately apparent. She had prob-ably not been invited there as often as she would have liked, and on reflection, James found it difficult to picture Prince Tassilo taking her to his bosom.

'Would it not be a nice idea to have some coffee instead of standing out here?' The suggestion was plainly a command. They turned to go in.

Her son fell into step alongside James after a smirk of ill-defined greeting. James tried to remember his name. Bubi, or something equally dire. With a tweed jacket of the sort only Continentals regard as typically English, a widow's peak of dark hair, restless eyes and sawtooth nose, he looked the type to live off gossip in one capacity or another.

Inside, the decoration was mainly modern with the odd, carefully chosen antique of the Coromandel screen variety. More or less what a designer might do for an industrialist who hoped to see his home featured in *Interiors* or *Ambiente*. That Christina could have had anything to do with this sinister elegance was impossible to believe.

'How long are you planning to stay in Munich?' Bubi's question interrupted his scrutiny.

'Oh, a few days probably. Difficult to be sure with so much to visit.' The black comedy of the exchange incited him to play things up even more. 'Munich is obviously a very beautiful city.'

The phrasebook banality extracted a similar response, but just as James was beginning to enjoy himself, he noticed a look flash from mother to son.

'Would you like to see over the house?' Bubi quickly asked. James hesitated for only a moment. Christina was going to have to face the old dragon alone at some point, and prevarication on his part would simply risk unnecessary suspicions. In any case, a good look round was exactly what he had wanted. 'Yes,' he said. 'Thank you very much.'

'You know,' Bubi confided on the stairs, 'I think my mother and Christina want to have a little chat alone. It's been so long since they saw one another.' As if relieved of a burden, he suddenly became magnanimous. 'It is good you spend a few days here, James.' He then wagged his finger. 'But you must not be just a tourist!' He made it sound as though the Alte

Pinakothek and the Nymphenburg should be left to the vul-
garians.

'Ah, but that reminds me!' he added a moment later with
unconvincing spontaneity. 'We are having a party tonight to
celebrate my cousin's wedding. You, as a friend of the family,
must come too. We would be so pleased.'

Friend of the family! That's really pushing it, James thought.
But since Christina was bound to be press-ganged as well, he
agreed. To spend the evening alone in a Munich hotel was far
too depressing a prospect. Besides, a closer look at the Retzen
family could be of great interest.

'You have a smoking with you?'

'A dinner jacket? Yes, I do.' He had not needed it in Austria,
so this would at least justify its journey.

'That is excellent!' Bubi's smile was enough to make anyone
think they'd just agreed to buy shares in a fictitious mine. 'I
will fetch you at nine thirty then. Which hotel are you at?'

James was about to say that surely Christina could bring
him along, but at that moment Bubi drew his attention to a
portrait of Georg at the end of the passage. What a likeness to
display, thought James. Or had he really looked like that? The
brutal good looks were shamelessly romanticized.

The tour included all the bedrooms. Almost devoid of personal effects, they had an air of abandonment, as if the house
had been rented to tenants.

'And this is the room of Christina's daughter. Have you met
Steffi?'

'Yes, I have met Stephanie,' said James, acutely aware of
being watched. His reply sounded more priggish than intended.
He glanced round at the unnatural tidiness. There weren't
even any posters on the wall. 'Tell me, how long have they
lived here? Everything seems so new.'

'Oh, only about a year. The architect and designer was a
close friend of my brother.'

On hearing Bubi's mother call from below, they went down.
The large white kitchen had a triple oven with a black display
panel where the clock's digital figures flicked noiselessly. The
whole thing looked like something out of a space laboratory.

Christina concentrated on putting out the coffee cups. To judge by the way she avoided James's glances, she seemed deeply embarrassed about something – he suspected the house. But then Bubi announced that James had agreed to come to the party that night. She shot him a look of betrayal.

Utterly confused, he turned to Bubi. 'Honestly, you don't have to bother about picking me up from the hotel. It'd surely be much simpler for everybody if I came along with Christina.'

'Christina?' He laughed. 'But the party is what I think in England you call a stag night.' He turned to Christina with one of his smiles. 'You don't mind, do you? It would be so amusing for your friend to see a little of Munich life while he is here.' Under their challenging stares, and unable to ask James to change his mind in front of them, there was little she could say.

To his subsequent dismay, James stood there in bewilderment, and missed the chance to back out on the grounds of misunderstanding. But he was also puzzled by the intensity of Christina's concern. Perhaps her convent training conjured up unspeakable depravities, although the fate-worse-than-death was far more likely to consist of crippling doses of alcohol and Bavarian bonhomie.

As soon as mother and son had left, he explained how Bubi had made it sound like a family party.

'*That* was not hard to guess.' She stood there looking as if she wanted to throw something against the wall. 'What I want to know is how they managed to find out about our arrival. Both of them being here like that was no coincidence!'

'Listen. Do you feel like telling me a bit about the background to all this?' He waited in vain for an answer. 'Well, then perhaps you'd prefer me to go to the hotel now and leave you on your own? I know you've a lot to get on with.'

'I don't blame you for wanting to get away from this place!' she said, her eyes averted. Once again, the bitterness was directed against herself. He put a hand on her shoulder hoping to calm her, but she reacted to his touch as if from an electric shock.

'Hey! Things aren't that bad. You can soon be out of here yourself. *For good!* Just grit your teeth over the next few days and don't let them get to you. Stephanie's at school in England, so why don't you move to London? There, you could ...' He stopped. 'But of course! She came here to have a go at you about her.' Christina turned away. 'Is that it?' he persisted. 'The old battleaxe is fighting the whole idea of Stephanie being away from Munich?' She nodded. James began to wonder what else he might have missed.

'Right,' he said abruptly. 'Let's both get out of here. We'll drop my stuff off at the hotel, then have some lunch. That'll make us both feel better.' After surveying the room listlessly, she assented.

In the car, he watched her out of the corner of his eye. The apathy disturbed him. 'Listen, as soon as we get to the hotel, I'll ring Bubi to say that I really don't feel up to the party. Instead, we can have a quiet dinner on our own somewhere. That'd be infinitely nicer from every point of view. What do you think?'

'It is too late now.'

'You mean you'd be blamed?'

'But of course. It would be better to grit my teeth, as you say, and not provoke them.'

'All right,' he sighed, and frowned dubiously. 'If that's what you really feel.' A minute or two later, he tried to lighten the atmosphere with a remark about buying a carton of milk to line his stomach before the party.

'James ...'

'Yes?'

'No. Nothing.'

'Don't *worry*. I'll be all right, I promise you. First thing in the morning, I'll give you a call to tell you all about it. That is, if my brain doesn't feel like it's been split down the middle by a meat cleaver.'

❧ 7 ❧

In spite of his jesting, James experienced the odd wave of trepidation while preparing himself that evening. He sipped from his carton of milk in between each stage. The deliberate rhythm was broken when he pulled on his trousers only to find one fly button missing and another hanging by a thread. Luckily, he had remembered to bring a supply of safety pins.

In his ancient dinner jacket, he was not only going to be the least fashionable man there, but also the sweatiest. Thick as a blanket, it had been made for freezing English houses. Down in the hotel lobby, Bubi's eyes glinted in amusement when he caught sight of it. He wore a mohair creation and one of those fake wing-collared shirts, which was then the latest thing. Nobody, thought James, can beat the aristocracy for vulgarity when they put their mind to it.

'We should have much fun tonight, James,' Bubi said with an emphatic chuckle, and led the way out to his car.

The large, shark-shaped BMW coupé appeared the perfect symbol of his preposterous posing, and, emphasizing its newness, the interior smelled of new leather. James watched as he went through a form of cockpit drill.

'Ready for take-off?'

Bubi glanced at him, then forced a laugh. 'It is the latest thing. I have only just bought it. A beautiful machine, don't you think?'

'Very impressive. By the way, where are we going tonight?'

'First to the Vierjahreszeiten. Have you heard of it? It is a rather good hotel.'

James had indeed heard of it, but mainly for other reasons.

His interest in Rilke had led him to study the Bavarian revolution that dethroned the Wittelsbachs in November 1918. The hotel had soon become the headquarters of embittered reactionaries like the Thulebund, a group of Aryan supremacists with the swastika as their emblem. Even Count von Arco Valley, the assassin of the socialist prime minister, had been refused membership due to a hint of Jewish blood. And it was the Thulebund which smuggled fellow plotters such as Rudolf Hess and Ernst Rohm through the lines when the White Freikorps forces massed to attack Munich in the spring. James wondered if Bubi and his friends would end up with marching songs over the brandy.

In the hotel, they were directed to a private reception room where a dozen young men, also in dinner jackets, were talking and drinking champagne. As Bubi led him forward, James eyed the short haircuts.

Hans-Dietrich, the young bridegroom, greeted him warmly after an embarrassing eulogy from Bubi. Already flushed, Hans-Dietrich looked stolid, amiable, and almost certainly gullible. Poor bastard, thought James. I wonder what they've got in store for him tonight. A thunderous burst of laughter from behind made him wince. He just managed to turn it into a pained smile as Hans-Dietrich said something in ponderous English. Pushing his spectacles back into position and leaning closer, James asked him to repeat himself.

'I said, what is it that you write?'

'Luckily for you, nothing to do with stag parties.'

Hans-Dietrich took a moment to understand, then laughed immoderately. James, who felt a little like an Englishman on the Grand Tour at the court of a German princeling, smiled politely in return.

Bubi, who clearly enjoyed his role as the raffish elder cousin chosen to organize such events, signalled to a waiter to top up their glasses and took James off on a round of introductions. Except for one other member of the Retzen family, also in his mid-thirties, they were mostly about ten years younger.

How predictable it all was, James thought, and how ridiculous his earlier fears had been. He studied them over the top of his glass as he drank. Bavaria's version of the Hooray Henry. Yet it was still difficult to forget his image of those junior officers in the spring of 1919 – those *hochgeboren* defenders of the old order only too capable of a Jekyll and Hyde transformation. From the punctilious formality of a Guards mess to gunning down Eisner and beating to death an old pacifist like Gustav Landauer.

And what did your Daddy do in the war? he silently asked Bubi. Don't tell me. He served on the Russian front just like every other Wehrmacht veteran west of the Elbe. Defending us from fresh genes, James added without thinking. His burst of xenophobia collapsed, and with a slight shock he discovered that his hand had been clenched around the glass.

After about an hour, everyone crammed into taxis. Their destination was a large nineteenth-century house in the French style set back from the road. The shutters were all closed and no light showed from inside until the door was opened by an elderly manservant in a white jacket. They entered a gloomy, old-fashioned hall, mostly taken up by a double-return staircase with black iron balusters, brass hand-rail and red carpet. James wondered if this was Munich's answer to the Athenaeum.

He followed Bubi upstairs to a long salon hung with large allegorical paintings in heavy gilt frames. The mock Renaissance furniture had been pushed back into the dark extremities. And in the middle of the room, under a chandelier dimmed to an amber glow, was a circular table almost ten feet across, with a heavy damask cloth draped to the floor. Fourteen places were laid for dinner. Each had six ornate glasses ranged diagonally outwards. Unable to read the menu cards in their silver holders, James counted the forks to estimate the number of courses.

Bubi looked round with satisfaction at the arrangements. 'One seldom finds a house like this anymore. It has a truly original atmosphere, don't you find?'

'Indeed,' said James. He could easily imagine a forgotten room full of stuffed creatures in glass cases.

Once everyone had arrived, Bubi announced the *placement*.

To general applause mixed with raucous comments, Hans-Dietrich was given 'the throne', a large open armchair upholstered in dark red velvet. Bubi put himself directly opposite with James on his right and then Wolfi, another English speaker, beyond him. On Hans-Dietrich's right sat the only other member of the elder generation – his brother Otto, according to Wolfi. A closer look revealed an unexpected resemblance to the Georg of the portrait.

James immediately liked the pale and studious-looking Wolfi. His round, gold-rimmed spectacles were slightly askew and his bow tie half undone. Although a little drunk and dogmatic, his comments on those present were entertaining. And when Bubi urged the future bridegroom to take more caviar on the grounds that it was just as effective as oysters, Wolfi groaned loudly.

He leaned over as the waiters began to serve the next course, an over-generous slab of *pâté de foie gras*. 'For once it isn't German gastronomic patriotism which is liable to prove fatal. Tonight, in case you have not realized it, the term "conspicuous consumption" is almost certainly going to take on a more specific, and quite disgusting emphasis.'

'Yes,' James replied. 'I can easily imagine that by the end we're going to feel like the poor geese that produced this. Not that that can be a very satisfactory revenge for them. But tell me, what are you doing here?'

'Hans-Dietrich was a friend of my childhood, and I could not really refuse him. He is a trusting fool, much nicer than the rest of them.' His eyes lifted past James in Bubi's direction. 'And you, I was told, are a friend of the family.' Wolfi grinned sceptically.

To stop the waiter from topping up his glass with hock, James quickly put out a hand, but the gesture was ignored. And when he turned to ask for some water, the man stared back without replying.

Wolfi had meanwhile become engaged in argument with his neighbour on the other side, so James carried on eating very slowly and as sparingly as possible from each course. He kept track of progress, using the menu card rather like the service sheet at an interminable wedding. The *foie gras* was followed by a champagne sorbet, then a rather metallic-tasting poached salmon, and then guinea fowl stuffed with mango, which was not a success. There were still tournedos to come, another sorbet, and finally *La Première Surprise*, which was presumably some extravaganza of a pudding.

Grateful that Bubi was still deep in conversation, James passed the time observing the company. He tried to imagine their womenfolk, especially Hans-Dietrich's bride-to-be, who was probably spending the night giggling with girlfriends. Would she turn into a dragon like Christina's mother-in-law? And as for the other men, mostly red-faced and sweating, and roaring the odd joke across the table, what would married life be like with them? If this was the Retzens at play, then no wonder Christina used to escape back to Lotzingen.

'Well, my friend,' Bubi said, finally turning to him. 'And how do you find Munich so far?'

'Oh, very interesting. It seems to be a city full of surprises for the traveller. How about that for the guidebook?'

Bubi flashed a smile in reply, then looked down at his napkin as he wound it round three fingers. 'And how are you enjoying the company of my brother's widow? She is beautiful, is she not?'

'Yes,' said James evenly. 'She certainly is.' Bubi's prurient interest appeared to confirm his suspicions.

'Ah, but how well do you know her?'

'We only met quite recently.'

'Now, James,' he said with a confidential leer. 'Let us have none of that *pudeur anglaise*. You know what I mean. Come on, my friend. Between men.'

'Bubi, for your information I do *not* know her biblically. And even if I did, it wouldn't be any bloody business of yours!'

'Answered as a true English gentleman!' Bubi exclaimed, pretending it had been a test all along. Then he turned back to the man on his other side.

Speechless with anger, James would have walked out at that point if he had not told himself that having survived so far, it would be stupid not to see the evening through. The whole reason for being there was to avoid problems for Christina. And he, after all, was the one who had been dishing out advice about gritted teeth. He looked at his watch. It was getting on for midnight and they still had not finished. Following the example of several of the others, James slipped out to the lavatory.

Finally, the *Première Surprise* was brought in on a huge platter to cheers and thumping on the table. The ice-cream sculpture was supposed to represent a woman's torso with chocolate shavings as pubic hair and rocket breasts topped with glacé cherry nipples. 'How really gross!' he muttered to Wolfi. 'It's worse than schoolboy graffiti.'

'Just you wait,' he replied. 'There's probably more to come.'

Wolfi was right. Hans-Dietrich, as a variation of blowing out the candles in one blow, was called upon to lick up the chocolate shavings in one mouthful. With good-natured embarrassment, he half rose from his chair, puce and sweating, to do as he was told. But as he stretched forward, his elder brother suddenly rammed his face down into the monstrous confection. This produced yells of laughter, and Hans-Dietrich, after cleaning himself off as best he could, had to grin and pretend to be having fun.

'We really call this the *Frauentorte*,' said Bubi as they were served from the breasts at the less damaged end of the torso. 'You know,' he added when James failed to react, 'like the cathedral.'

'I'd got that,' James replied, wondering what the servants thought of it all. And a little later, with an enormous sense of relief, he watched them clear the table before bringing round coffee and liqueurs. He accepted a cigar and even managed a grunt of thanks when Bubi passed the matches. It can't be long now, he told himself. But then he sensed an excited tension round the table. The laughter became even more strident; it also had an anticipatory edge.

He asked what was happening, but Wolfi lurched to his feet and mumbled: 'Need to go again.'

Bubi, who had overheard the question, put a hand on James's arm. 'Wait and see, my friend. Wait and see.' He signalled to the head servant, who nodded and left, taking the two waiters with him. Bubi then laid his cigar in the ashtray and rapped his glass with a knife. The most significant part of his speech, to go by the coarse cheers, appeared to be about *die Grosse Bertha*.

'Who, or what, is Big Bertha?' James demanded during the uproar.

'She!' Bubi smirked. 'We are about to play a game.'

'Well, where is she, then?'

In a pantomime of mock secrecy, he pointed under the table. His delight at James's surprise was particularly galling.

'All right. So what is this little game of yours?'

Bubi regarded him as if he were naive. 'We call it Russian roulette. But it has a big difference. Eros not Thanatos. The little death instead of the big one.' Comprehension dawned. His failure to suspect something of the sort made him feel foolish. 'Yes, my friend. I'm surprised you have not come across such a contest before.'

James felt distinctly uneasy. He suspected a nasty sort of initiation ceremony. The brutal look in Georg's portrait came to mind, followed by those earlier fears of another Thule Society. Remembering the story of Count von Arco Valley, it even occurred to him that this might be a way of discovering Jews in their midst. He told himself not to be ridiculous.

Only then did he realize that Wolfi probably had not gone to the lavatory at all. He must have sensed what was afoot and cut out in time. James wondered whether he could still do the same. But if Bubi was setting him up, as he suspected, this would give him just the excuse he wanted. He could call on the others to grab the deserter and punish him with an even worse humiliation. The general drunkenness offered his best hope.

'Now, James. The rules. If you betray what is happening to you by your expression, or any other lack of control, you have to pay a forfeit.'

'Do you take American Express cards?' he asked sarcastically, but Bubi, pretending to find this funny, repeated it to his neighbour on the other side.

'No, James. It is Bertha who chooses the forfeit. All depends on her mood. It is not always very nice, you know.' James found that easy to believe. One could hardly blame her for wanting to exact a pretty horrible revenge.

Once again Bubi rapped his glass. '*Alle fertig?*' He turned to James. 'Ready?' Then, he sat back in his chair. '*Berthe! Fangen Sie an!*'

The oppressive silence was broken by the odd drunken giggle. James wanted to mop the sweat from his face and neck with his napkin, but did not dare move. Cross your legs and think of England, he told himself, hoping that such an uninviting posture might deter her.

But either it produced the opposite effect or else, to go by Bubi's sideways surveillance, the target had been fixed in advance. James could not stop himself from grinning inanely when he felt a pair of hands take hold of his knees to prise them apart.

Bubi eyed his fists clenched on the tablecloth. 'Are you enjoying yourself, my friend?'

The pressure on James's knees relaxed, but the fingers groped beyond to his flies. They fumbled and tugged. He became panic-stricken. But then he heard a muffled curse from below and the hands withdrew abruptly. It took a moment to realize that Bertha must have encountered one of the safety pins. He began to shake with laughter.

'James, I challenge you!' Bubi screamed in triumph. The demented denunciation only made him laugh more. 'You must stand up! It is the rules!'

Hands raised in mock surrender and blinded by tears of merriment, he pushed back the chair to stand up. His challenger's eyes widened in disbelief.

Bubi found it even harder to be a good loser since anyone issuing an unfounded challenge received their own forfeit. From under the table, Bertha's sepulchral voice pronounced judgement. Bubi was to wear her scarlet and black frilly knickers as a dunce's cap until dawn. Although a mild sentence, James did not object. He considered himself lucky not to have been penalized for an illegal defence system.

Soon afterwards, things turned very nasty. Hans-Dietrich's elder brother proved himself a drunken pig by relieving himself when selected by Bertha, and then laughing. After a muffled shriek of rage from under the table, he was propelled backwards off his chair. Bertha, blonde and huge, her unhealthy white flesh squeezing from a black leather corset, exploded in chaotic fury from under the tablecloth, nearly pulling the whole thing with her. She looked set on exacting a savage retribution.

The uproar while those nearest tried to grab hold of her presented James with the perfect opportunity. From the door, he looked back at the scene of pandemonium with Bubi screaming and gesticulating to restore order. The knicker headgear had slipped down on one side of his head like a drunk's carnival mask.

There was no sign of the elderly servant as James slipped through the deserted hall to the front door. Outside, he paused to enjoy the taste of fresh air. But on feeling his shirt damp and cold against his skin, he set off in search of a taxi.

After about fifteen minutes he found one and sank gratefully into the back seat. Thanks to that final, ludicrous vision of Bubi, the evening's nastiness was largely effaced. James began to shake with suppressed laughter once again. At first the taxi driver appeared to fear that the noise came from his stomach and that the interior of the Mercedes might be fouled. But then he relaxed, although at each eruption of mirth he raised his eyes to the rear-view mirror. Eventually he said something indecipherable.

James leaned forward. '*Bitte?*'

'*Amerikaner?*'

'*Nein. Englander.*'

'Good party?' The Bavarian accent was very strong.

'*Ja. Sehr gut. Danke.*'

The man inclined his head sardonically. Ah, thought James, sitting back, if you only knew what went on in your city. But on reflection he admitted that taxi drivers probably had a very good idea. That was the most likely reason for their dyspeptic view of humanity.

At the hotel he asked for his key at the desk. The night porter

passed it across and nodded dourly over towards the corner of
the lobby. Fuddled by drink, James turned in a deliberate
movement, propping himself against the counter. There, half-
curled on an armchair, was Christina. At first he suspected
some sort of alcoholic mirage. In amazement, he walked over
and gingerly touched her shoulder. She shook herself awake,
then blinked at him with decreasing rapidity. Suddenly, she
remembered where she was. 'James. You are back. Are you all
right?'

'Yes. Here I am. Sound of limb.' Her concern struck him as
endearingly comic. [*Later – probably the next day – the scene
reminded me of an old film. I'm fairly sure that Claudette Colbert
played the heroine, but I cannot remember the title.*]

'I was so worried.'

Ignoring the porter's stare, he helped her up. She clung to
him to gain her balance. For a moment he even thought that
she had been drinking too. 'Come on. Let's move from here.'
He led her to the lift. She shivered involuntarily and he put his
jacket round her shoulders.

By the time they reached his floor, Christina had woken up.
She took the key from him when his ill-aimed stab at the lock
ended in the point skidding away.

'Are you very drunk?' she asked once they were inside.

'Not as bad as the others, thanks to my wise virgin precautions with the milk. However, I think it would be fair to
admit that I'm not entirely sober.'

'But are you at least in a proper state to tell me what
happened? No doubt it is very silly, but I have been worried
all evening.'

'As things turned out, you were quite right to be suspicious.'
He doffed an imaginary hat. 'It was indeed a set-up.'

'Oh, please! Tell me what happened!'

The role of modest hero was too tempting to resist. 'Listen,
just give me a moment to clean up first. That dinner jacket of
mine was a portable sauna. If you're cold, you can always get
into one of the beds. I'll only be a moment.'

James returned in a towel robe, drinking from a tumbler.
The toothpaste had made his mouth burn after the cigar.

Christina had switched off the overhead light, leaving on the twin reading lamps above each headboard. She sat forward impatiently. He perched on the bed beside her, leaned across to put down the glass, then turned to hug her.

'Come on! Tell me!' she ordered, her mouth beyond his ear. He kissed her neck through the mass of hair. It smelt of warm honey.

'Once upon a time,' he began, having remembered the first story he told her, 'there was a knight in a shiny old dinner jacket. He loved a princess very much indeed, but he was a silly fellow, and didn't believe her when she tried to warn him against her wicked brother-in-law, known as Sir Bubi of the BMW.'

She chuckled. 'I like this.' He kissed her cheek.

'Where was I? Oh, yes. Well, the wicked brother-in-law invited our knight of the ridiculous countenance to this deserted castle, where he planned to compromise him ... actually, "compromise" isn't a very fairy-tale word.'

'Set a trap.'

'That's better. Trap him into making a bigger fool of himself than he was already. So when Sir Bubi led him to a banquet in this deserted castle, he feared nought. There were gathered in this place some dozen other knights, in the main, relatives of Sir Bubi. And they all sat down to sup at a large round table, like in the days of good King Arthur, only this table was covered with a white silken cloth draped to the floor. Together the knights ate and drank heartily and there was much merriment. But after the servitors had cleared the platters and charged the goblets, Sir Bubi announced a tournament for the valiant company present.'

'A tournament? Oh, my God!'

'It was to be a special tournament. Not skill of arms or strength, but of reticence. Not danger of death or injury, but of humiliation. Sir Bubi warned the noble knights of the rules, and of the conduct expected of those with gentle blood coursing in their veins, the very flower of Christendom. Then, Sir Bubi called for the trumpets to be sounded and the tourney to commence.

'The knight of the shiny old dinner jacket was sore afraid.He at last saw the plot prepared for him and heartily cursed himself for not having listened to the warnings of his beloved princess.' Christina was so eager for him to continue that his kiss was returned most perfunctorily. 'Well, to cut a long tale short, under the table lay concealed a dragon in the form of a maiden – well, ex-maiden to be precise – who went by the name of Big Bertha and lived at the sign of the Red Light.

'In the cavernous darkness below the lily-white cloth, this fire-breathing maiden advanced upon the knight of the ludi-crous countenance without delay. For she had been bribed with gold by Sir Bubi, who ardently desired the innocent knight's abasement before his beloved princess. Anticipating the danger from the dragon maiden, the good knight girded his moth-eaten armour about him and prepared to defend his honour to the end. Whatever the evil trickery of Sir Bubi, he still felt obliged to obey the rules of the tournament.'

'But you haven't said what they were!'

'They were that throughout the ordeal, the knight selected by the dragon-maiden must betray no feeling. So when our knight felt her claws upon his legs and her fiery breath directed upon his loins . . .'

Comprehension transformed Christina's expression. 'James, you're making this up!' she exclaimed aghast.

'Fairy tales aren't exactly made up. They're a symbolized portrayal of a wider truth.' A giggle escaped him. 'García Márquez once said . . .'

'Be serious! Was that really what the evening was all about?'

'Scout's honour. And that was why Bubi was so damned pleased with himself at your house.'

Christina was speechless. James thought that if he were in Bubi's shoes at that moment, he'd have preferred a dozen of Bertha's forfeits to anything she might dream up.

'Now before you burst a blood vessel, let me get to the end. I'll tell it straight and you'll see why revenge is unnecessary. All that's needed is for Bubi to know that *you* know.'

After he had finished – in the interests of peace he glossed over the drunken pig's contribution – she still could not quite bring herself to believe his story. So he leaped up and fetched his trousers from the bathroom to show her the safety pins.

That Bubi had been made to look such a fool appeared too marvellous for her to take in. Then came an incredulous joy. 'My dearest, dearest James. You are a *genius!*' The kiss which followed felt the most exhilarating of his life.

'But credit where credit's due,' he said when they finally disengaged. He nodded at the bedside table. 'Don't forget the safety pins.' And she leaned round him, laughing, to blow them a kiss.

To have stumbled into glory through sartorial deficiency struck him as the summit of poetic justice. The only problem was that whenever Christina thought of Bubi crowned with Big Bertha's frilly knickers, she had to break away to smother her face in the pillow. The occupant of the next-door room had already thumped on the wall twice.

The next time she turned away, he grabbed her head out of the pillow, forced it round and swallowed her laughter until they both choked. He struggled out of his bathrobe and clambered into bed beside her.

As they finished making love, she began to shake from sobs of breath and muscular tremors. Then he felt the dampness of tears on his shoulder.

'Hey,' he murmured, and stroked the back of her head. 'What's the matter?'

She attempted a laugh, but had to sniff. She raised her head above him. He craned up to kiss her cheek and tasted the salt. She blinked to clear her vision. 'I could never explain. It's too complicated.'

'What is?' he asked. She shook her head, then lowered it out of sight. 'You mean there's something you think I won't understand?' There was no reply. 'Please say.'

'I can't!'

'Why? Because it's to do with your marriage to Georg?' After a moment she nodded.

Eventually, he coaxed her into telling him. This had been the first time for her in nearly five years. His initial scepticism dissolved with the certainty that something so painful would never be invented. He lay there staring past her hair at the shadows on the ceiling. The enormity was difficult to assimilate.

'I must be squashing you,' she said in a lifeless voice.

He followed her movement and twisted round onto his side to hold her closely. 'But what the hell was wrong with the man? Didn't he like women, or what?'

'That depends what you mean by "like". There were many others. He just did not seem to want me anymore. Once, he even said he had only given me Stephanie, because he thought I needed a child to keep me occupied.'

James was dumbfounded. How could anyone come out with something so cruel? Three times he started to speak but fell silent. He simply did not have the words to comfort such a disfigurement.

'But why on earth did you stay with him?' he said eventually. 'Was it because of being a Catholic?'

'It was not as simple as that. You see, I was about to leave him when he was killed in that crash. You'll think it stupid, but when it happened, I felt responsible in a way.'

He stopped himself from pressing the point. Confessions, like vomiting, had their own rhythm. In any case, this insight into her marriage gave him more than enough to think about. Several things were at last clear – the lack of confidence, the gratitude, her desire to get away from Munich, even the desperation when she made love. The damage to her pride must have been massive, almost irreparable. And he was just lying there saying nothing while God knows what ideas of inadequacy were going through her mind.

He began to kiss her neck. 'The man must have been mad. Stark raving mad.' His mouth nuzzled in aimless exploration, until he felt her body galvanize in spasms like silent hiccups. She was trying to stifle her sobs.

He raised his head. 'If only I'd been able to take a photograph of Bubi in his exotic headgear. We could have sent it to his mother. I'd give anything to see her face!' Finally, he obtained a muffled laugh. 'I've just thought of something. What shall I do if Bubi turns up with his tail between his legs begging me not to tell you about the party?'

'Tell him the truth!' She pushed herself up onto one elbow. 'Tell him how I was waiting here for you, and that we spent the night together.'

He looked at her for several moments. 'No regrets, then?'

'None!' Then she added quietly, 'And you?'

'Never.'

Next morning, James awoke in confusion. The memory of his dream slipped through his grasp like water into sand. He opened his eyes, trying to remember where he was. A pale grey light seeped round the curtains at both sides. Then, resting his eyelids, he tried to sort out the previous night's adventures. They would have felt little more than another of his fantasies if it had not been for the gentle heat from Christina's body.

He turned gingerly to avoid dragging the bedclothes and raised himself above her naked shoulder. He bent to inhale the fragrance of warm flesh. Her cheek was camouflaged by a mesh of hair which he longed to brush aside with his fingertips. And as he slid out from the bed, his gaze lingered on the dark blonde mass.

The haggard sight that greeted him in the bathroom mirror prompted a grimace of commiseration with his reflection, yet underneath there bubbled an irrepressible self-congratulation. His luck was incredible.

He had nearly finished shaving when sounds came from the bedroom. With a towel round his waist, he opened the door to say that the bathroom was all hers, then turned back to the basin to rinse off the remaining lather. From the doorway, Christina gasped. He looked up at her in the mirror. She was wearing his dressing gown.

'Did I do that?' she said.

By twisting his neck, he managed to admire the weals on his back in the full-length glass opposite. 'Do you like steak tartare?' he laughed.

'Don't! It is too awful!'

He reached out for her. 'They're the loveliest scars the knight in the shiny old dinner jacket could have ever hoped to bear.' He squeezed her to him.

'You're just being nice again.'

'I am not!' He sighed emphatically, then, he took a deep breath. 'Christina Dorothea Marie-Louise Sophia,' he recited, having learned the names from her passport. 'I have already told you I adore you, but I haven't yet asked you to marry me.'

She stiffened, pushing him back as she withdrew her arms. 'Is that another of your jokes?'

For an instant, he almost lost his head and was on the point of recanting when she began to pull away. He gripped her shoulders. 'It was no joke. I mean it seriously. I promise you!'

She searched his face. Her silence was even more unsettling than the distrustful stare. But then she slowly shook her head. 'I really believe you do. Is it true?' He nodded. 'Oh, James. Are we crazy?'

'You maybe! But I don't think I am. It's probably the only decent decision in my whole life.' She began to laugh and cry at the same time. 'Is it that bad?' he teased.

She wiped her eyes on a sleeve of the bathrobe. 'James, I'm so glad you asked me now.'

'Now? Why now?'

'No. You'll think me so silly if I tell you.'

'I'll be furious if you don't.'

'Well.' Her mouth bunched and she blushed, hiding her head. 'We didn't take any precautions last night. And you see, I would never have an abortion. So I'd have hated it if you'd asked me later, because then I would have suspected you had, only because you felt obliged. Oh, damn! I am saying all the wrong things!'

He stared at her, then ran a hand through his hair. There seemed to be only one reply. He took her by the hand to lead her back to bed, but she firmly extricated herself from his grasp. 'You said the bathroom was all mine.'

After running Christina home to change, then back to the city centre for her meeting with lawyers, James returned alone to the hotel feeling light-headed and weak-kneed. The previous night had at last caught up with him. He flopped onto the bed. If nothing else, it was time to consider things in peace.

Engagement, wedding, married life. The whole sequence appeared so momentous that it lacked conviction. Then there were the details of daily life together. She certainly wouldn't want to live in his flat, which, apart from the bachelor squalor, was far too small. So would they buy a large house? It would have to be with her money. Then remembering her present meeting, he wondered whether the Schwanemberg family lawyers would insist on a marriage contract with property settlements discussed like a treaty between nations, and every stage reported back to Prince Tassilo. James started to feel a little out of his depth.

A trace of Christina's scent reached him from the pillow. He rolled over to bury his nose in its insubstantial softness. Soon, on the edge of sleep, images began to mix in his mind. Christina naked over him, shoulders back like the Winged Victory of Samothrace, face straining up as she bit on her lower lip. Then, slowly, her mouth opening. A silent cry, which made him think of a genie's escape.

He drifted off and dreamed that he was under the table with Big Bertha. But somehow Prince Tassilo knew they were there and had raised the white cloth to jab at them with a sword.

The ring of the telephone beside the bed jerked him awake. He had to ask the receptionist to repeat himself. There was a man to see him. James, still half asleep, at first assumed that it must be Christina's father. Then, having gathered his wits, he guessed his visitor's identity. He said he would be down in a few minutes.

His hands were feverish with anticipation as he straightened his tie in front of the mirror. 'Right, you bastard!' he muttered.

In the lobby, Bubi sprang up from a low armchair like the one in which Christina had been asleep the night before. His sickly complexion made the hail-fellow-well-met manner particularly gruesome.

'Good to see you, James! How are you? Such a pity you

disappeared like that. You know, things picked up marvellously.'

James found the free-fire zone irresistible. 'Quite frankly,' he said, 'I've never been so happy to get away from a party in my life. But it was well worth it when I told Christina what happened. I've never known her laugh so much as when I described you with the frilly knickers round your head.' Bubi's horrified expression encouraged him to twist the knife all the way.

'Oh, yes. She was here when I got back. And while we're on the subject, I thought you'd like to be the first to know. We're going to get married.'

Bubi stared at him not knowing what to believe, and probably unable to decide which was worse: James's betrayal of male freemasonry, or the engagement. 'It is quite obvious,' he said, summoning up every particle of aggrieved self-righteousness, 'that you are not a gentleman.'

As he swivelled away with the air of having issued a challenge to a duel, James let out a contemptuous laugh. But then, through the tinted glass of the main entrance, he spotted Christina. She was paying off a taxi. Bubi, in his furious dignity, had failed to see her. The two of them came face to face when the automatic doors opened.

Christina, mastering the initial shock, gave Bubi an icy look. Then she caught sight of James over his shoulder. Bubi followed her glance. 'You degrade yourself consorting with such a person!' he said loudly in English, and walked straight past.

James joined her and together they watched his progress to the BMW. A man in the passenger seat twisted round. It was the drunken pig from the night before. Hans-Dietrich's elder brother.

'Do you know Bubi's companion in the car?' he asked with a grin.

'Oh, that's Otto Retzen. A first cousin of Bubi and Georg.' She flushed slightly at mentioning her husband's name after all that had been said the night before. What a family, he thought. Perhaps Bubi would now challenge him to a *schlager* duel. He began to laugh.

'What's so funny?'

'I was just wondering who I could get as a second if Bubi calls me out? I know, Wolfi! He'd do an excellent job sending the whole thing up.'

'Oh, James, you are ridiculous.' She kissed him on the cheek-bone. 'The role of knight in shining armour seems to have gone to your head.'

'Don't knock my finest hour.' He cocked his head towards the hotel to suggest they go in. 'Well, don't you want to hear about my little encounter?'

She slipped an arm through his and squeezed hard. 'Can't wait!'

❖ 9 ❖

While Christina continued to meet with lawyers, James wandered round the Alte Pinakothek in search of ideas for his book on the image of power. But, dizzy with erotic exhaustion, the slightest reminder would divert him. His mind seemed no firmer than the swirling ice-cream flesh of the huge Rubens figures. And reaching the Fragonard of a naked girl on her back holding up a small dog with its white, fluffy tail between her thighs, he abandoned himself entirely to memories from the last three nights.

They had moved to another hotel, smaller and more discreet, near the Maximiliansplatz. The notion of hiding from the Retzens heightened the excitement, for Christina had summoned up her nerve to put the house at Starnberg on the market. During the drive back to Munich with the last of her belongings she had kept looking round to make sure they had not been followed.

The last problem with Georg's estate was sorted out after lunch on the Thursday. This enabled Christina to sign the papers and authorize the sale of the house. She rushed back to join James at the hotel and, although only half past four in the afternoon, they celebrated this final act of secession in bed with a bottle of champagne.

Next morning, they drove in convoy to Munich airport. James returned the hired Opel and took a plane to London, while Christina carried on in her own car to Austria to tell her parents.

During the flight, he endured horrific visions of an accident on the Salzburg autobahn like Georg's. To lose her at such a moment and in such a way would be typical of fate's vile twists. Yet having worked himself up into an even worse state of silent panic after an unexpected delay at Frankfurt, he arrived home to find a message already on his answering machine to say that she had arrived, that she loved him and would ring again after dinner. Limp with relief, he ridiculed his fears. Fate evidently didn't work that way. Only fiction.

James looked at his watch to estimate the time in Austria. He pictured Christina and her father alone together in the dining room at Lotzingen with the candles lit although it was not yet dark outside. Once again he became certain the old man would disapprove of their marriage. You can hardly blame him, he warned himself. Especially if he thinks she's on some sort of rebound from losing her last husband.

While waiting for her call, he kept lifting the receiver for an instant to check the line was all right, then went back to rearranging books on shelves. The first ring still made him jump.

'Papa's just gone to bed,' she told him. 'We had a long talk.'

'Well, don't keep me in suspense. Tell me exactly what he said. Didn't it come as a bit of a shock? I mean, he must think it's all a bit sudden, to put it mildly.'

'Oh, no. He wasn't surprised. He seems to have suspected already. But then he knows me very well! And although he feels it would be better if we left it a little longer, he does see that selling the house in Munich makes that difficult. But James? Do you know that he immediately guessed the one thing I wanted above all?'

'What's that?'

'To have the wedding here at Lotzingen – in the chapel!'

'But my love,' he laughed, taken off guard, 'I'm still a heathen, you know.' He had been counting on a quiet registry office affair in London. And yet her enthusiasm touched him deeply. He knew how much the castle's baroque chapel meant to her. The wedding to Georg had presumably taken place in Vienna to accommodate the hundreds of guests. Wall to wall Putzis, Sisis, and Gotfis. At least he would be spared that.

'Oh, James, I know we never had a chance to talk about . . . well, the question of religion.'

'Now just hang on a moment! You're not about to suggest I actually become a Catholic, are you?'

'But would it really be asking too much of you? You cannot imagine how happy . . .'

'You don't know what you're asking! It's not just a matter of making a Catholic out of a Protestant. I'm an agnostic, for God's sake!'

The last remark reduced them both to helpless laughter. All his arguments collapsed, and when they returned to a modicum of seriousness, he could only fall back on feigned truculence.

'I've never heard anything so shameless,' was his reply to the suggestion that if religion meant so little to him, then surely it could not hurt to pretend.

'What do you honestly expect me to do?' he ended up saying. 'Look in Yellow Pages under Churches? This isn't America where no doubt they have "Dial-a-Conversion, All Charge Cards Welcome!"'

'Please. Just trust me and I will arrange things. There is a very nice old priest in London called Father Hoyos and he can give you instruction.'

With a good deal of accuracy, as it turned out, he pictured an urbane Jesuit, the *branche cadette* of some grand family, who had known half the Lumbering Procession from the font. James didn't know whether to be amused or recalcitrant.

Christina came to London after her week at Lotzingen, and James, in a great state of excitement, met her at the airport. He had spent the last three days shopping and spring-cleaning for her arrival. But to his dismay he found she was booked in at Claridge's again. Trying not to show his hurt, he probed without success for the reason.

After lunch, she came back to the little flat in Notting Hill and surveyed everything with an air of wonder which he found unsettling. All the spontaneity between them seemed to have frozen. And Christina's nervousness compounded his own when they made love, rather unsatisfactorily, in his bed.

She seemed to be suffering from some sort of claustrophobia. And on the totally unconvincing pretext of an important telephone call, she escaped back to Claridge's, doggedly refusing his offer of a lift.

Having found her a taxi, James returned to stare at their untouched cups of coffee. He became convinced with a quiet despair that everything was over.

An hour later, she rang to apologize and assure him that her feelings hadn't changed. He had to be patient. She was scared. This was a big step. Probably much bigger for her than for him. They should think of this visit for the moment as a purely practical one. She had come to find a new home.

Far from reassured, James lay awake most of that night. In the morning, she was supposed to go down to Ascot to break the news of their marriage to Stephanie. She might have already changed her mind. Insomnia magnified his fears out of all proportion and her absence, lying in another bed less than two miles away, tortured him with its unfairness.

Daylight brought a sober resignation. Christina's attack of doubt was entirely justified. They hardly knew each other and she perhaps suspected that he might have made her into a vehicle for his fantasy. Presumably, from a woman's point of view, that wasn't very much better than being a vessel for male lust.

But to complete his confusion, she rang that evening as though there had been no hint of a problem between them. She had taken Stephanie for a walk in Windsor Great Park and told her about their plans. Once again he felt limp with relief. The return of hope erased all questions.

The following day, Christina found the house on Brook Green. She immediately telephoned James and another tour was arranged for early in the afternoon. Her excitement and trepidation produced in him a surge of affection. 'Now *don't* allow them to see how interested you are,' he said, knowing the advice was useless.

Mrs Pears, the owner, cornered James at one end of the

sitting room. She was a plump, short divorcee who clearly believed in elaborate femininity, overheated rooms and heavy doses of scent. But worst of all, she had a confidential manner which was both smug and ingratiating.

'As I told your wife-to-be this morning, the whole place has only just been refurbished from top to bottom by a very famous interior decorator.' She mentioned some name which meant nothing to him. He nodded and quickly looked away. He felt tempted to say that since he would not be signing the cheque, her estate-agent buzzwords were rather wasted. How frightful, he thought, the way people feel obliged to imitate professional jargon. Later, he debated whether this was some sort of counterpart to Sartre's theory from observing waiters: that we play at a role in order to distance ourselves from it.

The unusually large rooms were well-proportioned, yet the famous interior decorator had produced the worst sort of prissy extravagance with pink walls, ruched cerise blinds and huge powder-blue curtains of stiff silk like a debutante's dress in the 1950s. James could not see Christina lasting a day surrounded by such confections.

'As the agents should have made clear,' Mrs Pears persisted, 'the asking price of course reflects the very considerable expense lavished on the decor. Fittings like carpets and curtains, however, can of course be ...'

'Oh, no, don't worry,' said Christina from the other end of the room. 'I am not interested in any of the decoration. The whole thing needs to be stripped completely and the walls painted white. Don't you agree, James? That is the only way to start.'

The look of horrified disbelief on the owner's face forced him to bring out a handkerchief and pass off his guffaw as a sneeze.

Once out of the house, Christina too laughed at her gaffe, but not as much as James. She was impatient to get to the agents. There, she informed them she was willing to pay the full asking price on condition contracts were exchanged within ten days and vacant possession obtained by the end of the month. James had never seen people fall over themselves so much to satisfy a customer. This produced a mixed sensation; more of unease than satisfaction. The outrageous price disturbed him most of all. Particularly when she was obviously intending to spend another fortune on redecoration. He began to feel out of his league again.

'I presume we are of course talking of a straight cash transaction,' said the manager. His smile, both sycophantic and knowing, mirrored the woman's manner of half an hour before.

Christina frowned in astonishment. 'You mean Mrs Whatever-her-name will *not* accept a cheque? That will be a lot of money to carry around.'

'Er, no, Madam,' the man tittered. 'I simply wanted to be certain that there was no mortgage financing involved.'

James, despite his desire to remain in the background, had to explain what a mortgage meant.

That night, on Christina's insistence, they celebrated at a very expensive seafood restaurant. Afterwards, he accompanied her back to the hotel, and to his delight she hesitated in the hall, then suggested he come up to her room. All the tensions of the previous two days were effaced. James was reminded of their first night together in Munich, only this time he was the one to burst out laughing from time to time. The image of Mrs Pears's expression kept coming back to him. 'Sorry,' he said. 'I'm obviously in a silly mood.'

They lay together for hours discussing the different ways to arrange the house. James would have the top for his study and books, and Stephanie most of the second floor. Christina wanted a small sitting room for writing letters and telephoning, and a large dressing room with her own bathroom.

'Quite right! The Queen's apartments. What a good thing it's such an enormous house. We'll call it Schloss Hammerschmidt.' He kissed her shoulder. 'Honestly, you are amazing. I've never heard of anyone coming to London and bagging just what they wanted straight off.'

'Oh, but the lawyers at home had already obtained a list of all those which matched what I was looking for. There were only three or four worth seeing.'

'Ah, well, yes,' he said. 'I suppose that does tend to make life a little simpler.'

As he fell asleep he tried to work out why she was so reluctant to spend the night at his flat. It wasn't just the scruffiness and its size. The problem was more complex than that. She had also been rather evasive about her day with Stephanie.

Christina saw their wedding as a purely family occasion. James firmly agreed with the idea of keeping it small, but his unusual dearth of relatives produced a sensation of comparative nakedness. In need of moral support, he invited David and Antonia. Both writers and probably his closest friends, they tended to get on well with everybody and, most important of all, Christina had liked them immediately.

'Even though you're witnesses,' he hurriedly reassured them, 'you won't have to do anything during the service except sign the book at the end.'

'Oh, what a pity,' said David. 'I was looking forward to giving you away. Even so, it's still worth the trip just to see you put all that religious instruction to good use.' During one of Christina's absences in Austria, James had entertained them over dinner with descriptions of Father Hoyos.

'Pay no attention,' Antonia told James. 'I'll make sure he behaves. In any case, I think it all sounds the greatest fun.'

The wedding was fixed for the first weekend in September, just before Stephanie came back to England for the autumn term. She had been spending the summer holidays at Lotzingen while Christina returned to London to oversee the builders and decorators. Then, for the last week in August, mother and daughter flew to Greece for a week at the villa of Andrea Bourbon Valdemar.

James had been invited to join them and would have liked to go, but after careful consideration he reluctantly decided to invent a rush of last-minute things in London. The week in Greece was Stephanie's only chance to be alone with her mother before the wedding. And to judge from Christina's equivocation about their day out together, her daughter's reaction to the prospect of a stepfather could not have been very enthusiastic. But then Christina's uneasy manner with Stephanie had probably not helped.

Accompanied by David and Antonia, James finally flew to Vienna three days before the wedding. Christina met them at the airport and took them to the Schwanemberg Palace, behind the Burgtheater. Most of the building was leased out to various companies including a market research organization and a public relations firm, but the family retained one side of the courtyard.

'So what's the plan?' James asked as they strolled arm in arm round the Hofburg garden before lunch. Their steps went in slow unison on the macadamed path under the chestnut trees. Having circumnavigated the Theseustempel twice, they headed towards the twin equestrian statues in front of the Neue Hofburg. In the background, there was a steady sound of traffic from the Ring. 'Apart from an energetic sightseeing programme with David and Antonia – and keeping out of the way while you finish whatever still needs doing – am I going to see anything of you?'

'Today, do you mean? Because tomorrow, you know, I have to return to Lotzingen.'

'Well, actually, I was thinking more of tonight. I noticed that we don't seem to be sharing a room. Now is that just for form's sake, or would the servants be truly shocked if they found that I had somehow sleepwalked my way to your bed?'

She laughed, slightly embarrassed. 'Oh, James, darling. You will probably consider me very old-fashioned ...'

'No! Really?' He looked over the top of his spectacles, then took them off to clean them on the end of his tie.

'Oh, *please* don't tease. I know you'll think it's silly, but would you mind so very much to wait until after the wedding?'

He sighed, then chuckled. 'Honestly, my love, you are amazing. They just don't make 'em like you anymore.' He raised her hand and kissed it. 'Of course, if that's what you want, then I will indeed respect this pre-bridal sanctity. But you must admit, it does rather give you the air of a recycled virgin.'

'Oh, you are horrible!' she burst out. David and Antonia up ahead turned in surprise. 'I have never met such an unromantic man!'

'*Un*romantic? If only that were true. Scratch a cynic, and underneath you'll find a frustrated dreamer.'

She glanced at him as if to assess the degree of truth behind his jest.

❧ 10 ❧

The day before the wedding, Christina's brother Alexander came to the Schwanemberg Palace to take James, David and Antonia to Lotzingen.

'I have come to collect the English delegation,' Sasha announced with mock formality, and promptly focused his attention upon Antonia with *Handkuss* and compliments. The spectacle reminded James how compulsive the exercise of charm could become. But Antonia accepted the game with merriment and gave her husband a wink when Sasha was not looking.

At that time, Sasha had recently separated from his second wife and retained the effortless good looks which James had first seen in the portrait photograph beside Christina's bed. The only difference was that his dark hair had become frosted at the sides.

Antonia again glanced at David as they settled into the back seat of the Mercedes estate and they both had to look away to stop laughing out loud.

James, obliged to maintain an air of propriety, sat in front next to Alexander, who paused in the act of starting the car to give him an ironic look. 'Nervous?'

'No. Not especially. Should I be?'

'Oh, yes. On these occasions, always.'

This mild flippancy irritated James. It left him feeling curiously flat, and to his further annoyance, he could not understand how something so trivial could have the power to affect him.

From the Ring it did not take long to join the Wiener–

96

Neustadt autobahn. They followed the same route James had taken the first time with Christina, past the same villages and the same baroque spires. But the countryside had changed from a bright nascent green to the dryness of late summer with the occasional field of sunflowers, their withered heads drooping.

Then they followed the road up between the Fischbacher Alpen and the Hochschwab. Antonia commented on the banks of flowers along the balconies of houses and the heavily laden apple trees. And when they finally ascended the valley of Lotzingen, Alexander greeted the first glimpse of the castle with a forward nod over the steering wheel just like Christina. The gesture made James think of bowing to the new moon. The last trace of his bad mood lifted and an end-of-term exhilaration came over him too.

In the courtyard by the steps, they climbed out of the car and breathed in luxuriantly, blinking in the sun. The air tasted so good after the city.

'It *really* is beautiful up here,' said Antonia.

Malte bounded down the steps yapping in excitement. Then Christina appeared. She kissed David and Antonia first, saying how wonderful it was to see them at Lotzingen, then, under her brother's gaze, she gave James a self-conscious peck.

'What a welcome for your bridegroom!' said Alexander.

She coloured. 'My welcomes are given in private.'

'Quite right,' said Antonia. 'We don't want him getting even more of a swollen head.'

'Thank you very much,' said James. 'With friends like you, I shouldn't be in too much danger of that. Anyway, knowing Christina's respect for wedding custom, I'll probably find myself out in a tent tonight so as to be under a different roof.'

'Not quite!' She quickly squeezed his hand and they turned to go inside, but at that moment Stephanie materialized beside them. The sun in Greece seemed to have transformed her. She looked several years older. James jerked back his head in a show of surprise.

'Gracious!' he exclaimed, guilty at having forgotten her.

'Where did you spring from?'

'I was here.' Arms by her side, she leaned forward to kiss him on both cheeks.

'That's really quite a tan you've got. I'm sure you'll be the envy of all your schoolfriends ... who are no doubt scattered in lobster pink patches all round the Mediterranean. Probably the last bits of British colouring on the world map. Anyway, enough of that. I don't think you've met David and Antonia.'

Stephanie shook hands gravely. Afterwards, as everyone moved towards the steps, David made a face of disappointment at James. He had greatly enjoyed his account of the curtsey in Claridge's.

Prince Tassilo was waiting for them in the hall with the old portraits and the chamois horns. Although lunch should have started twenty minutes before, his manner betrayed little sign of impatience while he greeted the new arrivals. James had already spent enough time at Lotzingen to know how much he disliked meals being delayed. A few moments later, the majordomo put in his fleeting appearance, and Prince Tassilo indicated the way to Antonia.

The rest of the family, including a dozen of Christina's nephews and nieces, some of whom were already married, turned up during the latter half of the afternoon. David and Antonia were bemused by the crowd at tea, when one after another, the polite, fair and good-looking Franzis, Hansis, Ettis and Loulous came up to introduce themselves.

David leaned towards James. 'But they all look the same.'

'Yes, they do a bit, don't they?'

'Shall I test you on their names?' he murmured out of the side of his mouth. 'Or more to the point, on exactly how everyone's related?'

'No. Please! My general-purpose smile is about to crack, and I haven't got a clue who to kiss or who to shake hands with.'

'Why don't you compromise and kiss hands like the rest of them? I think Antonia's getting quite a taste for it.'

'It may be boringly English and unsporting, but I refuse to

make a complete fool of myself.'

'Coward!'

The volume of chatter and laughter did not diminish even when tea was cleared away. James steered Christina aside to suggest that he take David and Antonia off for a walk as they all felt in need of some exercise.

'I wish I could come with you,' she said, looking around. 'But as you can see, I obviously can't. Please, do take Malte, if you can find him.'

On the way out they came across Stephanie, about to slip upstairs.

'Are you escaping too?' said James, surprised to find her avoiding all her cousins.

'I have some revision to do. School goes back in three days time and we have tests.'

After a glance from James, David and Antonia moved on.

'Wouldn't you prefer to come for a walk with us?' he said. 'It's too nice an afternoon to be inside. Besides I'd like the chance for a bit of a chat. Tomorrow's going to be busy, to say the least, and then we disappear off in different directions.'

She looked up the enormous wooden staircase for a moment to consider, then turned back, although still avoiding his eyes. 'Is it all right if I only come part of the way?'

'Of course it is. Do you need to change your shoes, or anything?'

'No. It's perfectly dry. I can go like this.'

In the inner courtyard they found the other two playing with Malte, his barks echoing in the confined space. They set off together under the arch and then turned out of the open courtyard down the hill. After a little James slowed his pace so that he and Stephanie hung behind out of earshot.

'Do you mind flying back to England with David and Antonia, and staying the night with them? They'll take you down to Ascot in the morning. It's just that it seemed the simplest solution from every point of view.'

'No. That's fine. I understand.'

'We'll come down as soon as we're back and bring you up to London for a proper look at the house. It should be nearly finished by then. Have you yet thought about any particular colours, or wallpaper for your bedroom?'

'No. Not really. White will do perfectly well.'

He remembered her blank room in the house at Starnberg. 'Are you sad not to be going back to Munich?'

'Not very.'

'What? It doesn't make much difference one way or the other?'

She shrugged. James sighed inwardly at his failure to dispel her distrust.

'Listen, I know this upheaval can't be easy for you. By that I mean the whole idea of living in another country, and in a new home with a strange man in it. Especially since you haven't had much time to get used to the idea. But basically what I'm trying to get across is that I don't want you to feel pushed aside by my arrival on the scene.' His words sounded depressingly hackneyed. I bet that's what they all say, he told himself.

Her evasive mutter did not surprise him. He grunted in what was supposed to sound a humorous way. 'You don't appear very convinced. Anyway, what's your role tomorrow? Have you been roped in as a bridesmaid, or are you going to give your mother away?'

'I'm to be the bridesmaid.' Then she glanced over her shoulder. 'Do you mind if I go back now?'

That evening the whole party, over twenty strong, assembled in the Blue Drawing Room. The removal of dust covers had dramatically revealed its old magnificence. Dominating the scene from one end was a large, heavily framed portrait of the Prince Windisch Grätz who crushed the 1848 rising in Vienna. History, thought James, must seem much more cosy when it's a family affair.

The mixture of generations and their facial resemblances made the gathering look like one of those vast conversation pieces of *fin de siècle* royalty. Except for Prince Tassilo, who wore white tie and tails, the men were in dinner jackets and the women in long dresses with family jewels.

James insisted on wearing his old faithful from Munich as a sort of talisman, even though Christina, in an attempt to change his wardrobe completely, had taken him to her father's tailor in London. 'I'm not sure I want to be next in line for stripping and redecorating,' had been his semi-reluctant protest.

For most of the time before dinner, James chatted with Christina's eldest brother. At fifty-four, Eberhard was already a grandfather and he joked about the idea of Christina as a great-aunt. Yet even with all this affable family chat, James just could not picture him as a brother-in-law. Or Sasha for that matter. Or the elder sister Lore who was married to a Schönborn something or other. Only then did the real implausibility of becoming part of their world sink in.

He had made enough jokes about the Lumbering Procession's incestuous nature with David and Antonia. And he was well aware that whatever his progress in German, the cousinly nicknames and family reference points in almost every conversation were enough to exclude anyone not brought up in their circle. Yet, with the ingenuous, or perhaps arrogant, assumption of love, he had never really considered what an outsider he was.

His equanimity at this discovery surprised him almost more than the discovery itself. On earlier visits, his orphan side had yearned to join that central sense of security which Lotzingen represented. But the family's claustrophobic potential, when en masse like this, had not occurred to him then. He felt a sense of relief. To orbit the Schwanemberg nucleus rather than join it was probably the best solution after all.

When the majordomo opened the double doors the assembly lined up in their pairs and, led by Prince Tassilo with Christina on his arm, proceeded to the White Dining Room. James escorted Eberhard's wife, a rather regal matron, who was to sit on his right. Conversation followed a predictable pattern. She asked about his books and the house they had found in London, then he asked about her children.

'And afterwards, James,' said Prince Tassilo across the table, mopping his great moustache with outward pushes of his napkin, 'shall we have a little game of chess like the last time you were here?'

'With the greatest of pleasure,' he replied. 'Providing of course that tomorrow doesn't depend on my winning.' Christina laughed at his little bow in her direction.

In the Blue Drawing Room after dinner, they sat down to play at the ebony table inlaid with tulipwood. Others pulled up chairs and another circle of spectators peered over their shoulders. James, despite his joke, still sensed an element of doing battle for a daughter's hand. The old man was a deceptive player: slow and dogged, yet wily. James reminded himself not to move so fast this time.

While Prince Tassilo considered the response to his opening, James became mesmerized by the beautifully carved ivory pieces. He wondered to what degree chess, with its queens and kings and towers, was a game of symbolism. Not Oedipal exactly, but there must be something in the way the queen was the most powerful piece and the king had to be trapped, not killed. Chess as a political statement, he thought lightly, and braced himself to concentrate.

To James's surprise, he won after a good game. The possibility that his victory might be a form of wedding present had already struck him, yet this time he really had played better than usual. Christina's blown kiss of congratulation and the applause from the onlookers gave him great pleasure.

'Thank you, James,' said Prince Tassilo, rearranging the pieces with his enormous hands. 'That was very enjoyable. And now,' he sighed, 'I think it is time for some rest. Where has Christina disappeared to?'

'I'm here, Papa. Right behind you.' She rested her hands on the shoulders of his old tailcoat. He reached up to pat one of them.

'Will you walk with me up the stairs?'

'But of course.'

Everyone stood up to say goodnight, and Prince Tassilo, a hand raised in acknowledgement, wished them the same. Does the role create the actor? thought James. But then he contrasted the gesture with the laconic flourishes of Sartre's waiter.

The question should in fact have been: does only a central role *convince* the actor?

The day of their wedding passed so quickly that its separate stages seemed to merge into ceaseless motion.

When Eberhard came to call him at seven for Holy Communion, James scrambled up from the bedclothes in confusion. He had been dreaming that Stefan Valkus arrived at the last moment to marry Christina and somehow persuaded him to act as witness.

James reached the chapel slightly dishevelled and out of breath. Prince Tassilo greeted him with a stern nod, and James, directed by Eberhard, ducked into the confessional. There, with the help of a crib sheet in German prepared by Christina the day before, he sweated through the formulae with the local bishop. Father Hoyos had taken a fall in Paris three days before and broken his leg.

During the short service afterwards, James looked at the Schwanembergs around him. They were all on parade except for Sasha, and Christina, whose confession would be heard in her room. The thought of breakfast made his ordeal feel almost pleasurable in retrospect.

On the way back – a complicated route of corridors and stairs – he lingered at a window over the valley. In a clear hint of autumn, yet with the promise of a beautiful day, the pines were dark silhouettes in the mist, while above, the sky was a perfect blue. He longed to go out for a walk in the damp, mysterious silence of such a morning.

Barely had he poured his coffee when Eberhard arrived to remind him that he should be fully dressed and ready by nine thirty. James looked at his watch. The service had taken much longer than he realized. David grinned at him across the table.

'I don't want any remarks from you,' said James.

From then on, everything became more blurred: the long wait at the altar, self-conscious in morning coat and not daring to look round; his restless glances at the chapel's cream and gilt decoration while he silently rehearsed the marriage vows in

German; then, the sound of the congregation rising to their feet behind him. At last he felt able to turn.

Christina, who wore no veil, approached slowly on her father's arm. She looked incredibly young and beautiful in ivory silk, her hair magnificent under a pearl tiara. Behind came Stephanie, slim and dark and serious in her bridesmaid's dress.

All he remembered of the High Mass were Christina's presence at his side and the necessity of mouthing the responses because he never really knew what point had been reached. The service, with its apparently illogical rhythm, seemed to have no good reason for ever coming to an end. A couple of unexpected pauses raised false hopes, but for the most part, he lost all notion of time as his mind drifted with the spellbinding sound of the Mass. The beginning of the marriage ceremony itself took him by surprise.

At last they came out into the courtyard, squinting against the glare. The sun had risen fully and the last trace of valley mist long since evaporated. James and Christina were led off to the main steps where the photographer took pictures of them, first on their own, then with Christina's father and Stephanie, and finally with all the Schwanembergs and the witnesses. As soon as that was completed, everyone crowded round kissing and congratulating and taking pictures themselves. Antonia hugged James. She had tears in her eyes.

'Wow!' whispered David from beside her. 'You must feel well and truly wed after that lot.'

Antonia turned on him in exasperation, but James only had time to make a face as he and Christina were swept up in a rush of younger Schwanembergs – another blur of faces – to be led off in triumph to the Hunting Hall for toasts.

In spite of Christina's presence at his side, James felt curiously alone and distant. Even his euphoria possessed a tingling numbness. That sensation of being outside his own body had returned, almost as though everything were happening to another self next to him. Oh, God! he thought. Don't say it's the wandering twin back again. Today of all days.

'Come on,' whispered Christina. 'Now we must slip away to

see Mama. She will be waiting for us.'

Once the nurse had finished rearranging the pillows, her mother was ready to receive them. She appeared much weaker than the last time James had seen her, and her blessing on their marriage had a valedictory air.

She gestured feebly towards the bedside table, and the nurse passed her a flat, semi-circular case of faded morocco leather stamped with an imperial crown and monogram. Pushing it across the bedclothes, she indicated the case with her eyes. Christina reached over. She obviously knew the necklace inside, for she greeted it with a familiar smile.

James watched the case open to reveal an unwearable necklace of topazes set in heavy nineteenth-century gold filigree. Although clearly not one of the main Schwanemberg pieces, which must have already been given to Eberhard's wife, this present appeared to be symbolic in its way. Christina's mother had presumably been left it by her mother, and she was handing it over now rather than including it in her will. And Christina would leave it to Stephanie. But Stephanie? What would she do? The chain had to stop somewhere.

As they drove away from the waving and cheering, James turned on the windscreen wipers to clear the drift of flower petals used as confetti. They exchanged glances of wary affection. To be alone together felt strange.

For something to say, he again asked about their journey. From Lotzingen, she told him, it would take about three hours down through the Carinthian mountains. That night they would spend on the south shore of the Wörthersee, where her uncle had put his house at their disposal. Then, the following day, they would carry on to Venice.

❧ 11 ❧

Although the mountain peaks still floated in a luminous haze, night had fallen in the valley of the Wörthersee. Christina indicated a cluster of lights on the north shore of the lake. 'That's where most of the hotels are,' she said. 'Klagenfurt is too far to see from here.'

They had wandered down to the landing stage before dinner. James inhaled, luxuriating in the stillness. The notion of lakeside hotels produced a Noël Cowardish sensation, but when he finally identified Klagenfurt in his memory, the mood was dramatically reversed. This was the frontier area where Russian prisoners had been handed over to the Red Army. The clash of images made him wonder whether every beautiful spot had a sinister link.

'Shall we go in?' she said. 'Dinner should be ready by now.' His enthusiasm was so abrupt that she gave him a look of humorous surprise.

The path ascended through the trees. Ahead of them, concealed lights along the terrace cast upward shadows on the façade. A mixture of schloss and hunting lodge, it had a faintly absurd charm with balconies of rustic woodwork and turrets at each end.

The elderly couple who looked after the property had known Christina all her life, and for the newlyweds nothing appeared to be too much trouble. There were even little vases of wild flowers in their room, because Christina as a child used to wander off to pick them in inconvenient quantity, certain that everyone else wanted arrangements throughout in the house. Life there must have become lonely for the two of them, thought James. The place had the air of a royal retreat, kept ready for a master who never came.

Dinner was served in a room of eighteenth-century painted panelling. Like at Lotzingen, the food was much lighter than most Austrian food, and wonderfully fresh. The trout had apparently been caught that morning. Replete and sensuously tired by the end of the meal, James ran forefinger and thumb up the stem of his glass. He contemplated its golden contents, a Tokay from before the war. 'Your uncle must be something of a connoisseur,' he said. 'But I certainly get the impression that he doesn't come here often.'

'I know. It is such a pity. And now that he is ill and old, he may not see this house again.'

James nodded reflectively. He could not help wondering where Christina and Georg had spent their first honeymoon. She had been eighteen – only five years older than Stephanie. He could not ignore the streak of irrational jealousy. Perhaps envy would be more accurate, he reasoned; a piercing regret not to have known her at that age. And yet in those days, she would never have considered him for a second. That alone was enough to show how everything depended on good timing.

'What is going through your mind?' she said, intrigued by the changes in his expression.

He raised his eyes and grinned. 'Voluptuous thoughts of sliding in between fresh sheets.'

They had breakfast the following morning out on the terrace. Through the trees, the lake was already dotted with the triangular sails of small boats and windsurfers. A strong breeze was blowing out there, ruffling the surface of the water, a deep blue-green far more substantial in its way than the pale, distant mountains.

Christina looked at her watch.

'Is it time to hit the road?' he said.

'I think we should be off fairly soon. I said we would arrive about four. Do you want me to drive?'

He lifted her hand from the table to kiss the back of her

wrist. 'Only if you feel sufficiently recovered from the shock of yesterday.'

'Only if I have recovered?' she laughed. 'You were the one who looked dazed! You should have seen yourself in the chapel.'

'Oh, dear. Was it really that obvious?'

'Yes. To me at any rate. But my darling James. I have not properly thanked you for ...' She hesitated and looked down at the coffeepot. 'For making it possible to have the wedding there.'

'There's no need to be bashful,' he said. 'However much I may have grumbled at the time, it was hardly a major sacrifice. Poor old Father Hoyos. I hope he's not too sad at having missed the result of his handiwork.'

'Yes,' she said with the sudden animation of someone relieved of a small load. 'We will send him a postcard when we get to Venice.'

On the autostrada from the Austrian frontier down towards the Adriatic, hardly a word was spoken. James watched over a landscape in which Alpine houses were abruptly replaced by meridional farmhouses with terracotta tiled roofs and green shutters. Almost without warning the mountains had given way to the coastal plain of vineyards and fields of maize. Inside the car it had become much warmer.

'Is anything the matter?' said Christina, glancing sideways. 'It feels strange when you are silent for a long time.'

'Oh?' He uttered a quick laugh. 'Sorry about that. But I wasn't miles away, whatever it may have looked like. I was trying to imagine you at eighteen and wondering how you'd changed.'

A flicker of her eyes betrayed an instinctive wariness. 'I was probably what you would expect at that age.' She shifted her position behind the wheel. 'Romantic and impossibly naive. And of course I refused to listen to advice.' Her quick smile was evasive. She nodded down at the map open on his knees.

'If you look along the coast towards Trieste, you'll find Duino, where Rilke wrote his elegies.'

'So I noticed. Do you want to go there?'

'No, not particularly. Let's get on to Venice.'

'I agree.' He folded up the map and put it in the glove compartment. So, he thought, the past is still locked out of sight. Probably from herself more than anyone else. Maybe with me, she's hoping to wipe the tape and start again. The idea appealed to him in a strange way.

Christina's plan was to leave the car at the airport and take a water taxi across the lagoon. She wanted them to have their first view together from the Adriatic side. The idea of such extravagance made James uneasy. Although he knew he had to jettison his Scottish attitudes, or rather his contradictory bouts of parsimony, the dramatic change in his fortunes had aroused a deep, almost superstitious, distrust. But one look at Christina was enough to remind him that any dissatisfaction with his lot would be totally perverse.

Standing in the back of the launch as it accelerated away from the jetty, he put an arm around her shoulders and hugged her gratefully. She rested her head against his for a few seconds, then, holding on to the varnished wood of the cabin roof, she gazed forward across the lagoon.

After a while, he sat down to one side. From that angle he could see more of her profile than the horizon or the industrial landscape of Mestre. Her eyes were narrowed against sun and wind like that first day at Lotzingen. She bent to search in her shoulder bag for the tortoiseshell dark glasses he had come to regard as her trademark.

On Christina's instructions, the driver took the long route out beyond Murano. She pointed ahead eagerly when Venice began to rise from the water, and James stood up to join her. Her anticipation stirred him. It struck him as a mature and complex desire, quite different from her childlike excitement at that first glimpse of Lotzingen. But he quickly mocked such an idea. Venice, he reminded himself, had a funny effect on lots of people. Not least, the temptation to rush into purple metaphor. Yet when the *campanili* and domes took shape above the shimmering water like a mirage of the sea, he once again surrendered in awe to the sheer improbability of the place.

Past San Marco, the launch slowed at the mouth of the Grand Canal. This gave them more time to admire the façades ranging from wedding-cake marble to umber stucco with Gothic windows. Beyond the Accademia bridge, they rolled on the wash from a vaporetto, then turned into a side canal. A little way down, the driver swung alongside the flood-stained landing steps of a palazzo. The bell was rung, and a manservant came to open the wooden gate. He wore a white jacket with epaulettes of twisted braid. James kept his remark about the Lumbering Procession's private hotel chain to himself.

The servant took their suitcases and led the way through a short passage permeated by the smell of the canal. They came out in a half-open courtyard of brick laid in a herringbone pattern. To their left was the main door from the street in a wall surmounted by terracotta castellation, rather Moorish in style. Ahead, a staircase in white Istrian stone, pitted with age, ascended to the *piano nobile* of which the front part rested on massive wooden beams supported by pillars. This formed a sort of *galleria* below.

Upstairs, the corridors were tall, whitewashed and high-ceilinged, the floors a diagonal chequerboard of white and russet-pink Verona marble. In their huge bedroom, a bouquet awaited them on the writing table. Christina examined the card.

'Oh! They're from Andrea. How sweet of him! "*Aux jeunes amoureux*",' she read. '"I am so sad to have missed the wedding. But to make up for not seeing you then, you must allow me to take you out either for lunch or dinner." It looks as if he is staying at the Cipriani.'

'The ubiquitous Andrea,' said James, inconsequentially. He had wandered over to the open window and was watching a tourist couple reclined self-consciously in a gondola.

'You do not sound very keen, but we really should see him. He was so good to Stephanie and I in Greece ...'

'My love, that is not what I meant, honestly. It'd be fun to see him.' He looked over his shoulder then. 'But I must admit I can't help wondering how many other relatives of yours we're going to bump into here.'

'Oh, James darling.' She came up and put her hands on his shoulders from behind. 'How terrible for you.' She kissed the side of his neck. 'Would you prefer to be on a desert island?'

'I doubt if we'd be safe even there.' He pretended to sound lugubrious. 'A yacht full of Lottis and Sigis would be sure to turn up after a couple of days.'

'Now you do exaggerate!'

'No? Really?' He arched back to kiss the side of her face. 'Anyway, we must remember one thing above all. We are also here to work! "The Image of Power and Authority", or whatever we're going to call it, awaits us.'

'I have not forgotten,' she replied. 'We will start in the Accademia first thing tomorrow.'

James had not meant her to take him seriously, but she fetched the guidebook from the writing table to look up the opening times.

Her enthusiasm at the idea of their partnership moved him. And to do the research together would be much more enjoyable than on his own. She also had a greater knowledge of art history as well as a better eye. Some of her ideas for the book were wide of the mark and some appeared very interesting, yet almost any comment or question was useful, if only to clarify his own thoughts on the subject. After several months of very interrupted work, his ideas had hardly progressed beyond the original instinct.

[*The theory I wanted to explore ran more or less as follows: patronage of the arts had created mirrors to flatter the self-esteem of powerful men and their families. But in time, this had a corrupting effect strangely similar to that of interbreeding. In other words, was there any similarity between the illusion of dynastic immortality and genetic repetition?*

I was also intrigued to see if the mirror notion had any link with another pet theme of mine: that however dramatic the decline in the power of kings and princes, their influence still lingered in a sort of cultural subconsciousness as the paternal 'imago' of the fairy tale.

Of course I knew only too well that these two different aspects did not really fit together. But in Vienna, just before the wedding, my enthusiasm had revived because of a coincidence, which I no doubt took too seriously. On Antonia's urging, Christina gave the three of us a full guided tour of the Schwanemberg Palace, including the parts the family no longer used. This visit had also been my first. On my two other trips to Austria that summer we had spent very little time in Vienna because Christina always wanted to rush back to Lotzingen at the first opportunity.

The Palace's main reception room turned out to be a long white drawing room with gilt plasterwork and looking-glasses down one side to reflect the portraits which had hung opposite. The unexpectedness of this Salon der Spiegel was, I suppose, bound to have an over-impressive effect considering my state of nervous exhilaration at the time.]

Christina made sure he was up in good time for their first day's work by ordering breakfast for a quarter past eight. James thought this excessively zealous, but restrained his reaction to a teasing grumble.

Their route through the Dorsoduro took them along canal walks, past barges with tarpaulins still coated in dew, over bridges with worn steps, then down an alley smelling of damp stone into an unexpected square, diagonally divided between brightness and shadow. Christina, finding she had mistaken the way, became irritated with herself.

'Don't worry, my love,' he said. 'It's hardly going to matter if we miss a few minutes. We *are* on honeymoon, you know.'

In the Accademia, they split up and wandered round making separate notes on any pictures which might be relevant. And shortly before the gallery closed at two, they crossed the bridge to the Campo Morosini, where they took a table in the sun outside a trattoria. James was so hungry that he finished off the bread sticks before the waiter arrived to take their order.

'I'd forgotten how many wonderful pictures they had,' he said. 'But I must say I was a bit disappointed from the book's point of view. Even allowing for the way the Venetian Republic discouraged personal glorification, my list of possibles is pathetic to say the least. How about yours?'

'It is not even worth discussing,' she said dejectedly. 'Now that I think about it, probably the only good example in the whole of Venice is that equestrian statue by Verrocchio.' She made a long face. 'We seem to have picked the wrong city for our honeymoon.'

'Rubbish. We came here for our own pleasure, and the work side was purely incidental. Anyway, I don't know about you, but I enjoyed myself this morning.'

Christina relaxed with the admission that she had loved seeing Carpaccio's St Ursula cycle again.

'Is he your favourite Venetian painter?'

'Beyond any doubt. He was Malte's too.' She smiled but James looked blank. 'Don't you remember?' she said. 'Malte Laurids Brigge. In the first few pages it is mentioned that he wrote a study on Carpaccio.'

James blinked his confusion. 'Sorry! For a second I thought you were talking about Malte, the dog.' He laughed at himself and squeezed her hand on the table. 'But as for the book, I'm afraid I've forgotten most of it. In fact I remember you had to put me right about something the first time we met.'

He tried to catch the waiter's eye to order more bread. 'Tell me, was that also Malte you were quoting back on the bridge, just then? The bit about visitors abandoning themselves to the "rewarding swoon of the gondola" without ever attempting to know the city?'

She nodded, her smile one of eager complicity. Christ, he thought. She's even worse than me when it comes to taking novels seriously. But why that character in particular? From what he remembered, it seemed such an improbable choice. And for her of all people. A *déclassé* Danish aristocrat, morbidly introvert and rotting to death in a Parisian garret. Perhaps he had better read the book again when they returned to London; especially since it seemed to be some sort of sacred text. He looked round again for the waiter.

Tired after the long morning and sleepy from lunch in the sun, they returned to the palazzo for a siesta. And there, in the enormous bedroom, cool and almost dark behind the shutters, they made love.

'Do you think this is why nothing in Venice is open in the afternoons?' he murmured afterwards.

'Undoubtedly.'

'They're very civilized, the Italians.'

They fell asleep only to be woken some time later by the telephone. Christina picked up the receiver upside down. Her expression as she turned it round made James smile. The identity of the caller was not hard to guess. He lay there imagining Andrea's languid tone.

He raised his head slightly from the pillow when Christina put her hand over the mouthpiece. 'It's Andrea. He wants us to join him for dinner tonight. All right?'

James nodded, but inwardly he groaned at the thought of going out at all.

In the end, the evening was much more enjoyable than he had expected. Andrea took them to Montin on the grounds that James would prefer its literary atmosphere. Afterwards, the three of them strolled up and down on the Zattere while Andrea waited for a vaporetto to cross back to the Giudecca.

'Unlike you,' he said, 'I won't be kept awake by endless gondoliers singing "Santa Lucia" to parties of tourists. The *serenata* – or "night excursion" as they probably call it now – takes away all the pleasure of a room over the canal.'

On the vaporetto's approach, they arranged to meet again. After waving goodbye from the embankment, James linked arms with Christina and chuckled. 'I'd love to know what sort of deal Andrea's managed to negotiate at the Cipriani. He really is quite shameless.'

Two days later, the weather changed. A sea mist enshrouded the city, and in a curious reversal of expectation James found his sense of hearing far more disorientated than his vision. The creak of pontoons seemed louder and the lapping of water even more ubiquitous, while every other noise became muffled and eerily disembodied. Voices drifted, their direction impossible to judge, vaporetto engines blurred in an indefinable distance, and out in the lagoon foghorns sounded like the call of whales.

To begin with, the difference was beguiling. Venice felt descrted, a city of ghosts. James pictured it as one of those ancient civilizations suddenly abandoned for no clear reason. By the end of the morning, the effect lost its novelty and began to feel oppressive, even ominous.

'It's the sort of day on which masked lovers stab their rivals,' remarked Andrea when they met for lunch in Harry's Bar. 'But more to the point, it is the sort of day on which one has a Bloody Mary instead of a Bellini. Christina, *ma chère*. Do try something a little more exciting than your usual mineral water. Or is that why you always look so disgustingly healthy? How depressing. I'm sure James will join me in something stronger.' He looked at his watch.

'Are you expecting anyone else?' Christina asked, noticing the fourth place.

'Yes, as it happens, I am. I was intending to keep it as a surprise, but as you know, my effervescent nature never allows me to keep them for long. Anyway, you will never guess who I bumped into this morning. *Ton cousin, le grand Fritz.*'

'Fritzi? But how wonderful!'

'I told him you were here on honeymoon, and do you know, he was quite dumbfounded. He had not even heard that you two were engaged, let alone married. For the last few months, he has been in South America, and apparently quite ill, poor fellow. *Aha! Le voilà!*'

Fritzi, who was speaking to the receptionist, caught sight of them and came over. He looked even more angular than in Paris.

'But Fritzi! You've lost so much weight!' exclaimed Christina in German, genuinely upset.

'There is nothing to worry about,' he answered in English as she continued to fuss over him. 'I'll soon put it on again. By a stroke of extremely bad luck, I picked up a bug in Bolivia. And La Paz, I can tell you, is not the best of places to fall ill. Anyway, it is very good to be here. And much more important, I have been told that there is reason for congratulations.' He gave a little bow to include them both.

Over lunch, Christina told Fritzi about their research. The initial disappointment at the Accademia had been entirely forgotten once she revisited the Verrocchio statue. And now, with the fervour of a convert, she paid little attention to the reaction of her listeners. Fritzi asked one or two polite questions, while Andrea maintained an expression of mild scepticism from the moment he had established the point of the book. He soon grew restless.

James felt uneasy for a different reason. His doubts about the whole project had greatly increased over the last couple of days. Even to have contemplated such a work appeared mad. The subject's scope and complexity was far beyond them, and Christina's enthusiasm now made him feel terrible. Fortunately, Andrea managed to change the conversation, and the lunch was saved by a few of his anecdotes. Fritzi, meanwhile, seemed rather subdued, presumably as a result of his illness.

Afterwards, James found himself alone with Fritzi outside as they waited for the other two. Christina had been with Andrea and his farewell to the manager must have turned into a chat.

'So how long are you here for?' he asked to make conversation.

'I return to Paris tomorrow.' Fritzi looked at the pavement, then up again. 'James, I hope you do not mind my saying this ...'

Surprised at the gravity of tone, he laughed. 'I'm perfectly sure I won't.'

'You have not known Christina very long, have you?'

'No,' he said. 'That's certainly true. It all happened rather quickly, as you know.'

Fritzi did not return his smile. 'I am sorry. What I want to say is not easy to put into words. Above all when you are on honeymoon. But I have to tell you this. I am still worried about Christina. As much as when we first met.'

'Worried? In what way?'

'Well, to say things bluntly, she has a self-destructive streak. She can be obsessive ...'

'Listen, Fritzi. I think I know what you're on about, and I

can assure you that I do know a bit about her life. And what
it must have been like married to that bastard. She certainly
went through a very tough time, but ever since she made the
break from Munich and got rid of that ghastly house, she's
completely changed. I mean, isn't it obvious how much happier
she is?'

He tilted his head, unconvinced. At that moment, the door
opened and Christina appeared, followed by Andrea buttoning
his jacket across his paunch.

'Did you know,' Fritzi murmured, 'that she also came to
Venice on her first honeymoon?' He looked quickly into James's
eyes, then turned to face the stragglers.

'What are you two discussing?' Christina called cheerfully.

'What else does one talk about with an Englishman, but the
weather?'

The glibness of the reply irritated James and only confirmed
his suspicions. He remembered Fritzi's manner towards Christina at the party in Paris. That hadn't been concerned, but
blatantly flirtatious. And even if she had spent her first honeymoon in Venice, what did that signify? She might easily have
thought that returning to the same place was the only way to
wipe out Georg's memory. In any case, the choice of Venice
for their honeymoon had been a joint decision.

The real answer was perfectly clear. Fritzi had been carrying
a torch for Christina all the time. And to hear of her marriage
from Andrea like that must have been a hell of a shock. James's
anger subsided. He felt sorry for him.

By next morning, the mist had disappeared, and memories
of that strange day felt unconvincing, as though the city's
pervasive sense of unreality had managed to distort everything.
James and Christina were both in an excellent mood as they
crossed the lagoon again to reclaim the car at the airport. They
had planned to break their stay with a couple of days visiting
the Palladian villas of the Veneto.

'It's going to feel funny back amongst traffic and the rest of
the twentieth century,' she said. 'But it'll be good to see greenery again. The one thing I really miss in Venice is trees.'

'It'll be even stranger to return to London.'

'In what way?'

He considered for a moment. 'I suppose the idea of having left it single to come back married.'

'Oh, my poor James! I think you are lamenting your bachelor days already.'

'On the contrary. I just marvel at my unbelievable luck.'

She sighed and nodded. 'I too.' She slipped her arm through his and gazed at the horizon with a faraway expression.

'What are you thinking?' he asked a few moments later.

With a sidelong glance, she laughed, caught out. 'I was wondering whether the decorators had remembered what I told them about the doors.'

Part Three

❧ 12 ❧

James rather dreaded the evening ahead. He had again wanted to cancel the dinner party, but Christina, with a hint of disturbing obstinacy, insisted that they went ahead as planned.

In spite of her migraine, everything downstairs appeared to be under control, and Mrs Evans, their daily, had come in to help. Since both women clung to an old-fashioned dislike of men in the kitchen, James kept out of their way. Having brought up the ice bucket, he stood with his back to the fireplace and surveyed the sitting room before the guests arrived.

Even after almost three years in this house, he had not become blasé to the combination of elegance and inspired simplicity which Christina had achieved. This room was the best example, where a natural use of wood (something he felt the British had lost with the Industrial Revolution) managed to convey a sensation both of cleanliness and warmth.

He remembered their return from Venice to find that, in spite of all the builder's assurances, only the main bedroom and the kitchen were in a habitable condition. Christina's exasperation was hard to calm, especially when her furniture arrived in a pantechnicon from Austria and had to go into store. The upheaval had continued for another four months before the floorboards could be waxed, the furniture positioned and pictures hung.

From the beginning, James had tried to dampen her optimism about the length of time the work might take, but even he had assumed they would be finished by Christmas. During that period, Christina found it hard to share his fatalism and black humour. She could not stop cleaning up after the workmen, even when they were about to make more mess the next day, and she treated every detail with disproportionate seriousness. James, admittedly not a houseproud man, found her emotional investment difficult to comprehend.

One thing at least was clear. Christina's perfectionism did not come from any desire to impress visitors. In her funny way, nothing irritated her more than the compliment that she should take up interior decoration professionally. She tended to regard it as the first resort of the divorcee with vaguely creative aspirations.

But in early February, just as James thought that they had finished with workmen in the house and could start leading normal lives, Christina acquired a second wind. She took endless trouble over the design of bookshelves for James's two rooms on the top floor. He was touched, but also uneasy at the expense since she had already insisted on buying him as a wedding present the best word processor on the market.

Then once he was installed in his immaculate study – which David and Antonia admired with a good deal of banter – Christina decided that the bedroom wasn't right. James, not knowing whether to explode or to acquiesce on the strict understanding that this was the very last improvement, ended by doing both rather ambivalently since he teased her at the same time.

He also said that he would soon suspect she was following the example of Ulysses' wife, Penelope, secretly undoing her work at night as an excuse to hold off her suitors. Christina immediately promised with great earnestness and affection that they would have a child soon. But first she needed a little time to settle down in London and for Stephanie to get used to her new home. Of course, he had said. The last thing he wanted was to rush her. And since it wasn't her first child, they didn't have to worry so much about her age.

The front door bell rang. Before going out into the hall, James ran an eye over everything. He wondered how Christina's friend would react to Julian Darin, especially if he was in one of his provocative moods. But these first arrivals turned out to be Roger and Claire Trustram.

Roger was both James's and David's literary agent. Although tall and bespectacled, he did not fit into that category of academic Englishmen who always seem to be either diffident or apologetic. With quiet charm, surprising firmness and flashes of unexpected humour, he could disarm even the most intransigent publisher.

Claire was what the Victorians would have called a handsome woman. She acted as if she had been born to the role of an upper-middle-class social worker. Cheerful and ebullient, she had a largely undeserved reputation for putting her foot in it and then roaring with laughter.

When Christina came in, she turned from examining a set of early Viennese prints at the far end of the room. 'Do you know, I love your house more and more? I can never remember who actually discovered it?'

'Oh, Christina did,' said James, bent over the drinks tray. 'As soon as she found out that Brook Green had the Austrian Centre, there was no need to look any further.' The ritual joke sounded wrong this time. He avoided looking in her direction when he took over the two glasses of white wine.

'But it's absolutely huge,' Claire went on, 'and you've made it wonderfully un-English. I mean, except for the windows and the cornices, one really wouldn't think one was in London *at all*.'

Julian Darin arrived at the same time as David and Antonia. Julian, a well-known critic who often appeared with deceptive nonchalance on book programmes, was seldom seen in anything but the same grey tweed jacket and shapeless black trousers. His ambiguous manner, usually on the verge of mockery, disconcerted Christina, and he played up to this by greeting her with an ironic inclination of the head.

Claire went over to kiss him. 'Really, Jules,' she said. 'I can't think why you don't wear something a little more lively on television. It is in colour nowadays, you know.'

'Yes, but the programme director is such a tyrant. Nothing is allowed to clash with the book jackets.' Julian, although not gay, often affected a slightly camp manner. Parody had become compulsive.

She was about to reply, then stopped. 'Really, you're so infuriating! One can never tell when you're joking.'

James, on the point of talking to David and Antonia, found he had forgotten to give Julian a drink. Then the doorbell rang again. 'Ah,' said Christina, 'that must be Béatrice.' And while she went to answer it, conversation began with Roger asking David and Antonia how their books were going, and Claire telling Julian how much she had enjoyed his piece on Sunday.

'Did you read it, James? It was excellent.'

'No, I didn't. For some reason I never got round to the papers this weekend.' That's one way of putting it, he added silently as he went over to greet the new arrival.

James had only met Béatrice de Creignes on a couple of occasions. Although the sort of professional partygoer he usually abhorred, she was so uninhibited with her extravagant manner and dramatic *jolie laide* looks that he had taken to her after all.

Christina, who disliked eating late, soon had everyone moving downstairs. They stood chatting just inside the door of the dining room while she sorted out her *placement*. The dark blue walls and oil paintings illuminated with picture lights produced a striking contrast with the rest of the house.

James noticed David and Antonia either side of the convex Regency mirror in which a reflection of their backs showed. 'From where I'm standing,' he pointed out, 'you two look like the Arnolfini marriage.' They both glanced over their shoulders.

'Or what about Velázquez's *Las Meninas*?' said David.

'We're facing the wrong way for that,' his wife retorted.

'All right, perhaps. But wasn't he supposed to have pinched the idea from van Eyck in the first place?'

'Please! Can I finish?' Christina broke in. The strain in her voice brought an abrupt silence. 'I am sorry,' she said, then hurriedly indicated the remaining places.

'Poor Christina!' said Claire after the scraping of chairs was over. '*What* an undisciplined bunch to have to deal with!'

'But to go back to the two pictures,' Julian said, after helping himself to a piece of toast without offering the basket around. 'Does it really make any difference whether Velázquez pinched the idea or not?'

'Careful everyone,' said Claire. 'Jules is obviously in one of his argumentative moods.'

'All right, Julian, so what are you getting at?' asked Antonia.

He pretended to ward off their attack with a raised arm. 'What a reaction! And why such distrust? I am purely interested in a question which has often intrigued me. And which is particularly relevant after those accusations of plagiarism in yesterday's *Sunday Times*.'

'Didn't you think they sounded justified?'

'Before anyone can answer that, you have to turn the question round first. How does one define an original work, when, according to the experts, raw imagination doesn't exist? Dreams, for example, are supposed to be a kaleidoscope of images we've seen at some point and then buried in the subconscious. So one might just as well argue ...'

'Oh, come off it!' James interrupted, the bottle poised over Béatrice's glass. 'You can't say that there's no such thing as originality just because the components exist already. Obviously it's their arrangement which counts. The pattern which the kaleidoscope takes, if you like.'

'You almost make it sound like those poor notional monkeys knocking out the Bible on typewriters.' He extended an arm towards Roger. 'Let's ask the literary agent. I'm sure he can tell us a bit about that wonderful euphemism "derivative". Even if every romantic plot doesn't stem from *Pride and Prejudice* and every saga from *War and Peace*, virtually the whole fiction industry is plagiarism in one form or another.'

'And what about autobiographical novels?' said David.

'Yes, darling, but they can hardly be original in terms of imagination, can they? Unless of course you're referring to that old chestnut about a novelist's autobiography being the only bit of fiction he ever writes. Come on, Roger.'

Roger adjusted his spectacles and smiled as if at a private joke. 'Well, there's no doubt both agents and publishers would have an easier time if aspiring writers were a little less self-obsessed.'

'Yes, do tell us. Is it just a myth, or are you really besieged by hordes of nutters who are convinced that their innermost ravings are of world importance?'

'It seems to go in waves. But you can soon spot the manu-script which really belongs on a psychiatrist's couch. But then maybe we should regard ourselves as a public service.'

'Yes, you never know,' said Antonia. 'You might even get a subsidy from the Ministry of Health. More chance at any rate than from the Arts Council.'

Béatrice turned on Roger, her eyes wide. 'Darling, I forget your name, but do tell me. What these people write – is it enough to make you feel *very* embarrassed?'

Roger laughed with the rest of them and it seemed a perfect end to the conversation. Yet Julian, for some reason, would not allow the subject to drop.

'But doesn't it all go to show,' he said, 'that rather like lonely and masochistic forms of sport, writing fiction is basically an auto-erotic practice?'

James noticed David and Antonia exchange looks. With an unexpected pang, he envied their complicity.

'That sort of comment,' Claire emphasized to Béatrice, 'is just typically Julian. Come on, James!' she then called across the table. 'You can't let him get away with that.'

'Well, I would have thought,' he said, 'that the emotional state of writing is much more like a second adolescence. For most writers it seems to be a jumble of conflicting moods: lethargy then manic activity, daydreaming and nervous rest-lessness, depression then wildly over-optimistic excitement. David, what do you think?'

'But absolutely!' Julian broke in. 'Adolescence is the most intense period of sexual tension in our lives. Yet you left off your list all that self-contemplation everyone goes through which also happens when writing a novel. You think you're creating an original and individual character, but if it's not based on someone else, then it's usually a reverse image of yourself.'

David laughed derisively. 'Are you honestly trying to say that writing's little more than some sort of extended pubertal blockage?'

'Hang on! Let me finish. At one point, Freud describes how the child's tastes evolve from breast-feeding to thumb-sucking, then to kissing its own shoulder or upper arm. And how when it's eventually attracted to the corresponding part of someone else's body – the lips – it's really thinking: "What a pity I can't kiss myself."'

'What absolute balderdash!' Claire burst out.

Christina's attempt to change the subject to the latest production at Covent Garden never stood a chance. Béatrice turned to Julian. 'Now listen, darling. You say some wonderfully ridiculous things, and I adore it. But are you telling to me in all sincerity that when we go to bed with somebody we are really making love to *ourselves* in the depths of our imagination?' Her chin jutted in Gallic scepticism.

'I'm not a psychoanalyst, but . . .'

'Cop out!' called David.

'Don't interrupt him,' said Claire. 'He's not used to it.'

'Thank you,' said Julian, then turned back to Béatrice. 'I would never for a moment attempt to suggest that we're all raving narcissists.' He looked down at the two forks beside his plate, and straightened them. 'But at the same time there can be little doubt that some form of reflective mechanism plays an important role. Take the more obvious sexual aberrations. An exhibitionist is a voyeur in his subconscious, while a sadist is just a masochist at another level. And vice versa. Masochists are really inverted sadists. They want to inflict punishment and humiliation on themselves.'

'Well, only up to a point,' said Antonia. 'Not, I hasten to add, that I have any personal knowledge of these matters. But it all sounds a little too pat for me. For a start . . .'

'I agree!' Claire nodded emphatically across the table. 'Freud at times has a *very* dubious ring, particularly on anything to do with women. Much too schematic for a start.'

'Quite possibly,' said Julian. 'Although you must remember he was writing about women conditioned by a nineteenth-century ethos, not about women today. But even leaving that aside, wouldn't you accept that he's right on certain female phenomena?'

'Such as?'

'Well, the perverse bond a woman can often have with a man she has come to hate. He found that however much they try to direct their love to another kind of man, the image of the first will always come back and intervene.'

'And why did he think that happened?' said Béatrice.

'Apparently, because they have not "completed their revenge upon them".'

'Their revenge upon the man?' asked David. 'Or upon themselves, for having been stupid enough to fall for a shit in the first place?'

'James!' Christina called. '*Please!* Can you start carving before it gets cold?'

The interruption finally put a stop to the conversation, and others soon sprang up in its place since few of the standard questions had yet been completed, either between friends or strangers.

James, going round again with the wine after everyone had been served, noticed Julian and Béatrice deep in conversation. He suddenly remembered from the only other time he had met her, that Béatrice was a great thigh-grabber when emphasizing points.

'What's the joke?' David asked across the table.

'I'll tell you later,' he mouthed back.

After the main course, James fetched an ashtray for the two smokers. Julian, true to form, was cadging Béatrice's cigarettes. James returned to his seat and poured himself some more wine. Voices merged about him as he watched Julian turning on his controversial charm.

James had first met him at the party of some literary magazine, but whether five, six or even seven years ago he could not remember. The next link had come some time later in the form of Sarah. Although James had become involved with her while she was still supposed to be with Julian, the overlap had produced no jealousy on either side. James had felt both flattered and reassured by the idea of finally acquiring some sort of invulnerability. In the past, he had made such a fool of himself with women, always falling for the impossible, or imagining qualities which never existed.

Sarah was very different. A sassy New Yorker working for an English publisher, she relished directness and the wisecracking putdown. Their paths had crossed at a couple of launch parties and a dinner, but for some reason the idea of going out with her had never entered his mind. Physically, she was not really his type. An artificial blonde, with milk-white skin, she had a wide mouth and the sort of lips the French describe as *pulpeuses*. She was also tall, flat-chested, and flat-bottomed; the loose slacks she wore appeared to drop vertically from the waist.

After meeting her again at yet another publishing party, the speed of the evening's events had left him slightly dazed. They had gone on to an Indian restaurant, and by ten o'clock were in her bed. But at eleven he had been sent on his way, because she was taking the early flight to Paris.

On subsequent occasions, she had talked about the import- ance of 'having good sex' as if the whole business were a sort of clinical recreation; a necessary function which, in her own words, should also be 'a gour-may experience'. Once, when she started issuing instructions in the middle of making love, he had to suppress a fit of giggles. He felt a bit like a circus lion being put through the hoops. Curiously, this very American brand of seriousness coexisted quite happily with a good, debunking sense of humour.

Their mutually convenient affair had drifted on until James met Christina. When he rang Sarah to break the news, she had wished him luck as if for a new job.

'Ja-ames!' Julian's amused tone shook him out of his reverie. 'Béatrice and I were discussing childhood fantasies.'

'Oh, God,' he said. 'You're not back on that again, are you?' Claire offered him the cheese board. He shook his head and passed it on, then half rose to reach for a pear from the basket in the middle of the table. He expected a subtle dig of some sort. Maybe something to do with Sarah. But Béatrice diverted their attention.

'I find it all utterly fascinating!' she called to Christina. 'Don't you? It's so intriguing to imagine what people talk about when they go to their *psychiatre*. I mean, take my friend Maryska. Darling, you know her! Bibi's sister. Well, I would just *adore* to know if she was in love with her father. Not that I would blame her, of course. Everyone thought he was the best-looking man in Europe.'

Julian grinned at James as if to say, isn't she priceless? But James was wondering how to get Antonia or David on their own. He wanted to arrange a quiet evening to talk things through during Christina's absence. She still hadn't said when she was going.

Looking down the table, he noticed her distracted glances. She obviously couldn't take much more. He stood up. 'Right, everybody. Let's make a move. We'll have coffee in the sitting room.'

'I say!' said Claire. 'That's a bit abrupt.'

'We'll be more comfortable upstairs,' he insisted.

While they began to rise to their feet reluctantly, he eased round the back of them to see whether Christina was all right. In a whisper he suggested she slip off to bed but she insisted that it was not necessary.

After little more than half an hour in the sitting room, Claire signalled to Roger with her eyes, and heaved herself up. 'Usual old babysitter problem,' she announced.

To James's relief the rest of the party soon followed. Antonia asked Julian if he wanted a lift, only to be told that Béatrice had already offered him one. They lived in virtually opposite directions, but James was too tired to find such an unlikely match amusing. He had not even had a chance to arrange an evening with Antonia and David. That would have to be done by telephone the next day.

'Honestly, why don't you go to bed?' he murmured to Christina in a break from fetching coats. 'You look exhausted, and I can easily do any clearing up.'

But when he returned from saying goodbye in the street, he found her emptying the ashtrays, her face distorted with disgust. He knew she hated the smell of stale cigarettes but this appeared more complex. 'Please! Why don't you leave me to do that and get off to bed?' She almost shook him off.

He gave up with a shrug. 'Well, they sure smoked enough, those two,' he said and flopped into a chair, hoping to calm her with a display of composure. 'How convenient for Julian she brought two packets. Anyway, the evening didn't go too badly. They seem to have enjoyed themselves. And, most important, nobody stayed too late.'

'I am glad you think it was a success.' Her tone was not sarcastic, just disturbingly flat.

He sat forward, no longer able to contain his unease. 'My love, please. What is the matter?'

She chewed her upper lip, inhaled deeply and looked restlessly around the room to avoid his eyes. 'Perhaps there is something wrong with me. But I do not like it very much when people are so arrogant that they believe they have the right to dictate the subject of conversation.'

'Look, I know you've never really liked Julian. But then you do tend to take him much too seriously when he's just being provocative. Everyone knows that he's a bit of a stirrer, and accepts it. As it happens, he's not a close friend of mine – nor is he for that matter of David and Antonia's – but he is quite stimulating company. Anyway, as far as tonight's little performance was concerned, it's pretty obvious what he was up to.'

'I suppose you are going to tell me he was trying to impress Béatrice.'

'No, not particularly.' He decided to leave their departure together unmentioned. 'Knowing him, I'd have thought it much more likely that he's been asked to write a piece that's got something to do with plagiarism, and he just wanted to test out the odd theory and provoke some ideas. I don't really blame him.' He attempted a smile. 'I just envy his lack of scruple.'

There was a long pause. 'I see,' said Christina in a manner

intended to convey the opposite. 'I am going up. I think it will be best if I use the bed in my room. We might both get more sleep that way. You needn't do anything else in the way of clearing up. Mrs Evans will be back in the morning. Good night.'

He could only stare at her as she moved to the door. 'Good night,' he echoed, but she had already left the room.

As he sat there, listening to her steps on the stairs, the indigestion brought on by the combination of alcohol, caffeine and nervous exhaustion became acute. He began to experience a sensation of breathlessness. Christina was not merely homesick, but exasperated with her life in England. The extent of his self-deception alarmed him almost more than the revelation.

Her restlessness had been apparent, but she would not talk about it, and he had completely mistaken its reason. Once the book on the image of power had been abandoned, a decision she found hard to accept, she had gone from one shortlived interest to another.

James, not wanting to push her on the question of children, had tried to suggest various jobs. But alongside a refusal to consider herself employable, lay the quite genuine belief that to take work when others really needed the salary would be wrong. Eventually, they had found the perfect compromise, translating documents and project reports for a Third World aid programme.

Unfortunately, the work had been sporadic, and Christina's attempts to be involved in other charities had led only to committees for fund-raising events. These she detested because the members were expected to rope in all their rich acquaintances.

James fully sympathized with her in this case, but usually she tended to be at her most obstinate when defending the wrong position. In the past this had turned into a joke once she relented. More recently, however, she had demonstrated a brittle intractability which, in its most extreme form, raised the fear of a nervous breakdown.

He gazed blankly at the room until the photograph of Prince Tassilo held his attention for a moment or two. Had he ever found out about the baby? James wondered. Just before forcing himself to his feet, he experienced a claustrophobic, drowning sensation. It made him think of treading water in the dark, trying to keep afloat until daylight.

❧ 13 ❧

A smell of stale cigarette smoke lingered in the dining room, the legacy of Julian and Béatrice. Mrs Evans was already clearing up in the kitchen. Unable to face any conversation, James pretended to be in too much of a rush for breakfast, and left a message with her that he would be at the London Library for most of the day.

This escape was intended to give Christina a breathing space, but on his return he found her packing for Austria. Having not expected her to leave until Thursday at the earliest, the scene came as a shock. He needed time to get used to the idea of this trip. From the door of her dressing room, he watched with a sickly void in his stomach.

'I'm booked on the ten o'clock flight tomorrow,' she explained hurriedly, her eyes roving round the room as if to check on anything she might have forgotten. 'I thought I'd go home for a few days first. My father's not well.' She might have been talking to a stranger.

She continued to evade his eyes by pretending to rearrange the top layer of clothes in her suitcase. The one she had brought to London. [*It felt strange that such a small detail should finally bring home to me the possibility of her leaving for good. Until that moment I had managed to keep my fears indistinct.*]

'Are you just going to stand there staring?' she burst out.

'If only I knew what to say.' His attempt at a laugh sounded terrible. 'You make me feel like an intruder. Perhaps that's what I've become ... I don't know.' He shrugged to demonstrate his confusion. 'Not being told what's really happening to you is what scares me. In fact I'm doubly scared because in

134

your present mood you seem to be quite capable of destroying everything.' An instinctive refusal to accept what he saw as a terrible mistake made him react. 'I do know you pretty well by now! Enough at any rate to see the irony of this whole ghastly mess.'

'What do you mean?'

'I'm talking about the way the danger comes from you being an utterly monogamous woman. Some sort of Catholic guilt is making you dramatize the issue out of all proportion. Let's face it, an infatuation can happen to virtually anybody ... at least that's what I keep trying to tell myself. So for both our sakes, I beg you, don't allow the whole thing to turn into some emotional *Götterdämmerung*!'

She continued to stand there immobile, looking down at the open suitcase. He sighed. 'What I'm trying to say is please don't exaggerate any resentment you may feel against me to help you summon up courage for a crazy leap in the dark.' He played with the catch on the door, waiting in vain for a reply. The silence became intolerable.

'What time's the flight?' he said eventually. 'I'll run you to the airport.'

'You really don't have to. I've already ordered a taxi.'

The mask of politeness infuriated him. 'Well, you can bloody well cancel it then! That is, unless you've become totally allergic to my presence.'

The cheap satisfaction of seeing her flinch had worn off by the time he slammed the front door behind him. Chin on chest, he paced diagonally across the road without looking and onto the broad grass island of Brook Green. Suddenly, he swung round to look back at the house. He spied a movement at the window which told him his indignation had been unfair. That cold manner was a sort of armour. Inside, she must be cracking under the strain. His anger and fear only made the grotesque confusion of feelings even worse.

They did not speak on the way to Heathrow until almost half way there. The morning was heavy and overcast with a grey-yellow light and James remarked that with any luck the weather at Lotzingen should be better than in London. A little later, he overcame his suspicions to say how sorry he was about her father's illness, and asked her to pass on all his wishes for a speedy recovery. [*Even after three years of marriage, the idea of sending Prince Tassilo my love still seemed to smack of lèse majesté.*]

The stilted platitudes hung uncomfortably in the air between them. He avoided any reference to the wedding and only just managed to restrain himself from asking when she would be back.

On the slip road from the motorway to the airport, Christina became restless. He guessed she was steeling herself to ask him not to come into the terminal. She finally spoke as they emerged from the fume-laden air of the tunnel. 'Please, just drop me outside. I'll find a trolley.'

A reflex obstinacy made him want to object, but logic prevailed. They both hated airport goodbyes and this was certainly not the moment to change. They kissed, a brush of dry lips.

A few moments later, fumbling with the keys – having somehow relocked his own side – he waved again as she disappeared through the glass doors.

On his return to Brook Green, James wandered from room to room half-hoping to find proof that she would soon return. But the house felt vacated, as if already on the market. He returned to the sitting room and sank onto the sofa. After a while, he tried to call David and Antonia, but found himself sitting there while the telephone rang and rang in another empty house. To replace the receiver required a conscious effort.

The framed photograph of the wedding in Austria caught his eye. Two self-conscious smiles and Stephanie's slightly perplexed expression. He could not remember if she shared her mother's almost primitive dislike of cameras. So few pictures existed of his marriage to Christina. David and Antonia, on the other hand, had amassed almost an album's worth after a year. God, what a measure of comparison! he thought. The marital happiness photo index.

The sudden noise of the telephone at his elbow startled him. His immediate reaction was that, through some telepathic process, David and Antonia were returning his call. Then, he felt sure Christina had missed her flight, or else changed her mind at the last moment. But as he lifted the receiver, he became gripped with a terrifying certainty that the aircraft had crashed on takeoff.

'James? Is that you?'

To his confusion, it turned out to be Stephanie. 'Yes,' he said. 'Yes, it's me.'

'Your voice seems funny. Are you all right?'

'Surviving. Just about.'

'Doesn't sound like it. Is Mummy there?'

'No. She's gone. I'm just back from taking her to the airport.'

'She's left *already?*'

'I'm afraid so.'

'Oh gosh. Poor James! Are you feeling really down? I wish I knew what was going on.'

'You're not the only one!' he said with a harsh laugh. 'Did she give you an idea of what it was all about when we dropped you back at school on Sunday?'

'Not much. She was in such a state underneath.' Then, Stephanie hesitated. 'James, don't hate her. She's still worth that Mass.'

He relaxed gratefully. 'No. I don't hate her. Though at moments it feels as though things might be a lot less confusing if I did.'

'You know, if you want to talk about it, you could always come down again and take me out for another lunch. It was scrumptious. Thank you so much.'

'Stephanie, what would I do without you? Yes, I certainly will come down. That is if Sister Crossbones allows you beyond the barbed wire in such dubious company.'

'Next Sunday, then?'

'It's a date. I'll be there by half past twelve.'

❧ 14 ❧

Hardly a breath of wind disturbed the Thames. James became mesmerized by the rhythmic creak of rowlocks, the dip of the oars and the imploded circles left behind. Only a few sounds reached them – laughter across the water, the ghostly beat of swans' wings, the quacking of ducks. But then a jet, high overhead, reminded him of Christina's departure.

Face tilted towards the sun, Stephanie lay in the stern, her forearms dangling outwards as if from a deck chair. James feathered the oars, letting the boat glide.

'Cox, would you mind taking an occasional look to see if we're heading in the right direction?' He grinned at her expression of vacant sensuality. This was the first really hot day of the year.

Stephanie raised a hand to shelter her eyes from the glare. 'What's so funny?'

'The look on your face.' Her answering grimace was unconcerned.

Raising an elbow, he wiped his forehead on the crook of his arm. 'Why don't you take over now? Put all that convent PT to good use.'

Stephanie stretched, pretending to yawn. 'All right. But it's so hot, I'll have to strip off.' She peeped at him mischievously to observe his reaction. 'There's no need to look alarmed. I've got a bikini on underneath. I knew you wouldn't mind.'

'What's that supposed to mean?'

'Only that I didn't think you were stuffy. And it isn't as if we're going to bump into anyone who'll recognize us.' She stood up to unbutton the campanula blue dress which suited her so well. Then, crossing her arms, she lifted it right over her head and shook her black hair free. The boat rocked dangerously. She grabbed down at his shoulder to save her balance.

Embarrassed, he eyed the pale lean stomach in front of his face. 'Don't get too sunburned or Sister Bona's suspicions about my bad influence will be confirmed.'

'Come on, James. If you want me to row, then move over. Otherwise we'll both fall in.'

On reaching the small wooded island near the far bank, they spread the rugs and laid out the picnic. 'It was a brilliant idea of yours,' said Stephanie. 'And all my favourite things. I love it when you spoil me.'

'I love spoiling you,' he returned. They both knew the holiday mood was forced.

In silence with their own thoughts, they ate, contemplating the river. The wash from a cabin cruiser slapped against their boat, making it dance a jig. Stephanie took the wine bottle and raised it in a wordless request. 'If you're expelled,' he remarked, 'I know whose fault they'll say it is.'

'Poor old James. Always gets blamed unfairly.'

He sat up, unable to control his restlessness. The heat had become oppressive. 'One of the reasons for having a picnic,' he said, his face half averted, 'was to be able to talk on our own.' In spite of her bikini, Stephanie managed to match his seriousness. Lying propped up on one elbow, she twisted the glass round and round in her hands while he tried to describe Christina's restlessness.

'Are you afraid Mummy'll leave you for good?' she asked after a short silence.

Startled by the directness of the question, he glanced at her, then down at the ground. He picked up a twig, snapped it in two, and threw the pieces into the water one after the other.

'Yes. Yes, I am,' he said, dismayed by the rush of pain. 'Do *you* think she will?'

'I don't know. But I honestly and truly hope not. For her sake as much as yours or mine. But James?' He raised his head.

'There's still quite a bit that you don't seem to understand or know.'

'In what way?'

'Well ...' Stephanie exhaled. 'For a start, life at Starnberg was not exactly cosy.'

'I'm sure it wasn't! Don't forget I visited that house, and I could sense how heavy the atmosphere must have been.' Then, he noticed her pained expression. 'Was it really so bad?' She nodded. 'But I thought ...' He faltered, unable to repeat Christina's confession, and made an uneasy, throwaway gesture with his hand. 'Well, I was under the impression that your father more or less ignored her.'

'If only he had!' she said shaking her head. 'Mummy did her best to shelter me from the truth, but it was impossible not to find out sooner or later. I hated that man, James.' Her eyes rose to meet his. 'I absolutely loathed him. I prayed he wasn't really my father, and I longed for him to die. Once, I even took a knife from the kitchen and stabbed my pillow pretending it was him.' James stared at her, not knowing what to say.

'After the accident, I was terrified that it was I who'd killed him, through a sort of curse. I begged God for forgiveness, but I was convinced I'd still be sent to hell because deep down I couldn't repent. I was glad! Glad and terrified, if you see what I'm trying to say.' He nodded in earnest encouragement, amazed at the way both mother and daughter had suffered the same fantasy of guilt. 'But then you arrived. And that was a help, even though to begin with, it felt a bit as if I was playing gooseberry.'

'Yes, I know. But how did my presence help?'

'Oh, your scornful attitude to any idea of hell. That gave me hope. And in other ways as I began to get over my "Trappist mouse" days.' She smiled quickly at his look of discomfort. 'It's all right. I didn't really mind. The first time I overheard you call me that in a conversation with Mummy, I stole along to your study to look up "Trappist" in the dictionary. I was very good at tiptoeing round the house. In Munich, my great dream had been to be invisible as well.'

'You used to eavesdrop on what your father said?'

'And did,' she added, more to herself. She looked up at James, then quickly out over the river. 'In a strange way I felt it was my duty. I needed to know so as to be able to help Mummy somehow. There were a lot of words to look up in those days. I didn't even know what a whore was.' She tilted her head mirthlessly. 'One way of educating yourself.'

Disconcerted by these revelations after so long, James felt slow, if not stupid. 'You mean he actually called your mother a whore?'

'And bitch, and slut. All those things.' Her voice sounded flat, almost weary. 'One of the times he beat her, he started shouting that I couldn't be his daughter. That I must have been somebody else's.' She flicked at the fringe of the tartan rug. 'If only I had been.'

'He used to beat her? You saw this?'

'No, I never actually saw it. He would do it in her room, having locked the door. He used his polo whip.'

Stephanie smiled sadly at his speechless outrage. Yet part of James's anger was directed against himself. The possibility had occurred to him after his visit to the house at Starnberg and he had dismissed it, essentially because he could not imagine anyone wanting to hurt Christina. Oh, you fool, he thought. And to make it worse, he had suspected the warped possessiveness which lay behind it all, even Georg's rejection of her.

'Did it happen often?'

She thought hard. 'No, not often. It's difficult to say looking back. It may only have been a few times although it seemed much more. I feel he must have been mad in some way,' she went on. 'But at the time it was terrifying. I had nothing to compare it with. And I didn't dare ask girls at school if that sort of thing ever happened with their parents. You're the very first person I've been able to talk to about it. I've wanted to bring it out into the open with Mummy, now that it's all in the past, but ... well, as you can imagine ...'

'So that was it. I felt sure she acted as if she were almost afraid of you in a way.'

'Yes, she's never really relaxed when we're alone together.

Obviously she's worried I'll burst out blaming her for everything. Just *imagine* what she went through! And how she's felt
obliged to hide it for so long.'

'But your grandfather,' said James. 'Surely, he must have
guessed something was wrong. That's what I never quite
understood.'

'Oh, I'm certain *Grosspapi* had a pretty good idea of what
was going on. I think he was against the marriage from the
start, and only gave in after she went into a decline. Because
when Mummy's got a fixation she can't let go. Anyway, she
probably sensed that *Grosspapi* knew, but she'd never have
admitted anything. Not unless he tackled her head on.'

An unsettling idea occurred to James. Prince Tassilo was the
sort of person who had an informal network of spies. And to
have arranged Georg's accident would have been a vengeance
worthy of his beloved Medici. James hurriedly told himself not
to get carried away.

'But what I still can't understand,' he said, 'is how she stayed
with such a man. Was it because she would never admit to
her father how wrong she had been about him? Or was it
because she was somehow still in love?'

'What is love?' Stephanie said flatly. 'Is a sort of stubborn
blindness "love"? Or maybe she carried on like the nuns refusing to give up on a conversion. I don't know.'

To find a girl of her age so clear-eyed about the perversity
of human nature made James feel put in his place. But then
he became unsure what to believe. He looked up sharply and
frowned. Stephanie turned away to search in her bag and lay
back on the rug as if exhausted. Had Georg's violence been
imagined – the make-believe of a lonely childhood? He knew
only too well how easy that could be.

Yet if her version had been even partly made up, it would
have had lots of dramatic detail. That aspect alone was enough
to convince him. The really remarkable part was that she had
come through it without being seriously disturbed. Yet children
were unpredictable, he told himself. They could often show an
incredible resilience.

Conscious of his gaze, Stephanie rolled her head sideways

to look directly at him. 'I didn't exaggerate, James. I promise you.'

'What telepathy! That was precisely the conclusion I'd just come to.'

'Poor old Step-Papa James. I realize that it can't be easy for you. Particularly when there's nothing much you can do, one way or the other.'

He shook his head. 'Stephanie, you are an amazing girl. Christ, who'd believe you were only sixteen?'

'I suppose I was bound to grow up fast. And funnily enough, I think it gave me a sort of strength – Mummy's suffering, I mean. Although it seems a terrible thing to say.'

Suffused with admiration and affection, James drained his glass of wine. 'It's not a terrible thing to say at all.' His voice sounded distant. The wave of emotion had produced the dizzy effect of an unaccustomed cigarette. Christina's absence no longer seemed to hurt so much. Or at least not in the same way. The focus had changed.

Stephanie sighed in contentment at the sun's rays. She rearranged her limbs in a ripple of innocent pleasure. James had to force himself to look away.

'You must be baking,' she said, squinting at him sideways. He unbuttoned his shirt in a deliberately mechanical fashion staring hard across the river. Once it was off, he lit a cigarette and blew a couple of smoke rings. Then he realized he was holding in his stomach.

This is ridiculous, he thought, trying to dismiss the hazy sense of desire as a purely chemical reaction to sun and wine. He forced the muscles to relax, and picking at the remains of his bread, he rolled pellets in his fingers and threw them to a blackbird at the foot of a nearby tree. It twisted its head up checking for danger, then hopped forward to snatch one in its plastic-yellow beak, and flew away as if panicked by its own daring.

The silence grew as oppressive as the heat. James felt a headache coming on as a result of the wine. He filled his glass from the bottle of Malvern water.

'Can I have some too?' Stephanie asked.

'Of course. There's also a couple of mangoes we haven't yet touched. Do you want one?'

'Yes, please.'

He lobbed it over and she caught it awkwardly just before it hit her stomach.

Afterwards, sticky with yellow juice, Stephanie descended the bank and squatted to rinse her hands. James decided to do the same. His eyes were drawn down the bobbled curve of her spine to the bikini bottom stretched below the coccyx. She had not inherited Christina's rather majestic rump.

Noticing that she had stopped to stare pensively at the water, he peered over her shoulder. Stephanie smiled. 'It's like Eugene Onegin and Tatiana,' she said, referring to the ballet they had taken her to for her birthday. But reminded of something else, James recoiled in confusion.

Unaware of his reaction, Stephanie broke the water's surface with a brisk swishing, then she stood up and turned, flicking her hands.

'What's the matter, James? Don't tell me it's already time to leave our little island.'

'I think we'd better,' he said and nodded towards the west. 'Look at that dirty black cloud over there. That's quite a thunderstorm on the way.'

They reached the car as the first drops fell. The inside was stifling and smelt of warm plastic. James wiped his brow on an unbuttoned shirt sleeve. He wondered why women sweated so much less.

Within a few moments the rain was drumming on the roof and pouring down the windscreen. 'Christ!' he muttered. 'It's worse than a car wash.'

Stephanie wound down her window enough to slip a hand out palm upwards. He suppressed an urge to ask what she was thinking. Once the downpour eased a little, he turned the key and to his faint surprise the engine caught immediately.

By the time they reached the convent's main entrance, the rain had almost stopped.

'James,' Stephanie said after the ratchet of the handbrake

144

seemed to signal the end of their time together. 'Can I ask a very personal question? You honestly don't have to answer if you don't want to.'

The frenetic rhythm of the wipers was louder than the engine. He switched off the ignition to silence them both, and left his other hand on the steering wheel in frozen relaxation. Odd drops still spattered the windscreen. 'Fire away,' he said with a slight dip of the head.

'Why didn't you and Mummy have a child together?'

After a long moment contemplating the rainspots in front of his face, he glanced out of the side window at the red brick façade. There was another reason why he found this place so awful. It reminded him of Norfield and his father.

'We nearly did.'

'I don't understand.'

He regarded her for a moment with a painful smile. 'You remember her accident in Italy?'

'Yes. At the beginning of last year.'

'Well, she was pregnant when it happened. Nearly three months gone, according to the doctor.' He had to clear his throat. 'It was the first I knew of it.'

'Goodness!' Stephanie breathed. She gazed at the glovebox, wide eyed.

'Perhaps I shouldn't have told you ... even now.'

'Don't worry. I won't say anything.' She began to close and open the ashtray slowly. 'Did you want a child very much?'

'Yes. Yes, I did.'

'Not now?'

'I don't know.' He shrugged. 'It's beginning to seem a bit late, don't you think?'

Stephanie, still finding it difficult to assimilate the news, acknowledged the point distantly. 'What's going through your mind?' he asked in an embarrassingly husky voice.

This time the lift to her eyebrows was rueful. 'Whether I would have had a little brother or sister.'

James had to look away. The lump in his throat hurt. 'What a pair of orphans we are!' he tried to say lightly. At that moment Sister Bona appeared at the door staring in their

145

direction. 'Oh, hell! It looks as though the head warder's after you.'

Stephanie nodded, but did not move for several moments. Then, without a word, she threw an arm round his neck to hug him tightly. He watched her walking rapidly away, head bowed as if against the last of the rain. She ignored Sister Bona, whose eyes never left her.

When Stephanie reached the steps, the nun said something. She swung round to reply. A sharp retort, to judge by the reaction it provoked. Sister Bona, after a look of outraged accusation towards the car, turned to pursue her through the door.

James fumbled for a cigarette as he restarted the car. Tears began to burn his eyes, tears of unashamed self-pity. He did not know which loss would be greater. And when Christina took Stephanie away, she would probably leave him the house. To make up for the child they never had.

❦ 15 ❧

James woke late after a bad night. Once the previous day's events came to mind, he lay prostrate, unable to slide back into sleep. His hangover produced a mixture of mawkish sorrow and self-disgust. Eventually, he forced himself to put on some clothes and go down for breakfast. But afterwards, on the way up to his study, the coffee's strength brought on a slightly nauseous sensation of vertigo.

The notes for his book lay untouched alongside the word processor in its grey plastic shroud. He half-imagined the room deep in dust and hung with cobwebs like a chamber under an evil spell.

He experienced an overwhelming need to ring Christina in Austria. Nervous anticipation made his legs feel even weaker. But how would he start? He could just see himself gabbling out some ridiculous excuse for having rung, which would be followed by an excruciating silence.

Resisting the temptation to pry in Stephanie's room, he wandered disconsolately downstairs again. But on the way, he halted in the doorway from where he had watched Christina pack. He went in, and after a few moments gazing round, opened the cupboards. The shelves of neatly folded clothes contained the same sort of mothballs as the bedroom at Lotzingen. A smell transported into exile like a handful of native soil. He wondered whether the house at Starnberg had known it too.

Then, he noticed a pair of jeans Christina had bought a year ago at Stephanie's suggestion and hardly worn. Typically, she had cut off the designer label, the sole justification for their outrageous price. As he closed the cupboard, his glance came to rest on the bookshelf.

He squatted to look along the two rows of titles. Almost immediately he spotted *Die Aufzeichnungen des Malte Laurids Brigge* which he had never got round to rereading on their return from Venice. Inside on the flyleaf was written 'Christina v. Retzen' and a date some two years after the birth of Stephanie.

The book opened in his hands at a page near the middle and he read the passage marked in pencil, but all he could make out was something about women taking on the entire task of love. His German wasn't up to such prose. Then, to his frustration, he remembered that the English translation he had come across in a secondhand bookshop was still down at the cottage. He put the book back and stood up.

His presence there suddenly struck him as morbid. Almost as bad as going through personal effects before a funeral. The room had that empty look, the counterpane smoothed and surfaces cleared. It reminded him of dreams about his mother's death. As he went out, he shut the door behind him with slow deliberation, a bit like posting a fateful letter.

He returned to his study and went over to the window where he leaned his forehead against the glass and, staring out onto the trees of Brook Green, felt the faint vibration from an underground train. Not long afterwards, the sound of the front door reached him. Hope surged in a Pavlovian reflex. Christina had returned. The aberration was over. He charged down the stairs two at a time. But on reaching the last flight, he found Mrs Evans staring up at him in astonishment from the hall. He muttered an apology for startling her and said he had thought it was the post. Once more, he retreated to the study.

The door to Stephanie's room reminded him of the previous afternoon and her sadness for the brother or sister she had lost. Then the sensation of that ugly truth returned. A truth that he had managed to repress at the time, then avoid on the grounds that it must have been a momentary derangement. For Christina to have tried tobogganing when pregnant clearly represented some sort of self-destructive urge.

Any reminder of that time instantly brought back the lines fixed in his brain from the drive north to Turin following the telephone call. *Riding, riding, riding, through the day, through the night, through the day ...* The rhythm of the words had somehow managed to check the rising flood of panic. Trotting and cantering, blindly and repetitively, they gave a drugged purpose to his actions while thought remained dangerous.

[*When I first read them in the loft at Norfield, they had sounded indefinably familiar; almost as if they had been left in the silt of my memory to be rediscovered one day. Where I might have heard them before, I had no idea. But their cadence of an accelerated heartbeat tempted me at the time with the notion of preconscious knowledge – a fragment transmitted by a delirious mother while she died giving birth.*

After that, I returned to university obsessed with Rilke, and soon came across his maxim that 'we carry our death within us as a fruit bears a kernel.' This idea grew feverishly in my brain. Death reflected in birth. The future in the past. Consciousness in pre-consciousness. A slow irregular development up to the critical point – a momentary mirror image similar to a Rorschach test – then the metamorphosis, physical, emotional, historical.

I became convinced that this formed part of a larger, more complex truth. But after my father's death in a Harrogate nursing home a year or so later, I began to re-examine the myths of my childhood. He had been so pitiable during those last few months that most of my hatred drained away leaving me exhausted and confused. And when I revisited Norfield for the last time, just after the sale of contents, all beliefs and emotions from those years felt exaggerated. I almost doubted my existence there.]

Arriving in Turin's morning rush hour, James lost his way twice, and by the time he found the hospital, his sweat had an ammoniac reek. The pandemonium around the enquiries desk felt like the last straw. But his anxiety converted itself into ruthlessness and he shouldered his way through to grab the receptionist's attention.

She glanced through her list, still fending off a woman on the other side. They had no record of anyone of that name, she said, without looking at him properly, then bent to answer the telephone which had been ringing all the time. In desperation he grabbed her pen, wrote out Gaunt on the back of his cigarette packet, and thrust it under her nose, begging her to look again. Making a face of theatrical reluctance, she went through once more. All she could suggest, after a fatalistic shrug, was to find *il dottore* Barga, either in casualty or intensive care.

His dash through the maze of linoleum corridors, swerving in and out of people and trolleys with squeaky wheels, had a nightmare quality. Everybody he stopped seemed to have a different idea of where this Doctor Barga might be. When at last a nurse pointed to a white-coated man with thick eyebrows and a swarthy, pockmarked face, it was difficult to believe the search was over. Barga had the look of a *condottiere*, a detail that only occurred to James later.

Fortunately, Barga's English was good. Yes. A woman had been brought down from Sestriere after an accident on the slopes. A foreigner, but not English. Probably German. Her name was definitely not Gaunt. But what did she look like? Mid-thirties, slightly taller than average, dark blonde hair? Barga frowned, then twisted to reach into the small office for the clipboard of admission forms.

That she might have been registered under Retzen had never occurred to James. Evidently under pressure at the time, the cousins she was staying with must have forgotten her new name. In the mixture of relief at having finally found her, and worry over her condition, he gave it no further thought.

Barga told him not to worry. 'She is strong. She will recover.' He passed a hand wearily over his face. The pouches under his eyes suggested a busy night. 'And the leg will mend all right. It was a clean break, luckily.'

'Thank God!' James exhaled. He ran a hand through his matted hair. 'I was told there had been some sort of internal injury.'

Once again Barga had a puzzled look. 'But it was serious. She lost the baby and a lot of blood.'

'Baby?' James stared at him in disbelief. There was obviously some mistake. The woman couldn't be Christina after all. Barga began to lose patience. He took James by the arm to a door with a glass observation panel. 'Is that your wife, or not?'

Afraid of the truth, James looked uncertainly at him before leaning forward to peer through. There was no doubt. Although almost unrecognizably pale, Christina lay in the metal-frame bed, a tube fed into her forearm from a suspended container.

Barga regarded him closely. The exasperation had gone. 'That *is* your wife?'

'Yes.'

'She was at least two months pregnant. Maybe close to three.'

James began to shake his head slowly, a movement which had more in common with the repetitive behaviour of a caged animal. But when he noticed Barga's expression of pity, he came to a bewildered halt. The Italian obviously took him for a cuckold. He was according him the sympathy due to the bereaved. In any other circumstances the misunderstanding might have been funny, but at that moment an explanation was beyond him.

Subsequent events remained part of a malfocused blur broken only by the odd glimpse. The wheelchair at Milan airport with Christina's plastered leg sticking out in front. Then back in London on a chaise longue, with Mrs Evans fussing round at every opportunity.

During her convalescence, the subject of the accident was avoided. Christina would preempt any turn in its direction with distracted rushes of conversation, or a request for something she did not really want. James, also afraid to enter the emotional minefield, preferred to take her earnest affection and gratitude at face value. The night after the plaster came off, they went to bed inflamed with wine.

[*It is only now that I can appreciate how much we must have overplayed the role of refound lovers, probably more to ourselves than to each other. In any case, our life together seemed too miraculously restored to risk being upset by prodding below the*

*surface. Time was the great healer, went the old saying, and I did
not want to disbelieve it.*

*For some months after her return from Turin, Christina's deter-
mination to make things up was touching, although at moments a
little worrying. As part of this spirit of regeneration, she set herself
a heavy programme of study and reading. It even included a part-
time course at London University, but her concentration became
paralysed and she kept on having to go back to retrace the line of
argument. So, in spite of all my hopes that she had at last found
something to get her teeth into, I became a little alarmed that she
was punishing herself to no purpose. My greatest mistake, however,
was to have failed – probably refused – to recognize the significance
of the pattern: her exaggerated efforts on the house, the unrevealed
pregnancy and the accident at Sestriere, followed by those guilt-
inspired attempts to improve herself and be the perfect wife.*]

James noticed with a slightly shamed sense of relief that the
house was silent. Mrs Evans had not only finished with the
vacuum cleaner, but departed. To celebrate his liberation from
the top floor, he went down to the sitting room and flopped
onto the sofa's freshly plumped cushions. Bright sunlight made
a rectangle of white gold on the floor in front of his feet.

The telephone's ring once again startled him. The last time
that had happened the caller had been Stephanie, not
Christina. So this one should be the other way round. Or, more
likely, a wrong number. But instead, a woman's voice asked if
Mrs Gaunt had returned from abroad. 'No,' he replied. 'My
wife's still away. Can I help in any way?'

It turned out to be the Mother Superior of Stephanie's
convent. James frowned, then, remembering the contretemps
with Sister Bona, immediately assumed that a serious row had
developed.

'It's very urgent, Mr Gaunt. We must find her. You see, your
stepdaughter's been involved in an accident.'

He went cold. But to his subsequent surprise, he felt alert,
not numb. 'What exactly happened?'

The Mother Superior had obviously chosen her words in

advance. 'Stephanie fell on a stairway and gave her head rather a bang.'

The nursery euphemism irritated him. Why the hell couldn't she say things straight out? 'How bad is it?'

'She's under observation. It's too early to tell.'

'My wife's in Austria. I'll try to get hold of her right now. But where's Stephanie? In the san or in hospital?'

'Well, the ambulance took her to the hospital in Ascot ...'

He knew the one. Opposite the racecourse. 'I'll drive down there the moment I've got through. Goodbye.'

Unable to get a dialling tone, he jiggled the receiver cradle impatiently. The woman could not have hung up properly. Only after several tries was he able to punch out the number. The international connection clicked interminably, yet his emotions remained surprisingly controlled. Some reflex safety mechanism had automatically sealed watertight doors against the flood of visceral panic.

Josef answered. The *Gräfin* Christina was not there. He would put him through to *Fürst* Tassilo. James reacted too slowly to stop him. If the old man really was in a bad way, then he should not be told. Stephanie was his favourite granddaughter. After a good deal more clicking with the antiquated exchange, there was a pause, then a gruff clearing of the throat. 'Yes, James. What can I do for you?'

Needing a few extra moments to think, he enquired after his health, but Prince Tassilo dispatched the issue summarily. He regarded such questions as worse than superfluous.

'It's rather important that I contact Christina. Do you know where I can get hold of her?'

'I am sorry to have to tell you that she is not here. She left yesterday afternoon for Paris. I think she's staying there with friends. She promised to give me a ring this evening, so if you like, I could always give her a message then.'

James was at a loss. The seriousness of Stephanie's condition would be obvious, however carefully he phrased it. The old boy was no fool. After much dithering, James asked him to find out her number when she called, and he would ring back for it later. Prince Tassilo's rather brusque assent indicated how vexatious he found such complications.

As he rang off, James could not help wondering once again what he must think about their marriage. Was he torn between concern for his daughter and an old-fashioned conviction that she should stand by her commitments? No time for that now, James told himself as he dashed upstairs for jacket, keys and wallet.

❧ 16 ❧

'Paris?' James exclaimed after passing a sign to Heathrow. Wasn't the wedding supposed to have been in Germany? Perhaps her father had been confused. But one thing stood out clearly. There could hardly be a worse moment to start speculating about Christina's movements, or about whom she might be with. Not if he was to maintain any sort of self-control.

This particular stretch of motorway struck him as hideously ill-fated. It represented everything that had gone wrong over the last ten days. The return from that weekend with *Tante* Sisi – taking Christina to the airport – coming back from the convent yesterday – and now this. Yet what might have been the final straw had roused a fighting spirit. Even the car seemed to have risen to the occasion. He made an effort to relax his grip on the steering wheel. Then, to ease his neck muscles, he moved his head from side to side like a parrot.

The entrance to Heatherwood hospital he found opposite the end of Ascot racecourse's brick frontage. The place had a deserted, run-down air. No figures were visible outside the dilapidated concrete sprawl of early welfare state architecture and the car park was almost empty.

By a stroke of luck, the second person he asked for directions turned out to be the woman doctor who had examined Stephanie on arrival. Since Heatherwood was little more than a maternity unit, she had been sent on to the Radcliffe in Oxford, which specialized in head injuries. Stifling a curse, James thanked her and ran back to the car.

When he finally reached Oxford after nail-biting delays in

Slough, he was to regret his impatience once again. On the assumption that anything as complex as head injuries would have moved to the newer, and far larger, John Radcliffe Hospital on the ring road, he went straight there only to find that clinical neurology had remained in the old Radcliffe Infirmary.

'Why the bloody hell couldn't they call this place something completely different?' he stormed at the porter on reception.

He regretted the outburst back in the car, but his exasperation soon mounted again. The one-way system might have been specifically designed to prevent anyone reaching the Woodstock Road.

Without pausing to lock the door, James ran across the Radcliffe's front court to the main entrance. 'Clinical neurology?' he panted out at the desk. The porter, still sipping from a mug of tea, pointed down the corridor to the right with his free hand. Spotting the arrows to the Nuffield wards, James dashed off again.

He stopped in confusion when the trail appeared to vanish, but then, gazing desperately about, he caught sight of an arrow half way down the low, tunnel-like corridor ahead. It pointed up a staircase tiled to shoulder height in the typical style of a late Victorian institution.

On reaching the right floor, he spotted a staff nurse in a white uniform and broad blue belt. He said that he was Stephanie Retzen's stepfather and asked if he could see the doctor in charge of her case.

'Oh, yes, that's Doctor Aziz,' she said. 'He's in here with other members of the family.' James stared at her in disbelief as she crossed the corridor and opened a door. She impatiently gestured for him to enter.

Inside he found Sister Bona flanked by Bubi and his mother. The nun tried to ignore his arrival, but Bubi acknowledged him with a slight dip of that widow's peak. The Countess, formidable as ever, gave him a withering look. His forehead and scalp were soaked in sweat and then he remembered that he had not shaved.

'But how on earth did you get here?' James asked, too disorientated to care.

'Have you forgotten that Stephanie is my granddaughter?'

'I meant how did you manage to get here so quickly? Were you already in England?'

'No. We were in Munich. We took the very first flight as soon as we were informed.'

James turned to Sister Bona. 'But I don't understand. How long ago did the accident happen?'

'Just after dawn, Mr Gaunt. There was no reply when we tried to ring your home.' He remembered with dismay unplugging the telephone in the bedroom. 'Not able to make contact with the child's *mother*, we then of course tried the next closest relation, her grandmother.' Sister Bona punctuated her explanation with a little twist of the neck.

So, the Retzens had won her over. But how long ago? And for what? Just a watching brief? Stephanie had never mentioned an attempt to visit her.

'Did *you* manage to get in touch with your wife?' said Bubi, who appeared more vulpine than ever. His arch manner indicated little expectation of a positive answer. 'No? Well, in that case I think we'd better let the doctor finish what he was saying about Stephanie's condition, don't you?' With insolent politeness, he again inclined his head and turned to Doctor Aziz.

Although Aziz's expression gave little away, his restless eyes were assessing the battle lines. More or less the same age as Bubi and James, he had an intelligent face, the smooth brown skin complemented by an immaculately trim beard. 'I'm afraid I have very little to add.' His slight drawl seemed a little exaggerated. 'The X-rays show a fairly serious fracture as I said, but it is too soon to estimate any consequential damage.'

For James, the unspecified danger was too frightening to contemplate. He felt ashamed that instead of concern for Stephanie, his first reaction on entering the room should have been to recommence war with Georg's family. Why shouldn't the old dragon love her as any grandmother would? It was unfair to assume that she only acted in pursuit of family politics. But then the memory of Munich three years before brought resentment and suspicion seeping back.

'Now, I would like to see my granddaughter,' said the Countess, grasping onto her dignity. Careful not to brush against each other, they filed out of the office like mourners.

Stephanie was in a glass cubicle, her head tightly bandaged and her face pale. She could have been lying in state. The bandages made James think of Trotsky, an irrelevance which infuriated him. Wired as she was to electro-cardiogram and encephalogram machines, he might as well have compared her to Frankenstein's monster.

The Countess choked back a sob. '*Dornröschen*. She is a Sleeping Beauty.'

James frowned. Why couldn't the blasted woman get a grip? To wallow in pathos was typically German. A Latin would cry, but never descend to such cloying sentimentality. And in any case, she surely meant Snow White, not Sleeping Beauty.

They seemed to stand there for ever, perhaps half afraid that an abrupt movement might extinguish a last, imperceptible flicker of life. If anyone had spoken, it would have been in a church whisper. Rapid footsteps approached, then faltered. Somehow he knew it was Christina. After all the surprises, her arrival had acquired a bizarre inevitability.

Her gaze passed through him to fix on Stephanie's profile. She covered the last few steps in a sort of shellshocked slow march which petered out at the glass. The others made room for her, then closed round. Bubi glanced back at James as he put a comforting hand on her shoulder, then his mother embraced her from the other side.

James felt a stab of betrayal at the sight of the three of them hinged together. This unity of grief was not the occasion of their rapprochement. That must have happened already. And now, quite openly, Georg's family had closed in, flanking her to exclude him. Repossessing property. Reversing history. Day one of the counter-revolution.

Eventually the tableau was slowly broken with a movement like that stiff ripple after the priest's final blessing. There was no sign of Doctor Aziz. He must have slipped away. James found himself staring at Sister Bona making the sign of the cross. Her eyes rose as if to return a challenge. He looked away hurriedly.

Christina, still in protective custody, was being spoken to in low, urgent voices. James only caught the words *vom Paris*. He felt a wave of funk as he considered what to do. Should he try to assert some sort of marital authority, the only thing the Retzens might feel constrained to respect?

The idea of Christina publicly siding with them terrified him. He could not face it if she treated him like a stranger accosting her in the street. It would represent the most crushing denial of everything they had shared. His loneliness became unbearable. He could not continue to stand there, nor could he walk away. With a polite air of incomprehension, he turned to the only other detached figure. 'Sister Bona, I'm sorry, but I still don't really understand what happened.'

The old nun's head went back in a conspicuous gesture of scepticism. 'It would appear, Mr Gaunt, that Stephanie left her bed at dawn. She climbed out onto an iron spiral staircase that has *always* been strictly out of bounds.' Her tone gave the impression of distasteful evidence given in court.

'Another girl, who was awake, followed her out of anxiety at such strange behaviour. But she was only in time to catch a glimpse of Stephanie going down, faster and faster until she stumbled and fell forward, striking her head. The girl summoned help and an ambulance was called.'

'But why?' James muttered more to himself than to her.

'Perhaps *you*, Mr Gaunt, have a much better idea than anyone else.' The conversation in German ceased. All eyes were on him. 'Such behaviour,' said the nun in a voice to be overheard, 'was quite out of character, as everyone who knew the child agrees. She has never sleepwalked before, if that was what it was. And yesterday, she returned from an outing with you in what I can only call a highly emotional state.'

[*I still squirm in mortification and anger whenever I think of the way I must have stood there like a ventriloquist's dummy with its mouth jammed open. My confusion prevented me from seeing that Sister Bona's manner reeked of a guilty conscience, and that I only needed to ask about the row which must have taken place after*

Stephanie passed through that door.]

Outside the main entrance, however, the nun's presence worked unexpectedly in his favour, for Christina refused Bubi's offer of a lift after a glance in her direction. She made some excuse in German, then walked towards the Renault where James waited uncertainly. He quickly got in and reached across to open the door for her.

The barrier of resentment could be felt even before she fastened her seatbelt. All right, play it your way! he thought, still enraged by the sequence of humiliations.

But by the time they reached the motorway, his mood changed. He began to feel ashamed. Out of the corner of his eye, he glimpsed the signs of emotional strain behind the tortoiseshell sunglasses. Her celebrity incognito outfit, he used to call them.

'I tried to ring you in Austria as soon as I heard,' he said after making an unnecessary adjustment to the rear-view mirror. 'Josef put me through to your father before I could stop him. He told me you were in Paris. I didn't say what it was about. I thought it was best not to worry him.' Her only acknowledgement was a barely perceptible nod.

He imagined the load of guilt that must have piled upon her during the last few hours. He could even understand how she might believe Sister Bona's insinuation. Christina was not in a fit state to handle complex pressures. But her secret reconciliation with the Retzens he found impossible to forgive. Just to think of their reappearance on the field made his stomach knot with incredulous anger. He told himself to get a grip. He had to win this battle. For Stephanie's sake as much as his own.

'Well, anyway.' He shrugged unconvincingly. 'The main thing is the message got to you somehow or other.' In Paris, he silently added. The city of love had become the city of betrayal.

'Yes,' she said impatiently. 'Bubi rang me.'

'Ah, so that was it.' He forced a small laugh. 'I must say it was quite a shock finding myself face to face with those two. First time since Munich. At any rate for me.' He glanced across.

'I didn't know they'd kept in touch.'

Christina did not reply and a long, painful silence followed. 'Why was Stephanie so upset?' she said eventually.

The question, although expected, took James off balance. He tried to choose his words carefully. 'On Sunday ... well, yesterday, we hired a rowing boat and went for a picnic on the river. On an island to be exact. And as you can imagine in the circumstances, we couldn't help talking about you. Stephanie felt there were a lot of things I still didn't understand about the past.'

'What sort of things?'

'Mainly to do with Georg and the way it affected both of you. Stephanie spoke of the atmosphere in that house and the guilt you must have suffered from. Then and later. There wasn't a hint of disloyalty in anything she said, I promise you. She's amazing, that girl. Talk about wise beyond her years. Anyway, when I drove her back to the school, she asked why you and I hadn't had any children.' He paused. 'I told her about your tobogganing accident in Italy. After her frankness it seemed the least I could do.'

'What did she say?' Christina's voice was beginning to disintegrate at the edges.

'She wondered whether she would've had a little brother or sister. When you think about it, a reaction of that sort was hardly surprising, I suppose. It must've been a pretty lonely childhood for her.'

A strangled gasp made him look across in alarm. Her head was thrown back like a blind person in the street and tears rolled down her cheeks from under the dark glasses.

'I'm sorry,' he said. 'I'll shut up.'

She took off her glasses to press a handkerchief to her eyes. 'No. Please finish,' she said, then blew her nose.

After his description of Stephanie and Sister Bona on the steps, an uncomfortable silence fell between them. He felt she did not quite believe him. He didn't blame her. Even in his own ears, the story now seemed to have the hollow ring of self-justification.

* * *

When he turned the car into Brook Green, he snatched another glimpse of her profile. 'I'm afraid there's no food in the house, but I'll go up the road.'

She shook her head. 'I could not face the thought of eating in any case.'

'Perhaps not right now, but you must have something sometime. I know what. The water should still be hot enough for a bath. That'd make you feel better.' After the bitterness, to look after her made him feel better. Purified in a small way.

On his return from the shops, the distant hum of pipes indicated that she had taken up his suggestion. The telephone began to ring. He pushed the front door shut with his shoulder, propped the carrier bags against the hall table and went into the drawing room.

There was no reply when he picked up the receiver and said hello. Perhaps an international line had not connected properly. That happened quite often, especially from France for some reason. Otherwise it was one of those obnoxious cretins who waited in a war of nerves before hanging up.

'Hel-*lo!*' His exasperation mounted. Just as he was on the point of slamming down the receiver, a voice with a foreign accent said: 'Can I speak with Christina, please?'

'I think she's in the bath,' he replied. His stomach muscles had seized in dreadful certainty. He experienced a violent, fearful hatred of the voice's anonymity. 'Can I tell her who's calling?' There was a petrified pause. Come on you bastard! he yelled inwardly. Show your colours.

'Oh, do not bother her, please. If it is not a good time, I will ring back.'

But a click announced that Christina had picked up the extension in the bedroom. 'James, is it for me?' He had no choice but to replace the receiver. The idea of pressing the cradle and then eavesdropping came too late.

He paced about the room in impotent fury, pausing only to ransack a cigarette from his secret reserve at the back of a drawer. By the time he had found a box of matches, the telephone clicked faintly again. She had finished.

He needed three goes to light the cigarette, his fingers trembled so much. It felt as though his insides were being shredded. In a few hours he had gone from resentment to sympathy and back to rage again. She was destroying him with an uncertainty far worse than any *fait accompli*. The cigarette tasted disgusting. He bent to fling it in the fireplace.

When he straightened up, he found her standing in the doorway in her dressing gown.

'James, I am so sorry. With the bath running I didn't hear the telephone.' Her eyes pleaded for understanding and forgiveness.

'It was a friend anxious for news,' she added lamely. To have come down to apologize was an admission in itself. He stared at her unable to believe anyone could hurt him so much.

Choked by the obstruction in his throat he would not have been able to utter a word, even if he had known what to say. She did not cross the room to comfort him as his body begged. Instead, with the distraught air of someone unable to help a stricken animal, she fled upstairs.

That night, again alone in their bed, an idea came to him. He lay motionless thinking it over in the dark, then reached out, fumbling for the reading lamp. To his surprise, it was only half past twelve.

He crossed the room, gathering a towel around him and opened the door quietly. A crack of light showed from Christina's dressing room. She too must be finding it impossible to sleep. He crept along the landing to the stairs, and, wincing at every creak, continued on up to his study.

While searching through the bookshelves, his eye fell on the framed photograph of his mother. He remembered how Stephanie, on seeing it for the first time, had exclaimed that she looked just like her own mother. The remark had shaken him enough at the time to compare the picture afterwards with shots of Christina. But he had found nothing more than the most fleeting resemblance. Probably just a coincidence of expression. People saw such different things in faces.

Having found the volume he wanted, he returned to bed to leaf through it. Bubi's muttered *'vom Paris'* came back yet again.This time the connection was clear. She had lied when she said he had never met the man. He did not feel shocked, just surprised that he had managed to suppress his suspicion for so long. Fritzi had made his comeback at last.

This end to uncertainty provided its own relief, enough to allow him to sleep.

❧ 17 ❧

Soon after dawn, having shaved and dressed, James descended shoes in hand with the book under his arm. A nervous light-headedness, mainly due to lack of sleep, discouraged any thought of breakfast. Above all, he wanted to be off before the traffic began to thicken.

In the car he caught the end of the news on Radio Three. After a hazy start, the day would be sunny with a light breeze. Newfound purpose was the best fillip, he decided. The question of the caller's identity could wait.

He had already begun to have doubts about Fritzi. The idea now felt like one of those fallacious certainties which come on the edge of sleep. To his relief, the whole thing scarcely seemed important in the clear light of morning. And to find himself over the shock of Bubi's reappearance felt even more reassuring. In any case, the only thing that mattered was Stephanie's recovery.

At the Radcliffe, he had to hang around in the gloomy corridor waiting for Doctor Aziz. This time the journey seemed to have taken hardly any time at all. After looking aimlessly at the Impressionist reproductions provided by the Hospital Friends, he perched on an iron radiator of the same bulbous dimensions as those in Stephanie's convent. Soon restless again, he walked to the fire doors to peer down the ward. Without strip lighting, it was even darker. Only the colourless light from the window at the far end reflected a dull gleam on the linoleum. The surroundings probably depressed the staff more than the patients. To find such workhouse drabness behind a mag-

165

nificent classical façade struck him as typically British.

When Doctor Aziz finally arrived, he listened with a frown of concentration to James's jumble of apologetic enthusiasm. 'First of all,' he said when James had finished, 'I will be more frank with you.'

'You mean things are much worse than you said?'

'No,' he chuckled. 'That is *not* what I mean. On the contrary, we can tell from the encephalogram and other tests that she isn't paralysed or in a coma.'

'Thank God for that! But why didn't you say so yesterday?'

'We couldn't be sure then. You see, there's always the risk of residual damage after a severe concussion. And as it happens, this case is a little unusual. Although there is no evidence of brain damage and she is no longer concussed ...'

'She's just lying there as if ...'

'Precisely.'

'So don't you think my idea's worth a try?'

'From what you say of the circumstances, you may be right. And in any case reading to her could clearly do no harm. May I ask what you have chosen for her?'

James presented the book's leather spine. 'Carlyle's *Frederick the Great*. She's very keen on history. It's what she wants to study at university.'

Unused to reading aloud, it took time to ease into the majestic sprawl of Carlyle's prose. Every now and again, he would glance up at his immobile audience. But just as his self-consciousness was beginning to disappear, a nurse came in to ask if he would like a cup of tea. Probably another who thinks I'm crazy, he thought after thanking her. The interruption, however, was soon forgotten and he became oblivious to his surroundings.

He had been reading for quite some time when a sixth sense warned of eyes behind him. Bubi and his mother were watching through the observation panel. James acknowledged their presence with a dip of the head like Bubi's the previous day, then bent once more over the book. He wondered how long they had been there. And what they thought of the scene. He had to force himself to concentrate on the print and resist the temptation to look round – almost like a child determined not to breathe or open his eyes before a given moment. Finally unable to resist any longer, he turned to find they had gone.

Mid-morning hunger heightened by an early start soon exacted a break. In the corridor he met Doctor Aziz again.

'Ah, Mr Gaunt. Exhausted already?'

'Not exactly. More in need of a little sustenance.'

'By the way.' Aziz's manner became more serious. 'Were you aware that Stephanie's grandmother wants her flown to Munich?'

'You can't be serious!'

'She thinks she could "have the best possible treatment there". I rather have the impression that she is shocked by the shabby appearance of our ancient hospital.' Aziz's tone revealed little bitterness. Simply an ironic acceptance that the rich had to believe in the power of their money, above all when tragedy made them feel they were losing control.

'Anyway, there's nothing to worry about,' he quickly added to calm the outrage his news had provoked. 'I told her there was absolutely no question of moving Stephanie for the moment, but that she was of course free to fly in any specialist she liked.'

In spite of his own thoughts on the Radcliffe's dilapidated appearance, James was still incensed. 'But what does she bloody well think this place is? A first aid post in the jungle?'

'Please, Mr Gaunt. Perhaps I should not have said anything. You must understand that family disagreements in the background do not help our work at all.'

James attempted to swallow his anger. 'Of course you're right, and I promise I'll keep quiet. But *Christ* has that woman got a hide like a rhinoceros!' Another thought struck him. 'What about my wife, though? Did she support this ludicrous scheme?'

'Mr Gaunt, you are putting me in a very difficult position.'

'Oh, God, yes. So I am. I'm sorry. But please give me an idea. I'm very worried that she's being heavily pressurized. The one thing Stephanie's grandmother refuses to accept is her absence from Munich. And for reasons we needn't go into, leaving that place was the best thing that could have happened to both mother and daughter.'

'I see,' said Aziz cautiously. 'Well, all I'm prepared to say is that your wife said very little on the subject. But she did refuse to forbid you access.'

'Good on you, C!' James murmured fiercely. So she hadn't gone over to the enemy after all. He grinned at Aziz. 'Thank you, doctor. Thank you very much indeed. And sorry to have mixed you up in all this.' Aziz smiled politely, then went on his way, raising the clipboard in a gesture of farewell.

James went back to Stephanie's bedside with a fresh sense of purpose – an earnestness which turned Carlyle's prose into an urgent supplication for her recovery. Christina's trust must be vindicated. This second victory over Georg's family was as important as the first.

Christina seemed doomed to repeat her mistakes. A victim of her upbringing and early marriage, she could only react to circumstances. The difference between the two generations was incredible. The clear-eyed Stephanie seemed far better prepared for the world after the childhood she had survived. And yet she was the one lying there.

Aware of the stiffness in his back, James stretched, then shifted position. He became aware of another presence and twisted round. It was Christina. She gave him a shy, melancholy smile. He beckoned, and after a long moment of hesitation staring at Stephanie, she came in. He brought over a second chair.

'Thank you for not letting them stop me,' he said. She pretended not to understand and turned the book in his hand to see the title. Her drawn face seemed more beautiful than ever. He longed to say he loved her but it was neither the time nor the place. Aseptic and asexual, hospitals were devoted to the mechanics of life and death, not the mystery. And yet they retained the hush of a religious foundation.

'Go on reading,' said Christina. And he bent to the task with a resolution that surprised him.

Despite the hardness of the moulded plastic chair, she did not stir. Paradoxically, her stillness became distracting. It made him want to check she was all right. But as with an itch resolutely ignored, the temptation receded and he managed to regain the rhythm of the prose in time for one of his favourite passages – Carlyle's description of Frederick the Great's father.

'"Conceive a rugged thick-sided Squire Western, of supreme degree, for this Squire Western is a hot Hohenzollern, and wears a crown royal. Conceive such a burly *ne-plus-ultra* of a Squire, with his broad-based rectitudes and surly irrefragabilities; the honest German instincts of the man, convictions certain as the Fates, but capable of no utterance, or next to none, in words; and that he produces a Son who takes unto Voltairism, piping, fiddling and belles-lettres, with apparently a total contempt for Grumkow and the giant-regiment! Sulphurous rage, in gusts or in lasting tempests, rising from a fund of just implacability ..."'

Christina's hand gripped his forearm. He stopped in astonishment to look up at her. The expression and stare directed at Stephanie told him what had happened.

Her eyes were open. She gazed at the ceiling and blinked uncertainly. James, strung with emotion, made an effort to continue reading, but his voice cracked. Christina began to rise to her feet with the air of someone witnessing a miracle. He pulled her back. 'Shhh, nothing abrupt. Don't startle her.'

His voice restored, he bent again to the book.

❦ 18 ❧

The night of Stephanie's recovery, Christina rejoined him in their bed. They both felt so emotionally drained that the significance of her return was submerged in the events of the day. Their goodnight kiss after switching out the light was affectionate yet chaste. James, in spite of his determination not to exert any pressure, could not let such an habitual act mark the moment on its own. He reached across under the duvet to massage the crook of her neck. In response she stroked his hand, then kissed it. Although a signal to withdraw, the response more than satisfied him.

Stephanie was kept at the Radcliffe for further observation, and each day they drove down together to see her. At odd moments, the reversal of all disasters left him unsure whether to laugh or cry with relief and happiness. If not miraculous, such a turnaround at least represented a classic case of poetic justice. This appeared manifest in the departure of the Retzens the morning after he and Christina had made love again.

On her return from the airport, he could not resist asking if they had finally seen the back of them. He immediately regretted the smugness of his tone. Christina reacted with acute embarrassment. She turned to look through the post on the hall table. He cursed his thoughtless exploitation of her guilt and wanted to tell her that the last ten days no longer mattered. The War of the Bavarian Succession, as he secretly used to call it, had truly ended. But Christina, pretending to read the postcard of thanks from Claire Trustram, spoke first. 'I promise you won't be inflicted with them again.'

She laughed at his surprise. 'Come on,' she said quickly. 'Let's have some lunch. I'm starving!' He pulled her to him. She rubbed her head against his, then led the way downstairs.

The next morning they set off to collect Stephanie from Oxford. Christina drove as if every minute counted. James, still in high spirits, patted her thigh and grinned. 'It's all right. They won't let her leave without us.'

She slowed down reluctantly and he reached over to caress the side of her face. Christina's wary glance tempted him to remark that he wasn't going to molest her in the fast lane, but at that moment they passed the sign to Heathrow. This time it raised the question of Stephanie's convalescence, a subject which hadn't yet occurred to him. He had assumed they would stay in London or go down to the cottage.

He turned in his seat. 'Don't you think that Stephanie'd get more peace and quiet out of London?'

Christina glanced across, startled. 'What do you mean?'

James tried to maintain a nonchalance in his voice. 'Only that I thought it'd be a good idea if we all went down to the cottage.' He watched her profile. 'Stephanie loves the place and it's such a long time since we were there together.'

Her eyes flickered apprehensively. 'Oh, I'm sorry. In all the rush, I must have forgotten to tell you that I was taking her back to Austria.' The words poured out nervously. 'The mountain air at Lotzingen would be so good for her, and I am so worried about my father. He is not any better, you know. It would do him so much good to see Stephanie ...'

All James's fears surged up once more with a sickening pain. They were made worse by anger at his own gullibility. How could he have been so stupid as to believe the danger had passed?

'You *forgot* to tell me? Is there anything else you might have "forgotten" to tell me? Like when you were thinking of leaving, for example?'

'James, please! I'm so sorry!'

'This sounds like where we came in!' He shook his head in bitter disbelief. 'So when were you thinking of going?'

She did not reply. Her eyes filled with tears.

'You know, I bet you've got the bloody tickets right there in your handbag!'

She choked back a sob. 'I didn't have the courage to tell you. I'm sorry.'

'Jesus! This is unbelievable! So when is the flight?'

'This afternoon.'

'You certainly don't hang about, do you? And as for the tickets, when did you get them? No, don't tell me. I think I can guess because it's all becoming horribly clear. You picked them up when you took the deadly duo to the airport. Isn't that it?'

'I know you have every right to be angry . . .'

'Oh, indeed! But it's not doing me any damned good, is it?' He exhaled, his anger collapsing back into that confused pain. There was no pleasure to be had from hurting her in revenge. She was now crying openly.

'But why did you make love with me then?' he asked sadly. 'I thought it meant that everything was all right once more.'

She steered the car across onto the hard shoulder and brought it to a halt. He could not at first understand what she was doing. Then he realized she could hardly see through her tears. Shaking with sobs, she slumped sideways against the door, head in hands.

He touched her shoulder, but she shook him off. Motorway traffic continued to roar past and the car juddered with each slipstream. After what felt like a considerable time, he opened the door to get out. 'Let's swop places. I think I'd better drive the rest of the way.'

Doctor Aziz took them to Stephanie. He gave James an enigmatic smile when the two men stood back to let Christina enter first. Stephanie was seated on the edge of the hospital bed in mock primness. The neat bandaging resembled an incipient turban. Her mother, bending to kiss her, had to remove the dark glasses which concealed her inflamed eyes.

'Mummy, what's the matter?'

'It's only a bit of hay fever.'

Stephanie then offered her cheek to James as demurely as a

shepherdess in an operetta. 'Doctor Aziz tells me I must avoid all sudden movements.'

'If only all my patients were so conscientious,' Aziz returned. The two of them had obviously hit it off. 'By the way,' he said, turning to Christina, 'what are your plans for Stephanie's convalescence?'

Christina became flustered. She tried desperately to avoid James's gaze. 'I was thinking of my father's place in Austria. The air would be so good for her.'

'Perhaps later on, that would be fine,' said Aziz. 'But for the moment I must advise most strongly against travel. And flying is out of the question for at least a week.'

James did not have the heart to feel triumphant as she stood there not knowing what to say. In any case, the respite was only temporary.

'Mummy, I've thought about it carefully,' said Stephanie, 'and surely the best place is James's cottage. I'd have lots of fresh air and rest there. And Doctor Aziz has said I must also avoid reading to begin with, because apparently it might give me headaches. And since I don't want to waste time with exams coming up, James can be my history tutor. You could, couldn't you, James?' He bowed his head in acceptance. Poor Christina, he thought. She must think it's a conspiracy against her.

'And when I'm not working,' Stephanie asked Doctor Aziz, 'would it be all right for me to help with light duties? They're really very light at my stepfather's *Petit Trianon*. It seems that Marie Antoinette wasn't the only one to enjoy playing at gardeners and milkmaids.'

'Oh, dear,' James responded, feigning a sigh. 'That bump on the head didn't do any good at all.'

Stephanie raised her eyebrows, then, maintaining her Infanta role, stood up to leave. 'Honestly, Doctor Aziz, I can't thank you enough for everything.' James smiled involuntarily at the innocent gush. 'You and the nurses have been so kind.'

'It was a pleasure,' he replied quite truthfully, with a slight inclination of the head and shoulders. The obeisance syndrome must be catching, James thought. Or perhaps Stephanie had an unusual talent for inspiring it.

With Stephanie strapped in the front seat, and Christina at the wheel once more, they set off down the Woodstock Road into St Giles.

'Well, the Radcliffe may be a bit of a dump,' Stephanie said, looking out at the front of St John's. 'But Oxford is *definitely* where I want to be at university.' James leaned forward between the front seats to point out landmarks and direct Christina.

The city was at its best on that May morning. The golden stone glowed beneath a clear blue sky. Trees and grass were a lush green. A mixed group of undergraduates bicycled past, laughing. The girls' summer dresses billowed. No one really looked where they were going as they called to each other. How little things had changed. Perhaps his old Hercules with the wicker basket in front was still being stolen and restolen in Oxford's version of *La Ronde*. He so envied Stephanie. She would probably become the Zuleika Dobson of her year.

'Which way am I supposed to take?' Christina suddenly demanded in exasperation. Jerked out of his daydreaming, James frantically looked around to get his bearings.

The atmosphere in the car remained tense even when they were safely back on the right route. Stephanie broke the silence after her mother overtook a bus on Headington Hill in an unusually aggressive way. 'Mummy, *what's* the matter? If it's because you're upset about Austria, we can all fly over as soon as they say I'm fit to travel. It's only a bit of a delay.'

'Yes, of course.' Christina forced a painful smile. 'I'm sorry to spoil your homecoming. But I am concerned about *Grosspapi*. He's no better. If anything rather worse. And I must be with him.'

'Oh, no! I am sorry. But you should have told me.'

'I was afraid it might upset you in hospital.'

'Anyway, I'm sure Doctor Aziz'll give me the go-ahead at my checkup next week. But honestly, Mummy, if you feel you should go straight away, then you must. You don't have to worry about us at all. We can survive perfectly well down at the cottage, can't we James?'

'Yes,' he replied uneasily. 'Of course we can.'

Christina was clearly upset and confused, while he was torn between his reawakened suspicions and a longing to believe the story of her father's illness. Their glances met in the rearview mirror. Christina snatched her eyes away as if burned by the contact. Perhaps her real reason for avoiding the cottage was claustrophobia. With only two bedrooms, the sleeping arrangements lacked flexibility.

As soon as they reached Brook Green, Christina disappeared upstairs saying she must pack. James and Stephanie were left in the hall staring at each other. Their expressions of incomprehension masked unease and also resentment at being made to feel at fault in some way.

Stephanie followed him into the sitting room. 'Is *Grosspapi* really ill?' she whispered.

'He's not well, but at the same time I suspect he's not as bad as your mother implies.' He shrugged in frustration. 'On the other hand his condition may quite possibly be worse. That's the blasted trouble! I just don't know what to believe anymore.' He wheeled round and strode over to open the French windows to the garden. The baked air in the room felt suffocating.

Stephanie gazed at the carpet for a while, chewing the inside of her mouth. She raised her head. 'I think I'll go up and have a word with her.'

About half an hour later the door of Christina's room opened and he heard their voices unmuffled on the landing. He walked through to the foot of the stairs, and with a hand gripping the giant acorn of the newel post, he waited expectantly, his hopes boosted by an instinctive faith in Stephanie. But then Christina appeared in a pale grey dress, her favourite for summer travel.

With handbag and dressing case held in front, she descended in a slightly precarious, diagonal way. James had the impression that her eyes were avoiding him so acutely that she might even bump into him. He stepped aside.

Stephanie followed with her mother's coat over an arm. She signalled silently to let things be. He took another look at Christina and knew she was right. There really was no hope.

'I'll go and fetch your bag,' he said, his voice flat with despondency.

❧ 19 ❧

Apart from a last, linear halo along the horizon to their right,
darkness had set in by the time they turned off the main road.
In the narrow lanes, James drove fast, strangely stimulated by
the fall of night. Banks of cow-parsley, dazzling in the headlights, rushed by on either side. The inside of the car felt like
a driving simulator with the film accelerated, the world outside
no more real than a projection screen, a crash no more lethal
than a tinny sound effect to signal game over.

'Gosh!' said Stephanie. 'It's like the Cresta Run.'

'Driving fast is much safer at night. You can see the lights
of other cars a long way off.' He glanced sideways, but then
wondered whether Georg had taken her to St Moritz.

'What about bicycles, though?' she said.

On the point of retorting that hardly anybody rode them at
night in the country, he slowed down.

'Will you be getting up early tomorrow?' she asked.

'Very probably. But you can sleep as late as you want. I'll
even bring you breakfast in bed if you give me a yell.'

'That's sweet of you James, but you honestly don't have to
spoil me like that. In the country I love going out early, like
you. It's been such a long time since I've been down.'

'I know. And I only managed a couple of visits since Easter.
So I dread to think what state the garden's in.'

They reached a turning where the silhouette of a great, ivy-
covered tree served as landmark. Ever since his first visit to the
cottage as a child, its bleached branches sticking out of the
foliage had made him think of a skeleton's fingers poking from
a mitten. 'Not far now.'

'You know, you say that every single time we reach that horrible old tree.'

'Oh,' he said, slightly taken aback. 'What a creature of habit I must have turned into.'

'Yes, a crusty old bachelor,' she teased lightly.

He wondered if her throwaway remark was unintentionally revealing. Did she not see him as married?

Shortly afterwards, they reached the turning onto the farm track. He slowed the car to a walking pace as it began to roll and yaw in and out of the ruts like a ship in a heavy swell. At one moment the headlights swung up illuminating the candle blossom of the giant horse chestnut.

'It could almost be a Christmas tree,' said Stephanie. She broke into an extravagant yawn.

'Time you were in bed.'

'Yes, James. But first of all I insist on a tour of the garden by moonlight.'

'We'll probably get lost in the undergrowth. And anyway, I'm not sure there is a moon.'

'Goodness, you're a gloomy old thing. How could anyone be so prosaic and still be a writer? I love that word. Pro-saic. *Prosaisch!*'

With a final lurch the car swung into the entrance, and came to a halt five yards or so from the sitting-room window. The dark panes flashed back the headlights like answering torches. He switched everything off and leaned forward to look up through the windscreen.

'Well, it's still standing.'

They remained motionless in the silence; almost a counterpart to the old Russian custom of sitting down for a few minutes just before a long journey.

'Right,' he said, breaking the spell. 'I'll bring the cases in. Do you want a hot-water bottle or anything? What about some cocoa?'

'Cocoa? *Eeugh!* You're as bad as the nurses. Relax, James. For the moment, all I want is that walk.' He grinned lopsidedly and reached across her to open the door.

Out of the car, Stephanie breathed in deeply then exhaled

in contentment. 'Oh, the difference to be out of hospital! It smelt of death, that place. And everything here is so fresh and so alive. Is it true that some flowers smell more at night than during the day?' She looked up at the night sky, and with arms out to balance herself, she turned round and round, searching out the constellations. Her bandaged head gave her the air of playing blind man's buff.

'I think tobacco flowers are supposed to give off the most scent after sunset.'

'James, can we plant some tomorrow? Please! Oh, yes. And some sweetpeas?'

'If you like. Tomorrow I've got to go over and buy seeds and bedding plants in any case. But are you sure about the sweetpeas? I always think they have rather a sickly smell, a bit like a public lavatory. Although I agree they're very pretty.'

'Only *you* would come up with that sort of comparison. Anyway if I had a garden, I'd like to plant lots and lots of different things and go out every morning before breakfast to see what's come into flower.'

'Hah!' he cried in triumph. 'And what was it you were saying about me and my *Petit Trianon?*'

'Just listen to him!' she said, threatening his flank with an index finger. 'He's so pleased with himself! Savour your victories while you can, James. There won't be many of them.'

She exhaled again happily to signal a return to her interrupted reverie. 'How peaceful it is,' she said in wonder. 'Look at those stars and all that real midnight blue.' She laced an arm through his.

He patted her hand. 'You're sure you're not cold?'

'Oh, James, stop nannying me! I'm fine and it's a beautiful, mild night. There are so few of them in this country, so let's enjoy it while we can.'

Once Stephanie had been installed in the little bedroom, she hugged him goodnight and extracted a promise that he would wake her early. James went back downstairs. He poured himself a whisky and wandered out again onto the grass at the rear of the house. Everything was so still that the urgent drumbeat of a train could be clearly heard from the main line a couple of miles to the south.

The quarter moon was by now above the line of trees next to the field. Stephanie had spotted it apparently trapped in the branches of a dead elm. He smiled at the memory of her gleeful tone. Raising the glass to his lips, he turned to look up at her window. The light was already out.

Once the last of the luggage was out of the car, he tiptoed up the narrow staircase trying to avoid the creaks. To undress and spread himself between the cool sheets lent a sensual pleasure to his tiredness.

In this cottage bedroom with its low ceiling and low window, the double bed seemed to be squeezing outwards against the walls. Once again he experienced that Alice in Wonderland sensation of his surroundings fluctuating in size.

This had been Aunt Margaret's bedroom. On his visits in the school holidays, James used to sleep in Stephanie's room. And just like her, he would slip down early on the first morning to see what was new. In those days the garden was always full of foxgloves and hollyhocks. One saw them so rarely now. Tomorrow, he would ask if they had any at the gardening centre.

An owl hooted, probably from the copse beyond the dead elm. While drifting off to sleep, it occurred to him that since their arrival he had not given Christina a thought.

❧ 20 ❧

A sharp rapping noise out in the garden attracted James's
attention. Coffee in one hand and slice of toast in the other, he
moved to the open door. A thrush holding a snail in its beak
was trying to crack the shell on the brick path. Loath to take
his eyes from the scene, James bent his head to sip from the
steaming mug, but his spectacles misted up, and by the time
visibility was restored the bird had gone.

The early haze promised another warm day. His heart rather
sank at the thought of all the work to be done, although
admittedly the grass took much less time to cut now, thanks
to Christina's insistence on buying a baby tractor.

Her first visit to the cottage had been soon after their return
from honeymoon. Quite plainly she could not understand his
affection for its faded chintzes and cosy dilapidation. James,
recognizing the sentimentality of his attachment, and well
aware of his own hopelessness at decoration, had given her a
free hand.

She had redone the place in a similar fashion to the house
on Brook Green. Every wall was replastered and painted white,
and every piece of wood stripped to the natural grain and
polished. The transformation was finished with kelims on the
floor and curtains in strong plain colours – her favourite greys,
blues and greens.

Once again he had been impressed, but also disturbed, and
not just because of the expense. That such a fundamental
change could be effected by someone with her attachment to
the past had struck him even then as paradoxical, if not slightly
perverse.

James jumped on discovering a presence beside him. Stephanie had arrived barefoot in her cotton nightdress. Eyes still half closed from sleep, she gave him a perfunctory kiss.

'Sorry,' she said. 'Didn't mean to startle you. The smell of toast wafting upstairs dragged me out of bed.' She stuck her nose out of the door and sniffed luxuriantly. 'Goodness, it's going to be a lovely day. It's warm already. I slept so well you can't imagine.'

'I'm glad to hear it,' he said as she stepped out onto the lush grass. 'What do you want for breakfast?' he called after her. She looked different for some reason, then he noticed that the bandage had gone.

'Could I have some tea please, with a spoonful of honey? And a yoghurt. I'm going to try Mummy's regime. Who knows? I might even become a creature of habit too!'

Arms out to balance, she skated for a few inches on the grass, then slowly pirouetted. James looked up from the kettle. The sun silhouetted her body within its loose virginal smock. He blinked and studied the kettle again, waiting for it to boil.

'I would hardly describe your mother as a creature of habit,' he said when he came out with her breakfast on a tray. 'At least certainly not at the moment.' Stephanie did not reply. She followed him to the small terrace of old brick and flagstones. The rosemary bushes he had planted round it the previous autumn were beginning to show their tiny blue flowers.

James put the tray on the table and fetched a couple of the white garden chairs. Then, while Stephanie ate her yoghurt in a reflective rhythm, he craned his neck to examine the outside of the cottage. Although nearly two years since the work had been done, he was still unused to how smart everything looked, with the new Georgian paned windows and garden doors.

'You know,' he said, shielding his eyes from the sun, 'I once heard your mother say to a friend that the English must be very strange to dream of retiring to what she called "one of those dolls' houses in the country".' He uttered a quick laugh. 'It must have been a shock for her to find that the whole of this place could fit into the Hunting Hall at Lotzingen. One thing's certain about your Mama: she does need her space.'

Stephanie eyed him over the top of her mug. She then put it down carefully on the slate-topped table and gazed across the field. James changed the subject to plants and seeds.

Once she was dressed and he had shaved, they set off on their shopping expedition. In half a morning, they filled the car with everything from cleaning products to wine, food, plants and plastic sacks of potting compost. Then, after a lazy lunch outside, he persuaded Stephanie to rest in the shade, and once she was asleep he stole in to clean the house. He had almost finished by the time she woke.

'James, that was really sneaky. You might at least have let me help a bit.'

'Perhaps. But you're amazingly stubborn, and it was the best way to make sure you had your rest.'

'Well, it was sweet of you, but will you *please* let me do the cooking. I *really* want to. And I promise not to poison you.'

'All right. Since you *really, really* want to.'

'Don't mimic! It's not fair.'

'What, not fair because you're a foreigner? But who's the mimic round here? It's you. You picked up that voice at school, and now you can't stop taking the mickey out of it.'

She made a face at him, and he laughed on his way out to tackle the herb bed where only a sickly-looking thyme survived the weeds. A completely fresh start was the only solution, he decided, and began to dig everything up.

His eyes soon stung with sweat. Unused to such exertion in the heat of the afternoon, he stopped to mop his face and lean on the fork, just like old Fox, Aunt Margaret's gardener, who used to come from the village on his bicycle two mornings a week.

Through the kitchen window, he noticed Stephanie studying a cookbook, chin on hand and a frown on her face. She must have sensed his gaze, because a moment later, she looked up. 'What on earth are you finding so funny?'

'Your expression,' he called back. 'I've never seen such a picture of desperate concentration.'

'Oh, James. You mustn't put me off! All these pounds and ounces are driving me crazy.'

'Don't say that school of yours has gone metric? You'll be telling me next that the nuns are computer literate.'

'If you really want to know, one or two of them are. Honestly, your prejudices about the place are so exaggerated!'

'Come on. I was only joking. And I'm sorry the cookbook's so ancient. Your mother never really used them down here.' But Stephanie was not to be mollified. He shrugged ostentatiously and returned to digging. Perhaps her reaction had more to do with being interrupted. She was taking the job so seriously, and yet she had never shown the slightest interest before. Perhaps the novelty of cooking for a man appealed to her.

On further consideration, he recognized a touch of the newlywed stereotype with Stephanie playing at grown-ups. Maybe a sense of duty prompted her to take on the role of her absent mother. But whatever the degree of imitation, one thing was certain. That mix of genes, environment and timing which was supposed to define character looked as if it had given her an infinitely greater measure of control over her own fate than Christina could have ever enjoyed.

The contrast returned in a curious way a few hours later. Half way through their supper in front of the television, the telephone rang. They immediately knew who the caller was, and while James put down his plate and levered himself to his feet, Stephanie turned off the sound with the remote control. His gruff 'I'll get it' camouflaged a strange sensation of anticipatory guilt.

'Is your father any better?' he asked. 'What do the doctors say?' He was conscious of Stephanie's eye upon him until a voiceless argument on the screen distracted her.

He went on to assure Christina that they were both well, that yes, he was making absolutely sure Stephanie took things quietly. She had even spent most of the afternoon sleeping under the walnut tree. The weather was lovely. They were managing very well. Stephanie had cooked a delicious meal which they were eating in front of the television. And no, he wouldn't forget her appointment at the Radcliffe on Monday.

Throughout the conversation, Stephanie's expression had remained sceptical while her eyes lingered on the furious mouthing of the screen characters. But when she took the receiver from him, the hint of suppressed irritation vanished completely.

'How is *Grosspapi*?' she asked in unfeigned concern. The next exchange was in German. Christina must have switched languages.

After Stephanie had hung up, she returned with a troubled air. To forestall any questions she picked up the remote control to restore the volume, and only then sat down. James, trying to imagine what Christina might have said, could not stop glancing across. The conversation in German had rattled that other skeleton: how often Stephanie had been seeing her grandmother and Bubi.

When the credits finally appeared on the screen, he attempted a cheerful tone to ask if she wanted any more. 'I'm going to. It really was delicious.'

'No thanks.' Stephanie's smile was little more than a twitch of the mouth.

He took both their plates out to the kitchen, where he found that he could not face even a token helping. He returned to the doorway. 'You don't look too happy,' he said. She jerked her eyebrows without looking up. 'Is your grandfather's illness worse, then?'

'It's not so much *Grosspapi* I'm worried about. It's Mummy.'

'What is she up to now?'

'I don't think I'm supposed to say.' Her tone had an edge of disapproval.

'Is it about flying to Austria next week?'

Stephanie looked up at him for a moment, then back at the lager commercial. 'More or less,' she said, and with a fully extended arm, aimed the remote control to switch off the set. She watched the image implode and continued to gaze at the blank screen. James meanwhile remained standing in the same place, unsure whether to prompt her with another question or keep quiet.

'Oh, *scheise!*' she burst out. 'What on earth does she think she's doing?'

'But what is she doing?'

'My mother – assuming the Radcliffe gives its approval on Monday – wants me to take the very next flight to Munich.'

'Munich?' James perched on the arm of the sofa. 'So that's where he is.'

'Who?'

'The man this is all about. The one she's infatuated with. For a time, I thought it was someone else. Someone who lives in Paris.' He lowered his head and gazed at the floor between his feet. 'When she first told me of this mysterious character's existence, she said I didn't know him, and I believed her. Funnily enough, the most terrible part came when I spoke to him, but only for a few seconds. It was the evening after your accident. He rang and your mother didn't hear the telephone because she was running a bath.' He looked up. Stephanie was staring at him. 'Come on, surely you'd realized there was someone.'

She looked out of the window for a few moments. 'Yes, I suppose I did. Though I didn't want to, if you understand what I mean.'

'Yes! Only too well.' He scraped the fingertips of both hands back over his temples and down the back of his neck. 'What about you? Have you the slightest idea who he might be?'

'Absolutely none. I promise you.'

'But what did she say about Munich? I presume she's off to join him there.'

'No. That's the peculiar bit. She's not going there, at least not for the time being. The whole thing's crazy, but I could tell from her tone that there was no point arguing. She asked me to trust her and do what she said. She'd explain everything later.'

'But where are you going to stay?'

'Oh, James,' she sighed. 'Where do you think?'

'You mean with your grandmother?' he said quietly. She turned down her mouth in ironic confirmation. 'Have you ...' he began. 'Have you seen much of them, then? Since your mother and I were married, I mean.'

Stephanie looked at him sadly. 'I wondered when you were going to ask that.' He gave a sheepish smile in return. Then, in a brusque reaction, he leapt up to fetch his emergency packet of cigarettes. In addition to the sudden craving for nicotine, he needed a pretext to move around.

'Poor James,' she said. 'I can imagine how you must feel.'

He pretended not to hear. 'This reconciliation with your father's family. How exactly did it start?'

Stephanie pursed her mouth before answering. 'My grandmother began to send me cards and birthday presents to the school. Then letters saying how unhappy she was at being separated from her only grandchild. I'm sure you can guess the sort of thing. It was all rather treacly and embarrassing.'

'But what did you feel about her and Bubi? Did you hate them like your father?'

The question obviously discomfited her. 'No, obviously not as bad as that. It's so hard to describe exactly. But I certainly didn't like them much. Least of all Uncle Bubi. I *always* thought he was poisonous.'

'So did your mother push you into it, then?'

'Oh, James! For heaven's sake! You're the one who's pushing me now. It's not fair.'

'I'm sorry. You're absolutely right. I'll shut up.'

Her sigh of reproof also accepted the apology. 'This isn't easy for me either, you know.'

'I'm sure it isn't. I really am sorry.' He drew voraciously on his cigarette.

'Can we go outside? It'll get stuffy in here if you're going to carry on puffing like a chimney.'

They walked up and down on the grass in the stillness of the twilight. Every few moments the tip of James's cigarette glowed, illuminating part of his face. He told himself not to interrupt.

'Mummy told me that they were specially coming over to England to visit me. And we couldn't really refuse since she was after all my grandmother. Funnily enough, it was the nearest she got to admitting anything about our life in Munich.'

'But when was this?'

'Last year, at the beginning of the autumn term. We went out for lunch at the Berystede. It was pretty grisly all round. Mummy was as nervous as anything, Uncle Bubi his usual smarmy-charmy self, and Grandmama on booming form. The poor waiters didn't know what had hit them.'

'I can just see it.'

'What embarrassed Mummy most about the whole thing was asking me afterwards not to mention anything to you. She said you wouldn't understand.'

'Damn right I wouldn't!'

'James. Please?' He nodded earnestly and threw his cigarette into the flowerbed. Its glowing tip traced a red arc through the penumbra. 'Mummy said you wouldn't understand because you saw them as the enemy.'

'Because *I saw them* as the enemy? What about her? Did she happen to mention . . .' He reined himself in abruptly. 'Oh shit, I'm sorry.' He put a hand on her shoulder. 'I'm being unfair again.'

Thwarted anger he found the most galling of all. Christina's implication that he was obsessed about Georg's family might well have some justification. But what of her? Had she forgotten, or, more likely, managed to blank out the past completely? Not just Georg, but Bubi and the way he had behaved in Munich. And what about the way she hated that old battleaxe of a mother-in-law?

'No,' he insisted, returning suddenly to the attack. 'I most certainly wasn't imagining things! What really frightens me is the way she seems to have gone in for a rewrite of history.'

Stephanie continued to watch him closely. 'Can't you tell me a bit more about what happened?'

He felt a horrible constriction. As if the truth would choke him if he did not spit it out. He struggled with the urge to tell her, but then he knew that if he started, he would have to tell her everything.

'It wouldn't be fair on your mother,' he said eventually. 'Not now, at any rate. Maybe one day.' Stephanie took his hand and squeezed it and he smiled gratefully.

'You know, I can't help thinking, at times, that she must suffer from a sort of retarded guilt which has become all twisted up inside. Almost a compulsion to punish herself.' He felt Stephanie make a movement of hesitation. 'What do you think?'

'I don't know.'

'Are you sure you're not cold?'

'I'm fine, honestly. But can we go and sit on the terrace and look at the stars?'

'All right, but I'll fetch you a jersey just in case.' He began to feel calmer, and above all thankful that he had held his tongue at that crucial moment.

They settled themselves, one on each side of the table. James hunched to light another cigarette, his eyes squinting at the flame. Then he leaned back, legs stretched out, and paralleled her gaze up into the sky. 'It's too early to see many yet.'

'I don't mind. It's another wonderfully quiet night.'

After a short interval there was a scrape of metal on brick as Stephanie moved her chair. 'James, don't you think there might have been some truth in what Mummy said about exaggerating things in your mind?' She hurried on before he could reply. 'What I really mean, is that I can't help feeling that you – and Mummy too in her way – didn't know each other properly when you fell in love.' Stephanie reached across and put a hand on his forearm to soften the effect. 'Please understand that I'm not getting at you. I never would at such a time.'

'I know.'

'I'm just trying to help you see things a little more objectively. After all, it was you who warned me to be on my guard when I fell in love. And about distinguishing between an infatuation with one's image of a person, and a love that's based on the reality of friendship. Don't you remember what you said? "Love is a psychosomatic condition," and so on? Oh, yes. And you also quoted Goldsmith. Something about friendship being a disinterested commerce between equals, while love was "an abject intercourse between tyrant and slave".'

'Bloody hell!' he said with a bitter chuckle. 'You've got a

sharp memory. What other little squibs of mine have you got tucked away, ready to lob back at me?'

'Sorry, but it was too tempting to resist. Anyway, let me finish what I was saying. Mummy probably fantasized even more. After her life in Munich, where everyone only talked about money, scandal and parties, she probably created daydreams round you. I'm not sure what, but maybe of a literary salon in London with clever and witty conversation at her dinner table.'

'Oh, no! She can't have done,' he said, thinking of her reaction to the last party. 'She may love books, but she's never really liked publishing gossip. Mainly, I suppose, because she didn't have any friends of her own in that world.'

'Yes. Poor Mummy. In a way she doesn't quite fit in anywhere. Except of course at Lotzingen. And to make it worse, she's neither one generation nor another. That's what makes her so funny and old-fashioned about things.

'But to go back to what I was saying. At the crucial moment, when you and Mummy met, she was at a point in her life when things had to change. Perhaps you were too, I don't know. But what I'm trying to say is that you both probably appeared to each other as the heaven-sent escape from whatever had been getting you down. Gosh, that sounds a mouthful, but you know what I mean. Anyway, I suppose it often comes to that. At least that was more or less what you told me.'

When her message eventually sank in, James found himself lost for words. She had turned his most cherished belief on its head. That what he'd always assumed to be miraculous good timing – probably the only bit in his life – had in fact been disastrously bad. She was really saying that he and Christina should never have married.

Stephanie stood up, pushed back her chair, then quickly kissed the top of his head. 'I'm sorry. I feel very tired all of a sudden. I think I'd better go up to bed.'

'I can't believe this,' he murmured as she disappeared into the house. He did not know what to think anymore.

To raise the will and the energy to fetch a drink took him several minutes. On the way back with a tumbler and the bottle of malt whisky, the bookshelf caught his eye. He stopped, hesitated, then dropped to one knee to search along the rows for that translation of *Malte Laurids Brigge*. He recognized the faded blue spine.

Having switched on the lamp by the armchair in the corner, he poured himself a glass, and sat down to read. He skipped through the beginning. The description of the rue Toullier and its neighbourhood with the Hotel Dieu was more or less as he remembered. He came to Urnekloster, the house of Malte's grandfather, Count Brahe, inhabited by the ghost of Christine Brahe who had died giving birth to her second child. And back in Paris there is the lyrical description of the *Dame à la Licorne* tapestry which Christina had taken him to see at the Musée de Cluny the day after Andrea's party.

He jumped ahead, reading feverishly. Many of the resemblances were farfetched, the result no doubt of over-interpretation. Yet beyond the detail of vague and often mixed similarities, Christina's abyss-like fear of losing Lotzingen could be clearly pictured.

Far more important, however, was the marked passage he had found in London: 'For centuries now, women have undertaken the entire task of love; they have played the whole dialogue, both parts. Man has only echoed them and badly.' Then over the page: 'They have nevertheless persevered day and night, and have grown in love and misery. And under the stress of endless sorrow, have emerged those outstanding women lovers, who, while they called their man, rose above him ... and those women who remained with their bullies and their drunkards, because they had found the means to withdraw farther within themselves than anywhere else; and this they could not conceal when they came among people, but were radiant as though they had always moved with the blessed.'

Malte, she must have thought, was the only man to understand her. But then a deeply unsettling idea struck him. Had she somehow thought of *him* as another Malte? He tried to dismiss it as a ludicrous notion, merely the effect of alcohol or a sense of paranoia. But when he flicked back to certain

191

passages, reading them again with rapidly mounting dismay, the evidence could not be dismissed.

During that first evening at Andrea's, in conversation and later with the story of his childhood, he had, quite unwittingly, offered up enough coincidences to inspire this fantasy. He quickly made a rough list of points reflected in the book, such as Malte the writer, researching in the Bibliothèque Nationale. Then there were the details of his Danish childhood. The death of his mother, the subsequent importance of his aunt. The menacing patriarch in the God-forsaken house. The child left to the care of servants. Then came a strange and unnerving parallel, a detail he had never mentioned to her: the lonely child's creation of an alter ego.

For Christina, the most striking touch of all must have been his mother's fascination with Rilke. He had even quoted that line about the woman who loves transcending the man she loves.

'Oh, Christ,' he muttered. He felt weak and foolish and slightly sick.

After a long time slumped in the chair, he forced himself upstairs. Yet even in bed, the prospect of sleep seemed no nearer. Unable to move, he lay there breathless, empty and afraid. Finally, as a grey luminescence filtered round the curtains, exhaustion provided release. The dwindling dawn chorus could have been a sort of 'Nunc Dimittis'.

❧ 21 ❧

Moments from those last four days remained in his memory with an almost tactile intensity. The feel of sun-baked skin, the itch of grass against naked back, warm brick paths underfoot, then out of the vivid light into the dark coolness of the house. Images such as Stephanie in the old straw hat he had found for her, deep in thought, twiddling a dandelion under her nose. A squirrel's sudden ripple of movement on the lawn, freezing after each dash as though in a game of grandmother's footsteps.

And the sounds. The pompous buzz of clover-hopping bumblebees, the somnolent call of wood pigeons, and in the middle distance, a woodpecker's multiple rap, which could be mistaken for the creaking of an old tree.

It felt as though the outside world had ceased to exist, or at least lost the power to affect his life. Neither pain nor humiliation could reach him. His ratio to surroundings had finally become irrelevant. They might, as Stephanie remarked, stretching in the sun with a frisson of make-believe, have been stranded on an enchanted island.

To drive off to the shops on the Saturday morning, and find streets full of cars and people, came as a slight shock. But once they returned, this brief interruption was soon forgotten. Sprawled on the grass, James in a pair of old tennis shorts, Stephanie in her black and white bikini, and with a bowl of cream between them, they dunked the strawberries bought at a roadside stall and threw away the stalks.

James contentedly licked between his fingers. 'It's just like in *Elvira Madigan*.'

'Oh, yes,' said Stephanie, with a frown. 'I saw that on

television with Mummy once. She thought it very romantic.'

'It certainly sounds as if you didn't.'

'If you really want to know, I thought it was dated and yucky.'

'What precocious good taste,' he said lightly.

She eyed him, then reached across to right a punnet which had tipped over. 'Do all novelists compare everything to fiction?'

He grunted. 'Probably just the bad ones.'

'What made you want to become a writer?'

'That's a long story. But the flip answer is that I longed for a profession which required none of the qualifications my father believed in. In fact a lot of the pleasure I got from the success of that first novel was knowing how much it would have irritated him.'

'But why? I mean why should he have been? Wouldn't it have made him proud of you?'

'Proud? You must be joking! It would've stuck in his gullet!'

'Did you honestly hate him that much?'

'Yes, at the time I most certainly did. Quite frankly, he was a miserable old sod.'

Stephanie cocked her head in dubious consideration then, without further comment, rolled onto her back. She sighed to emphasize a change in subject. 'I wish summer would never end. I can't face the idea of going back to that school and boring old Sister Crossbones.'

'That's like wanting to remain young for ever.' He knew he sounded lugubrious – his Eeyore tone, as she called it – but at that moment he could not help it. He began to stack the empty punnets.

'I'm going to do the bonfire,' he muttered, suddenly too restless to remain in anyone else's company. As he scrambled to his feet, Stephanie raised her head from the grass and shielded her eyes with a hand.

The bonfire was one thing he preferred to do alone. Paper, twigs and matches were soon assembled, but there were no medium-sized pieces of wood to form a good core before piling on the greenery. He remembered the sledge. With its rusty runners, there had been no point in keeping it, but Christina's arbitrary decision to throw out everything in the garden shed had provoked him into revolt. [*Even at the time, I considered it strange that she should make me feel like a child allowed to keep a single shell from a holiday collection.*]

The irony was that this sledge, grudgingly built by Fox to Aunt Margaret's specifications and coated in the dull green paint used for potting-shed windows, had been impossibly cumbersome. Even when launched with tremendous effort, it would dig its front deep into the snow and halt abruptly like a pony refusing a jump. He remembered having to take it back to school after the Christmas holidays. All the other boys had small fast toboggans which their parents had bought in shops like normal people. James fetched a heavy hammer and smashed it apart, joint by joint.

Stephanie appeared, drawn by the crackle of the flames. Without speaking, they stood together watching the old green topcoat blister, blacken and then ignite.

'Why are you burning it now?' she asked eventually.

'Should have done it a long time ago. It was never any good.'

Stephanie made no comment to begin with. She just wrinkled her nostrils at the smell of burnt paint. But then she said: 'I hardly know anything about your childhood.'

'It wasn't very interesting.' He shrugged, took the fork, speared a load of weeds and heaved it onto the fire. Grey-yellow smoke belched up into the sky. 'Polluting the atmosphere,' he said lamely after returning to her side.

Stephanie nodded, a trifle distantly. 'You haven't really managed to write much during these last few weeks, have you?'

He glanced sideways, startled by her return to the subject. 'No. That's certainly true.' He uttered a harsh laugh. 'I've been thinking of writing the story of my life instead. I'm going to call it *Abort, Retry, Ignore?*'

'I don't understand.'

'It's what a word processor asks when you've made a mess of things. Sorry, not a very good joke. But to answer your question, it hasn't exactly been easy to concentrate lately, as you might imagine.'

'I certainly can. Poor James.' She put an arm round him and gave him a hug.

'Hey, I'm all sweaty,' he said, touched by the gesture and a little uneasy at the contact of bare flesh.

She turned her head to sniff him. 'You may be sweaty but you smell of wood smoke.'

'Like a charcoal burner.'

'In*deed*,' she said, both relishing and mocking the Englishness of the word. 'But to go back to your writing. I was thinking that perhaps all this worry and unhappiness over Mummy might give you a new idea for a novel.'

'What?' His surprise was genuine. 'Write about all that's happened? You know, I was only joking just then.'

'You sound nearly shocked.'

He pulled a dubious face, once again contemplating the flames. 'It's certainly an idea, I suppose.'

'I don't think I told you,' Stephanie added a few moments later. 'But I've at last read your book. The first one. Well hidden from Sister Crossbones of course.' She looked pleased at finally extracting a smile.

'So what did you think of it?'

'Oh, I thought it was rather good.'

He chuckled. 'Lucky I wrote it so long ago.'

'What is that supposed to mean?'

'I was referring to your air of surprise. The phrase "rather good", coming from a critic's pen, is usually called damning with faint praise. It's a bit like saying somebody is "quite nice".'

'Well, I'm not a critic, and I wasn't damning it at all! I simply said what I thought. It would've been much more insulting if I'd pretended it was better than *War and Peace*. By the way, I see you've got a copy down here. Would it be asking too much if ...'

He grinned, more against himself than in reply. 'Yes, of course you can. You must take it with you as a present on Monday.'

She gave him a look first of thanks then of commiseration.

'That's already the day after tomorrow!' She stared back at the flames. 'It feels we've only just got here.'

'Don't I know it,' he said.

❧ 22 ❧

The wind got up later that afternoon. Doors and windows banged in the house. The trees swayed and the young green barley in the field beyond ruffled and swirled like the surface of a lake. From the bedroom window James watched the smoke from the bonfire blow in different directions.

But the wind dropped in the night, and Sunday morning became increasingly oppressive. 'I bet there's going to be a thunderstorm later,' he muttered as they sat on the terrace trying to concentrate on the Congress of Vienna and the Holy Alliance. 'The weather in this country is truly unbelievable. You never know what it's bloody well going to do next.'

'But that's very considerate of it,' said Stephanie. 'After all, how else would England's favourite subject maintain its endless fascination?'

By two o'clock black clouds covered half the sky, and it soon became so dark that they had to turn on lights in the house. By half past three, they were watching a downpour of tropical intensity. The flashes of lightning were spectacular. One crash of thunder, which seemed to explode just above their heads, made James jump.

'I love dramatic storms,' Stephanie said, her attention undeflected. Following a sortie to retrieve some cushions, her black hair was plastered to the contours of her head and the campanula blue dress clung to her limbs. He had fetched a rug to wrap round her shoulders since she refused to go up to change.

The thunderstorm went round and came back, and James's mood became more and more melancholy. His plan for a farewell dinner with steaks cooked over a fire in the garden was now ruined.

The rain finally stopped at around half past six.

'Let's go out,' said Stephanie, by then changed and dry and wearing a long cardigan which gave her the premature look of an undergraduate. James prayed that when she got to Oxford she would not waste her time with the *jeunesse dorée*. He had certainly warned her enough on that subject. The thought of her in punts with boyfriends brought on a painful sense of loss.

Outside, the haze of moisture was broken with limpid streaks and the air had a freshly washed taste. The patter of water dripping from the trees produced the strange impression of rain falling all around while they remained untouched.

Arm in arm, they wandered slowly round to the front, their gumboots leaving imprints in the sodden grass. At the farm track, they came to a halt. There, the tractor ruts formed pools, even small ponds of *café-au-lait*-coloured water.

'We're marooned!' said Stephanie in mock despair.

'If only we were.'

'Come on, James. Cheer up! I'll be back soon.' She rubbed his arm in encouragement. 'Anyway, what's this top secret plan of yours for dinner? I'm starving! Must be the effect of the storm.'

'Well, Plan A has been rained off.'

'Oh, dear. What about Plan B?'

'The same, but inside. Anyway, let's carry on a little further for the moment.'

After they had both had baths, James fitted the grill over the fire in the sitting room and opened a bottle of claret. Stephanie, meanwhile, laid the table with a clean sheet as tablecloth and arranged the rain-battered flowers she had picked on returning from their walk. Finally she drew the curtains and lit the candles she had fitted in a pair of empty wine bottles. 'The Bistro Gaunt is what we'll call it,' she said. 'Don't you think that's the perfect name for a *cuisine minceur* establishment?'

'I really should have seen that one coming,' he called back

Antony Beevor

from the kitchen. 'What do you think of going into business together? But more to the point, if you've finished in there, you can come and do the salad.'

Once everything was ready, he brought the fillet steaks over to the fireplace, and with elaborate care, laid them on the grill which he had rested on short upended logs in each corner.

'Brilliant,' said Stephanie.

'And who thought it wouldn't work? Oh, ye of little faith.'

'Gosh, James, I never knew you were a wizard engineer *as well*.'

'Amazing what one picks up, isn't it?' He went back to the table to try the wine. 'You know, this really does taste rather all right.' He picked up the bottle to examine the label more closely. 'Anyway, a glass of this shouldn't set back your recovery.'

'But much more important, what about the meat? Come and have a look and tell me what you think.'

As soon as they both agreed that the steaks were done, she held the plates while he retrieved them. And with exaggerated quivers of anticipation they hurried back to the table. Stephanie was the first to cut a piece. She chewed voluptuously. 'James, you are a genius!'

'It ain't bad, is it?' The two of them grinned at each other in congratulation.

They ate and drank to the sound of the fire and of knives and forks. 'Heavens, you eat fast,' he said on noticing she had almost finished. 'Worse than me.'

'It was so delicious, I couldn't stop for a second.' She helped herself to salad.

After they had both finished, and James had poured more wine, she pronounced it the best meal of her life. '*Vive le Petit Trianon!*' she said, toasting him. 'I will never, *never* forget it.' He had already raised his own glass in reply when the implication of her words sank in. His eyes began to fill with tears. He tried to smile, but it was no good. On the feeble pretext of fetching something from upstairs he stumbled from the table.

Lacking even the energy to turn off the lamp, James lay in bed staring at the door and listening absently to the noises of the house. In spite of all the improvements, the cold tap in the bathroom still made the whole place vibrate. Stephanie was probably cleaning her teeth. Christ, he had made a fool of himself. Was it the wine that had made him so bloody mawkish? Apart from anything else, a performance like that just wasn't fair on her.

He heard the click of the light in the bathroom, one of those string-pull switches, followed by the creak of floorboards. To his surprise, then apprehension, they seemed to be coming in his direction. What was she coming to say? Not to be so pathetic. That was what he deserved. There was an even louder creak from the other side of the door. A pause, then the handle was firmly grasped. In a rush of irrational panic, James considered turning out the light or diving under the bedclothes.

The door opened. Stephanie stood there naked. For a moment it felt as if the fantasies he had not even dared to admit to himself had come back to haunt him. He took in no detail of her body, only the memory of a hazy, almost translucent form, lightly desexualized like a Victorian painting of water nymphs.

'Move over, James. I want to come to bed with you.' He obeyed, too mesmerized to notice how rehearsed her words sounded. 'It's cold!' she said, slipping in beside him with a shiver, whether of cold or trepidation he could not tell. She snuggled up against him, and he put an arm round her and gingerly rubbed the gooseflesh down her back.

He forced himself to try to see things clearly. He could not deny the excitement of the utterly unexpected, but to consider her motives seriously, even for a moment, produced the opposite effect. To his mixed relief, he felt touched and saddened by the generosity of her gesture. Perhaps the greatest anaphrodisiac was to remember that in certain peasant communities, if the mother should die or run off, it used to be the duty of the eldest daughter to take her place in bed.

'What's the matter, James. Don't you want me?'

He could not restrain a nervous laugh. 'Sorry. That wasn't directed at you, but against myself. Listen, it'd be damned hard not to find you desirable. Yet at the same time I'd hate to spoil things between us. In a way this makes me feel a bit like the wolf in "Little Red Riding Hood" when I should be the hunter, or whatever he was, who saved her.'

'What, you mean you should really be responsible and father-like and all that?'

'Well, yes. That's part of it, of course. But what I'm also trying to say is that if a woman or a girl offers herself in a spirit of sacrifice rather than desire, it's ... well, it's a bit like sensing in the middle of a game of chess that the other person's trying to lose just to make you feel better. I know that's a pretty terrible confession of male pride and so on ...'

'James, I *do* want to make love. I promise you I wouldn't be here if I didn't!'

'Ah, if only that were true. But don't you think I'm a little old to be your lover?'

'How old's too old?' she shot back. 'I remember one conversation when you said that no girl should lose her virginity to a callow youth since it risked putting her off sex for life. Mummy was rather shocked mainly because I was there. I bet she was a virgin when she first got married. Anyway, the point is that you're not a callow youth, are you James?'

'No, sadly I don't fit in that category anymore. All I can do is look back fondly at excruciating memories.'

'Such as?'

'Oh, above all of one's clumsiness. Such as fumbling and heaving at the double hook and eye of a bra strap. The worst was when the girl pushed you off impatiently and sat up saying "Oh, you'd better let me do that!" Has that ever happened to you?'

'Careful!' she threatened, then tickled him under the ribs making him jump as if from an electric shock. 'Now I've got you! No more stalling. You're no longer a callow youth, are you!'

'I probably haven't improved much,' he chuckled.

'Oh, poor James. Tell me. Do all men need their ego massaged as much as you do?'

'Bloody hell!' he said. 'Where have you been picking up all

these ... ?' But he knew the answer already. They had a disconcertingly familiar ring.

'I just keep my ears open.'

'Well, in future it looks as if I'll just have to keep my mouth very firmly shut.'

'Oh, don't be huffy.' She pulled back to check his expression, then glanced over at the bedside lamp. 'Do you mind if we have the light out?'

Before he could reply, she had lifted herself up to reach across him. One small breast quivered in profile just in front of his eyes. 'Yes, do switch it off. We must protect your modesty.'

'Very funny!' She settled down, with her head on his chest.

Gently, he blew away a strand of hair which tickled his face. 'Sorry,' she said, disengaging a hand to pat it down. 'You know, there are so many things I want to ask.'

'Like what?'

'Like why men give their penis such silly names – John Thomas and Willie. That sort of thing. It's the same in Germany.'

'Really? *Johann Thomas, und Willi?* I'm surprised they don't call it Siegfried.' He shook with suppressed laughter.

'You know, you really can be infuriating! How am I ever going to find out about these things except by asking?'

'Sorry,' he said. 'I seem to be in rather a silly mood tonight.' He played for time. Not out of reluctance, but because he was distracted by such a variety of thoughts and impressions. Her dramatic entrance and the nerve that it must have required. And then there had been no wriggling or nervous giggles. Her instinctive sexual awareness and absence of self-consciousness were amazing, yet paradoxically, a lingering reluctance prevented him from asking whether she was still a virgin.

In spite of his earlier relief that temptation was unthinkable, he realized that desire had infiltrated itself via a mood of jocular ambivalence. He was forced to acknowledge that there was something disturbingly sensual about innocence itself, not just the freshness of young skin. He remembered the Bolsheviks' prurient fascination with the little Grand Duchesses.

Stephanie became impatient.

'I suppose one of the reasons,' he began, 'in fact probably the main reason, for men inventing names for their willies, is to give them a separate identity. To invent someone else to take the blame and so avoid responsibility for their lust. Especially when it's either slightly shameful, or more often just illogical.'

'Honestly, James! How on earth is lust illogical?'

'All right then. Perhaps perverse might be a better word. Byron, who should certainly have known what he was talking about, wrote of "loving where we do not lust and lusting where we do not love".'

'I wonder if women are the same?'

'I get the impression that it's a case of some the same, but more different. It's hard to tell. I know what. In ten years' time you must let me know your conclusions on the subject.'

'All right. That's a promise! But I still don't quite get the point of this separate identity business.'

'Well,' said James, preparing his words. 'I think it all comes down in one guise or another to fear. Hemingway, although no coward, was always terrified of being afraid, just as he was scared for his virility. He even nicknamed death "the old whore" which was rather revealing. Then there's the virgin and the harlot, another pair of male extremes, or rather contrasts dramatized to manipulate choice. But the irony is that man has screwed himself up because often he secretly desires both, and hates and fears himself for it.'

Stephanie yawned. 'Sorry, James. You've lost me. I'm too sleepy. Can I stay here for the night?'

'*Indeed* you can,' he replied. 'My pontificating is evidently the perfect cure for insomnia.' He twisted his neck and kissed the top of her head. She lifted her face to reply with a sleepy brush of lips. 'Good night, James darling.'

He smiled in the dark. 'Good night, Stephanie darling.'

After she had fallen asleep, he lay thinking, not quite sure what exactly had happened or failed to happen. The strange mixture of feelings returned, relief at having rejected her gift, but also an ill-defined regret, a sense of loss.

He tried to examine her motives from other angles. Generosity had certainly played an important role, but at the same time she could easily have wanted to seduce him for a variety of complex reasons, which admittedly had little to do with straightforward desire. Then he thought of the thunderstorm and his persistent failure to notice the elemental force in her character. It now struck him as almost surprising that she had not stripped off all her clothes in Lawrencian ecstasy and run out into the rain. That would have been a wonderful sight.

Once again mystified by the strange contrasts between offspring and parents, then trying to imagine the dream which stirred Stephanie in her sleep, he too began to drift off, until with a start he opened his eyes. It took several moments to work out that the ethereal glow came from moonlight reflecting off the mirror. He felt certain there was somehow an important link. What with exactly, he was not quite sure. His mind struggled clumsily to remember. Something somebody else had said. Then, the question seemed to form of its own accord. Has man only looked into a woman's eyes in search of his own image?

❧ 23 ❧

James woke at about five, then dozed intermittently until the angry buzzing of a fly trapped between window and curtain ended any remaining hope of sleep. His mind went back to the strange experience with the looking-glass. He did not attempt to answer his own question – that was for later – but wondered if a series of others also needed to be asked.

He remembered seeing an ugly boy at prep school suddenly smash the mirror in the middle of brushing his hair. Those present began to taunt him. *Par-ker is bat-ty!* they chanted. But this reaction only betrayed their sense of awe when confronted with such a spontaneous act. The long-forgotten scene encouraged James to speculate whether man's destructive streak came from a sort of oedipal or sibling fear of his own image.

Concentration became difficult with an uncomfortably full bladder. He eased himself naked from the bed, looking backwards at Stephanie's head buried in the pillow, her dark hair against the white cotton. The sight made him forget to deal with the fractious fly.

Outside, while closing the bedroom door with immense care behind him, he remembered the noise the water pipes made. So he took the old towel robe of Christina's hanging behind the bathroom door and went down to greet the day in what struck him as a suitably rustic manner.

The sitting-room table had been cleared, the washing-up done and the kitchen tidied. Stephanie had only missed a crumpled paper napkin under one of the chairs. Ashamed at the memory of his lachrymose exhibition, he knelt down to retrieve it.

After a struggle with the bolt on the back door, he stepped out to find the brick path unexpectedly cold and damp underfoot. The air was so still the slightest sound carried for miles. In the distance he could hear a car slow to a halt. Although everything remained sodden from the rain, it looked as if the beautiful weather had returned already. Not that it made any difference now. They had to leave in a couple of hours. But first of all, he'd have to check the track was passable. They might need help from the farmer.

He walked across the wet grass to the far side of the old apple tree at the end of the garden, and took up position. As he began to relieve himself, he gazed at a dew-soaked spider's web. He thought it a little strange that Christina had not rung, if only to check they hadn't forgotten the appointment with Doctor Aziz. Unless, of course, she was planning a long-distance alarm call to get them up in plenty of time.

He focused, as best he could without his spectacles, on the curtains of the open bedroom window, and pictured Stephanie, fast asleep. His heart swelled at the thought of their night together. That consummation of complicity meant that nothing could really separate them now. But just as he was in the middle of shaking himself and considering whether to have a coffee before returning to her side, a dark figure appeared round the corner of the house. He froze, then, as an afterthought, leaned further behind the tree. To be caught having a slash in your own garden at this time of the morning seemed a bit unfair.

Their early caller had eyes only for the house. James could distinguish nothing more than her black dress. After stepping onto the grass and looking up impatiently at the bedroom window, she caught sight of the open kitchen door.

'Jesus!' he murmured as the figure set off towards it. The woman in black was Christina.

As the irreversibility of the disaster sank in, his limbs and mind suffered a nightmare-like paralysis. He could picture in detail the sequence of events about to take place inside those walls. Having found Stephanie's bed untouched, Christina would continue to the other end of the tiny passage and discover her daughter naked in her husband's bed. The symbolic nature of the evidence would be all. Technical innocence was utterly irrelevant. The only consolation was that she had not arrived ten minutes earlier and caught them *in flagrante delicto* like a bad farce. That thought alone was enough to make him feel weak. However much he feared to follow her, he could not bear to remain in ignorance outside.

As he hurried back towards the house, he desperately tried to think up excuses, like claiming to have spent the night on the sofa downstairs. Even that Stephanie's bed had been soaked by a burst hot-water bottle so he had put her in their room. But Christina would sense the truth immediately, and the fabrication would only condemn him further in her eyes.

He stood in dread at the bottom of the stairs listening to the exchange in German. Stephanie flung back a defiant reply. There was a silence, then Christina spoke in a hard, quiet voice that he barely recognized. Stephanie began to sob.

Christina left the room to fetch something for her to wear. From the top of the stairs, she caught sight of him staring anxiously up. She hesitated for a fraction of a second, then hurried on as if she had not seen him. He retreated to the kitchen and listened to the muffled footsteps of her return journey overhead. Then came hollow clumps as she began to descend the steep wooden staircase.

He did not know how to prepare himself for the onslaught. His nakedness under the dressing gown made him feel guilty as well as vulnerable. At the last moment, he decided to move out into the garden. Somehow it seemed less dangerous to meet her in an unrestricted place.

Close to, and in the morning light, Christina's appearance gave him a shock. Her face, usually so healthy, was pale and showed the effect of strain and exhaustion. The brown marks under her eyes resembled fading bruises. Her black suit was creased from travel and her shoes and stockings covered in mud. James could not piece any of this together. His mind felt as if it had lost all power of deduction.

'Stephanie said you made love last night.' It was more of a statement than the terrible accusation he might have expected.

'No, we didn't. We slept together, but nothing happened, I promise you. She only came to console me.'

With relief, James saw that she had not really believed Stephanie's outburst. But in the end it would make little difference. That the possibility could even arise was enough in her eyes to prove what a bad influence he must have been. Christina's anger was slow-burning. Sad, even fatalistic, but implacable. To argue with her would be completely futile.

She noticed his eyes on her shoes. 'The driver would not risk his car in the pools along the track. I had to leave him there and walk.'

'But I still . . .'

'You don't understand why I am here and dressed like this. Is that what you mean? Well, it is all because my father died yesterday.'

'Oh, Christ. I'm so sorry.' He did not know what else to say. Anything that came to mind sounded so inadequate or banal.

She acknowledged his condolences with an inclination of the head, as one might to a virtual stranger, then continued in a flat, controlled tone, which made her words sound like an official statement. 'I rang here in the afternoon to tell Stephanie the news and warn her of the changed flight plans. But it was impossible to get through. My brother then managed to obtain the use of a friend's private jet.'

'Of course. The telephone must have been out of order as a result of the thunderstorm.'

'So I was told. That was why there was no alternative but to come myself to bring Stephanie back for the funeral.'

'I see.' Everything he said sounded so pathetically lame and stupid.

'I must go up to check she is ready.' Christina regarded him for an instant in faint distaste. Her look and his nakedness under the robe now made him feel like a flasher, lucky to be let off with a caution. 'I think it would be best if you stayed out here,' she said.

He listened numbly to the exchanges in German which came from the little window above. What suitable clothes did she have in London? Had she packed her washbag? Was there anything else she might have left downstairs. They would not be coming back.

Although he was already resigned to the worst, this chilling lack of ambiguity ran through him. It suddenly felt as though everything had combined to produce an incontrovertible and crushing moment. One of those Rorschach moments he used to believe in. The catastrophe of Christina's arrival, although brought about by the thunderstorm, formed part of the general upheaval emanating from her father's death.

Almost as for the passing of a monarch or a great statesman, the effect extended well beyond those intimately concerned. 'The end of an era,' everyone would say, falling back on the reassurance of platitudes.

He thought of Christina. In a single, long-feared blow, she was losing her spiritual home and the most important person in her life. He also wondered about the requiem Mass at Lotzingen. Would it be packed with relatives from all over Europe, their Mercedes and perhaps a couple of helicopters on the meadows by the road below? Or would it be a simple family service, with old servants in black armbands weeping silently at the back? How strange to think of that baroque chapel now.

Christina's manner of farewell to Lotzingen was not hard to guess. Accompanied by Stephanie and Malte, she would take her favourite walk along the far side of the valley, then return to wander from room to room in farewell.

From the window above it sounded as if Stephanie were ready. James abruptly revolted against his banishment. He dashed into the house and took the stairs two at a time. He reached the main bedroom without a backward glance at mother and daughter in the little room at the other end of the corridor. He shut the door behind him and in great haste, pulled on trousers, shirt and shoes. In spite of the mad rush, he could not stop himself from wondering whether a scent of Stephanie lingered on the pillow.

As soon as he had retrieved his spectacles from the bedside table he presented himself, slightly breathless, at the head of the stairs. Christina was alone, Stephanie's suitcase beside her.

'Here, let me take that,' he said. 'It's a hell of a long way to the road.'

'It will not be necessary, thank you. I have sent Stephanie to ask the driver to come to fetch it.'

'But all that to-ing and fro-ing is ridiculous. It'll take him ages to get here.'

With considerable reluctance, Christina agreed. Delay evidently appeared a greater evil than the prospect of his company. He grasped the case and gestured for her to go first.

The grass beside the cart track proved even more slippery than expected, and he cursed the weight of Stephanie's textbooks. Trying to keep his breathing inaudible was the hardest part as he struggled to catch up with Christina. He was determined to brave the hostile silence.

'When do you think you'll be back?' he asked, attempting a matter-of-fact tone.

She did not look at him, but ahead to the road where the driver and Stephanie stood watching their approach. 'My lawyers will be writing to you.'

It had come at last. He wondered how that formula had entered the phrase book of ponderous statements. Or was it just another of those occasions when people needed a stock answer. He braced himself to pronounce the words. 'Does that mean you want a divorce?'

'No, not a divorce. An annulment.'

'An *annulment*? You can't be serious.' He came to a halt, then put down the suitcase. 'But how on earth could you hope to get it? And why do you want one anyway?'

'I would have thought that was perfectly clear.'

'Well, I'm sorry, but it's not! An annulment is presumably for a marriage that was never valid for some reason, or else has never been consummated. And that can hardly apply to our case.'

'Not necessarily.'

'But for Christ's sake! You can't even claim on grounds of infertility, as we both know from Turin!'

She flinched as she stood there rigidly. 'Please. We cannot discuss it here.'

211

'We damned well can, and we damned well will! Especially if you're about to disappear behind a Siegfried Line of lawyers. So tell me straight. Why an annulment ... for which I presume I would have to consent to some cock and bull story?' The implied threat forced her to face him at last.

'I am a Catholic, and I wish to remarry.'

The change in her manner, even in her stance, was enough to help him relax a little. He shook his head in confusion. Strangely, it was the idea of such an unpromiscuous woman marrying three times which disorientated him most at that moment.

'How soon is all this supposed to take place?'

'I don't know now. Obviously it will not happen while we are in mourning for my father. But fairly soon, I hope.' She was too proud and too honest to allow the slightest hint of supplication.

'I see. Well, who is he, then?'

'As I have already told you, you do not know him ...' She faltered as if remembering something.

'If I've never met him,' he said, instantly on the alert, 'then surely there is no harm in telling me his name. In any case, is it really so unreasonable of me to ask? Just put yourself in my shoes for a moment. Wouldn't you want to know?'

She looked at the ground between them, then back towards the road. Stephanie, now seated in the back of the car, was still watching them. 'Yes,' she finally admitted. 'I would.' She took a deep breath. 'His name is Otto Retzen. He is a cousin of my first husband.'

Her words registered in his mind while his guts froze in an instinctive disbelief. She simply could not mean what she said, and yet he knew her well enough to be sure it was the truth. The whole scene reprojected itself in his mind. Big Bertha's yell of rage, the chair toppling backwards, the confusion of shouting and Bubi trying to restore calm. The drunken pig. Hans-Dietrich's elder brother. The first cousin who looked so like Georg.

How could he have overlooked him? The whole idea had such a grotesque logic that it eliminated any trace of doubt.

Frantic to warn her, he searched for the best way. But his brain felt as numb as his body. He could not even put a sentence together.

Christina, from alarm at what his horrified expression might signify, now became impatient. She turned to make a move in the direction of the car. James pulled himself together, but as he opened his mouth to remind her of the stag night in Munich, he knew she would not believe him. She would think he was making it up. A last desperate, despicable slander to keep her.

As they approached the car, James was trailing several yards behind. The driver went round to open the boot, then held out a hand to take the suitcase. James staggered with the effort of lifting it towards him. He looked at Stephanie in the back, upset and guilty, and probably unsure how to react to a death which had not yet sunk in. She gave him a sad, apologetic smile, then tore herself away to face forwards again. He did not see Christina. She must have climbed in on the other side.